CONVENIENT MAFIA VOWS

A FORCED PROXIMITY DARK MAFIA ROMANCE

RUTHLESS BILLIONAIRE MAFIA KINGS

VIVY SKYS

Copyright © 2025 by VIVY SKYS

All rights reserved.

No part of this book may be reproduced in any form or by any electronic or mechanical means, including information storage and retrieval systems, without written permission from the author, except for the use of brief quotations in a book review.

PROLOGUE

VICTORIA

I'm hot, hotter than I ever thought it would be possible to be in New York in the winter. Sweat trickles down the front of my chest from beneath the black silk scarf wound around my neck, and I swear that if the line for the restroom doesn't move within the next three seconds, I'll whip off the blonde, curly wig I'm wearing and use it to fan myself. At this point, I don't even care if it ruins my costume.

I'm Sandy.

Or rather, I'm Victoria Callahan dressed up as Sandy from *Grease* for a costume party in a sleazy basement club in the Upper West Side on New Year's Eve. Scratch that. It's probably New Year's Day now although, if it is, I missed the countdown to midnight beneath the thump-thump-thump of hundreds of people in crazy costumes losing all ability to coordinate their movements into something that resembles dancing.

Beneath the blonde wig, my long brunette hair is pinned to my scalp and trapped beneath a scratchy net that isn't helping.

Well, it depends which way you're looking at it, I guess. My best friend, Sienna, was going to come to the party as Sandy, but being the sexy loyal best-friend-a-gal-could-ever-have, she suggested that it might work better on me.

Because Sienna has no trouble getting laid.

Not that I have *trouble* getting laid exactly. I mean, how do you define trouble when it simply never happens?

The problem is, the more time that passes without me finding someone worthy of spreading my legs for, and the older I get, the weirder it becomes. It's like, when a guy finds out that you're twenty-three and still haven't a clue what all the fuss is about they think you're either a lesbian in denial or there must be something inherently wrong with you that has deterred any other guy from scoring a home run.

Is there something wrong with me?

I don't think so. A girl's got to have standards, right?

You've only got to look at a classic fairytale to know that Prince Charming is worth holding out for.

Sienna thinks that I give off stay-the-fuck-away-from-me-unless-you're-prepared-to-go-down-on-one-knee-and-propose vibes.

I don't.

At least, I don't give them off intentionally.

I blame my mom. She read those goddamned fairytales to me and then went and ruined everything with a heroin addiction that made her see charming princes behind a slimeball with her next fix. She also left me with a little brother to take care of when I should've been fangirling over Zac Eron and Orlando Bloom.

Wednesday Addams comes out of the restroom, glaring at the rest of us waiting in line like we should've had the common decency to give her some space, and we shuffle along a couple of paces.

"Smile." Sienna's mouth lifts at the corners to demonstrate the concept, and I mimic her, knowing that my attempt hasn't quite reached my eyes. "That's better. You'll never bag yourself a stud while you look like you want to murder someone."

It's easy for her to say. After loaning me the costume she'd planned on wearing, she bought a leopard-print mini dress from a thrift store, teamed it with chunky blue beads and bare legs, and piled her naturally red hair up into a messy bun on top of her head. And voila: she's a gorgeously stunning Wilma from *The Flintstones*.

I know it sounds like I'm jealous of my best friend, but I'm honestly not. She's the kindest, sweetest-natured person I ever met, and I don't know where I'd be without her. I wouldn't be in this dingy club for starters, but I mean, I don't know where I'd be in life. Hopefully not chasing fixes around the city like my mom did until she met her new husband.

I peer around the club. Fred and Daphne are making out in a corner and, oh my fucking God, did she come here commando?

Blinking the vision out of my head, I avert my eyes and spot Cinderella strutting her stuff—literally—with Mick Jagger. I can't help smiling at them. I don't know if they arrived together, but it's pretty freaking obvious that they'll be leaving together when everyone else starts running out of steam.

This is what I don't understand, and I think this is the reason why I never 'bag myself a stud' as Sienna puts it. Not that there are any studs here tonight. Not that I've seen anyways.

Well, maybe there were some here earlier in the evening, but now that everyone's steaming, including me, all I can see is sweaty upper lips and drooping wigs.

But anyway, it's that easy confidence in their ability to attract a member of the opposite sex. Even in this blonde wig and wearing the tightest latex pants in the history of the world, I draw a blank when it comes to looking sexy and flirting. I must've been last in line—again—when they were dishing out the fuck-me-cowboy genes.

"You're doing it again." Sienna jolts me back to reality.

"Doing what?"

"Overthinking it. Vic—" she places her hands on my shoulders and forces me to look her in the eye "—you look incredible tonight. Any guy that gets the chance to slip inside those pants is going to think he hit the jackpot."

"Only if I pay out."

She tips her head back and laughs out loud, a sound that's contagious. "You will, trust me. You'll know when the right guy comes along."

We shuffle closer to the restroom entrance as a whole bunch of girls come pouring out, and suddenly, we're in, and I have to go through the rigmarole of peeling these pants over my hips.

I can still feel the music vibrating in my bones even if it feels good to have a few moments to myself to breathe while I'm shut inside the cubicle. My head is pleasantly fuzzy. I'm probably more chilled than I've been in months. But still, I feel like something is missing from my life.

Flushing, and then standing in front of the mirror, I touch up my lip gloss, and check that my mascara hasn't run while I've been boogying my butt off out there.

Deep breath.

I follow Sienna outside and realize, a beat too late, and when the space we've just vacated inside the restroom has already been filled, that I left my purse behind.

"Sienna, my purse!"

She doesn't hear me with the bass rocking the club, so I dash back inside, breathe a sigh of relief when I spot my purse next to the basin where I left it, and grab it quickly. I need to find Sienna before she gets swallowed up by a whole bunch of sweaty bodies and is lost to me forever. Or at least until we both sober up tomorrow morning.

Head down, I don't make eye contact with anyone in the line, and instead, collide headfirst with a rock-solid chest who isn't watching where he's going either. I tilt my head back and find myself gazing into green eyes framed by the thickest lashes I've ever seen on a man. His black hair is gelled back into an Elvis-style quaff, and he's wearing a beaten-up leather jacket over a white T-shirt.

"Danny?" I squeal like a teenager.

"Sandy?" His voice squeaks as he catches on quickly.

"Oh my God, I've always wanted to say that." My gaze travels down from Danny Zuko's wide smile and perfect white teeth to the broad shoulders and rippling chest muscles. I don't dare look any lower. Besides, chests have always been my thing.

He leans closer, so close that I can smell cinnamon on him, like he's spent the holidays baking cookies. I can't drag my eyes away. My body is refusing to cooperate, and my heart is going frantic inside my rib cage like I just bumped into the real Danny Zuko, and nothing else exists outside of those dark mossy flecks in his green-green eyes.

"Where have you been all my life?" he murmurs.

Wait. Even my fuzzy brain recognizes that this isn't a line from *Grease*. But I play along anyways.

"Waiting for you?"

It must be the right response because his smile grows, lighting up his beautiful face and crinkling the corners of his eyes, and I feel his hand slide around my waist as his lips press on mine.

His other hand entwines with the blonde curls and tips my head back, causing my brain cells to swim, and the ground to slide out from under me. I squeeze my eyes shut and concentrate on his tongue in my mouth. I taste beer and liquor, and it isn't at all unpleasant because I'm kissing Danny Zuko at a New Year's Eve party, and when my legs give way, he keeps me upright like it's what he was made to do.

He pulls his tongue from my mouth long enough to murmur, "You're so fucking gorgeous," and then it's back again, and I'm not fighting it because tonight, for one night only, I'm the Sandy to his Danny.

I don't know how long we stand there kissing like it's the end of the world. Time has stopped, and I barely even remember who I am or what I'm doing here.

When he pulls away, leaving my lips swollen and still parted, my tongue aching for his, I feel the crushing weight of disappointment. This is it. This is the moment when he realizes his mistake, that I'm not the Sandy he arrived with, and makes an excuse to get away from me as quickly as possible.

But instead, he looks me directly in the eye and says, "Come with me."

It isn't a question, and I don't even have a chance to answer before he grabs my hand and leads me through the club and outside into the freezing New York City night.

This isn't happening to me.

It can't be.

I'm Victoria Callahan, virgin extraordinaire, the girl who gives off all the wrong vibes for bagging a stud, and yet, when I climb into the back of a yellow taxi and Danny Zuko's lips reattach to mine, none of that even matters. He could be a psycho serial killer with a blonde wig fetish for all I know. But the ache between my legs tells me that I'm going to let him fuck me.

The cab pulls up on the curb, and Danny tosses some cash to the driver, his warm hand still in mine. He lets himself into an apartment building without a word. While we wait for the elevator, his tongue finds mine again, his hands roaming my body and touching me in places I've never been touched before.

He pushes me against the wall, the button dinging behind my back, and crushes my breasts with both hands, while he smothers my mouth with his own, his oxygen becoming mine. I'm breathless when we both roll into the elevator.

By the time we roll out of it and into his apartment, I can barely even stand, my legs are trembling so badly. "Danny, I'm—"

He tips my head backward, arching my neck so that it's hard to breathe, and then I feel his teeth digging into the soft flesh around my mouth, and I can't even remember what I was going to say.

"You're so fucking beautiful." His words caress my sore lips as he grips my chin between his thumb and forefinger.

Then, his tongue is tracing a line down my neck, and somehow, my breasts are exposed, and his mouth is closing around my nipples, his teeth nibbling the sensitive flesh. I gasp with the sheer pleasure of the sensation, pushing my lower back against the wall and inadvertently thrusting my nipples harder into his mouth.

His free hand fumbles with the latex pants, and I hear a low growl erupt from his throat as he finally manages to drag them down over my hips.

He slides a finger inside me, and I gasp out loud before I can stop myself. My hands are fluttering around his head, and I shove a fist into my mouth and bite down hard. I can feel his finger working around inside me, probing, exploring, and I instinctively open my legs, knees still trembling, to let him in deeper.

"Stay there." He reappears briefly, kisses my lips, a full-on tongue-down-my-throat kiss, and then drops to his knees, and oh my fucking God, when he spreads my sex open with both hands and inserts his tongue, I swear my eyes must roll back in my head.

Oh. My. God.

I feel... I don't know what I feel... My pussy is throbbing and tingling and writhing like it wants to escape his tongue which is dragging back and forth across my clit, when I know that escaping is the last thing in the world I want to do right now.

I'm almost there, my orgasm about to explode, when he pulls his tongue out. I almost collapse on him and press my spine hard against the wall to keep myself grounded. My pussy is twitching, desperate to feel his tongue inside me again, and I don't know what to do about it.

Danny stands and licks my lips with the tip of his tongue. I can't move. The pants are still around my ankles, and I'm conscious that my breasts and my pussy are exposed, and this is not at all how I imagined my first time would be.

But when he murmurs, "Do you want me to let you come, Sandy?" I find myself whispering, "Yes," huskily.

"Say it again."

"Yes," I breathe against him.

"Hmm." Danny watches me with those green eyes, and when I instinctively try to kiss him, he moves just out of reach. "Yes, what?"

"Yes, I want to come." I don't even recognize my own voice.

"Yes, Danny, I want you to let me come." When I remain silent, he grabs my chin again and nibbles my bottom lip. "Say it, Sandy."

"I want you to let me come."

He smiles, and I melt into a giant orgasmic puddle of wetness.

Danny rams a finger inside me, watching me closely. I keep my eyes on him even though I want to close them and lose myself riding his finger. He drags it out of me, pulling his finger across my clit and eliciting another groan, and then his finger is in my mouth, and I can taste myself.

And maybe this is it after all, everything I never dreamed of because I never knew I could be this freaking sexy.

This time, when he sticks his tongue in me, I don't hold back. I explode in his mouth, and for one scary moment I think he might drown in me because I never want this to end…

I don't know when or how we end up in his bed.

I'm naked, and he climbs on top of me, still wearing the white T-shirt, his cock bouncing in his hand as he frees it from his jeans and rubs it around my pussy.

"Tell me you want me, Sandy," he growls.

"I want you." Since when did I ever start being so meek and compliant?

"Louder."

I raise my voice a notch. "I want you."

He shakes his head and pulls away, withholding from me the one thing I want most in the entire world.

"I freaking want you!" I yell.

He smiles, and I've never seen anything so crazily hot and sexy in my life.

I spread my legs wide, and he studies me for several moments before guiding his length to my sex. I feel him pushing against me, trying to gain entry. Without thinking, I reach down and open myself up, holding his gaze the whole time.

"You're so fucking sexy, Sandy." I can see it in his enlarged pupils, and for once, I believe it.

Then he's inside me, and I start panting as he pushes, gently at first, and then harder, hitting that wall, surprise crossing his eyes. He lowers his upper body onto me and fills my mouth with his tongue.

Wrapping my arms around his neck, I hold onto him, burying my fingers in his jet-black hair. He moves slowly at first, grinding his cock inside me, gradually building up speed until our hips are pounding against each other, and I swear I can feel him hitting the bottom of my spine. Why did no one ever tell me that this is what I've been missing out on?

When he comes, I kiss him hard, crushing my lips against him until his body stops shuddering and he collapses on top of me.

He falls asleep almost instantly.

I don't move until I hear Sienna's muffled ringtone on my cell phone which is still somewhere in the other room.

Extricating myself from underneath Danny, who is snoring gently, spreadeagled across the bed like a starfish, I tiptoe across the bedroom and locate my purse on the floor near the entrance. I check my phone, guilt tearing my chest wide open when I realize that I've had twenty-three missed calls from Sienna.

"Fuck!" I left the club without telling her where I was going, and she's probably scared that she'll read about my battered body being discovered in a dark alleyway on the news tomorrow.

I try calling her back, but she doesn't pick up.

I try again, and the line goes dead.

Panic setting in now, I use the find-a-phone feature to locate Sienna's position, and don't believe it when I see that she's on the Interstate just outside the city. I start again, thinking there must be a problem with the app, but she's still there, and she isn't moving.

I don't waste a beat.

With one long lingering look at Danny sprawled across the bed, I drag my clothes back on, cussing myself for agreeing to the latex pants, and let myself out of the apartment. I might've just been fucked by the hottest guy in the entire city, but my friend is more important.

"I'm coming, Sienna," I whisper to myself as I step outside onto the frosty street and hail a cab.

1

VICTORIA

FIVE YEARS LATER

Chaos erupts near the end of my shift at a ritzy diner on the Lower East Side of Manhattan. It's coming from outside, and I instinctively know that my kid brother Mason is involved; call it intuition. Call it bone-fucking-weariness or reaching-the-end-of-my-tether, or how-much-more-of-his-shit-is-he-going-to-throw-at-me. Because even before Roy, our chef, comes striding in, his eyes seeking me out, I sense that this has nothing to do with the Irish bar down the street kicking some rowdy football fans out at closing time.

Ignoring the sounds of a crowd jeering a fight without even realizing they're taking sides, I set some drinks down onto a table of four—two couples—with a smile plastered onto my face and tell them that the bar is now closed.

Stay focused and upbeat until the last customer has left the premises, even if you feel like shit on the inside. I can't afford to lose another job. Mason sure as hell isn't bringing any money into the two-bedroom apartment we share since he got kicked out of his last place.

I hurry back to the bar with the tray of empties from the table I just served, but Roy takes it from me before I reach it. "Go, Vicky," he says, his dark eyes flashing at me from beneath bushy eyebrows. "Killian's spitting blood for your brother."

I knew it.

Killian owns the diner. He's a burly ex-boxer with biceps the size of rugby balls, and a temper to match his fiery red hair. He's almost sixty but still works out every day, and when he blows, everyone generally finds a quiet corner in which to cower. Including me.

But this is Mason, and despite all the hassle he causes me, I still feel responsible for him. Who else is going to look out for him if it isn't me?

I see the crowd gathered around the fight taking place on the sidewalk. Shoving through, I reach the ringside as Killian raises his fist and pummels my brother's face, blood spraying the front of my white shirt. I let out an involuntary shriek as Mason's nose seems to split, red smothering his nose and chin making him resemble a vampire at feeding time.

"Killian, stop!" I reach for his arm, but he shrugs me off and bats me away like I'm a fly who got in the way.

A young guy in green pants and a bowtie catches me before I hit the ground and stands me back up. "Stay out of it, lady, or you'll—"

But I'm not listening. Mason is curled into the fetal position on the cold sidewalk, and it's clear that no one else is going to intervene even though he isn't fighting back, and I left my cell phone back inside my purse in the diner. If I don't stop

Killian, the cops will be scraping my brother off the ground later.

"Killian, stop!" I'm trying to find a way to reach Mason beneath those swinging arms, but it's like completing an obstacle course of moving parts. "Someone, help him, please! He's my brother!"

Some folks turn away at the pleading in my voice—if they don't watch, they can tell themselves later that there was nothing they could do. Others stay behind but keep their distance, unwilling to get blood on their clothes.

Before I can talk myself out of it, I leap onto Killian's back, throwing my arms around his neck, and trying to steer him away from my brother as though he were a horse. But Killian wraps his meaty hands around my arms and flings me sideways, a minor inconvenience preventing him from finishing what he has already started.

I grit my teeth and wait for my body to slam into the sidewalk, but instead, with an unexpected whump, I hit the solid chest and arms of a guy wearing black motorbike leathers.

He catches me easily, the force barely even knocking him off-balance. "Are you hurt?" He sets me down and holds me at arm's length, scanning my face for blood.

I shake my head. His presence has halted the one-sided fight, and I realize that everyone is backing off now that the entertainment is over. Peering up into his face in the glow of the streetlamp, I understand why.

This is Caleb Murray. Owner of the Wraith, a sleek, black-mirrored, high-rise hotel in the city. Billionaire playboy rumored to have connections in all the right places, or wrong places depending on which way you're looking at it. He has to be one of the most photographed people in the States, and he just saved me from at least a couple broken bones.

With a nod in my direction to acknowledge that I'm alright, he turns his attention to Killian. "Why the fuck would you settle your shit in the street? You want the one-fifteen on your back?"

"No, Mr. Murray." Killian lowers his fists, muscles still twitching. I've never seen him look so sheepish or heard him speak with such utter deference to anyone before. "You're right, of course, Mr. Murray."

No, sir. Yes, sir. Three bags full, sir.

What the actual fuck?

I can't help staring at the wide shoulders and narrow hips clad in leather and wonder if the guy's cologne exudes some kind of pheromone that makes other men want to bow in front of him. Or maybe the rumors don't do the man justice.

Either way, Killian is still groveling—I almost expect him to drop to his knees and beg Caleb Murray to go easy on him—and I wish I'd taken more notice of his chest because, well, a solid chest *and* black leather...

"I'm sorry but the dumb fuck's been stealing from my place for weeks and I finally caught him red-handed."

While I've been staring, Mason has managed to slink away, crawling under the radar and waiting for it all to go away. But the truth is, if Killian caught him stealing, I know exactly how this evening is going to pan out, and I'll be the one who ends up paying for it.

I back away, silently, sticking to the shadows even though my senses are screaming at me to stay close to Caleb Murray because Killian won't try anything while he's around, but he isn't going to help me sort Mason out. I don't even know if I can sort out this mess, but I learned a long while ago that burying your head in the sand resolves nothing.

So, once I'm out of sight, I run.

I catch up with Mason at the subway entrance. Blood is still pouring from his nose, and his left eye is almost closed behind swollen purple flesh. I grab his arm, and he pulls away from me like he's expecting me to be a middle-aged beefcake.

His shoulders slump when he realizes that it's me.

"Mason, tell me Killian was lying."

His good eye darts all around as if I might've brought my boss back with me for more of the same. "Go back to work, Vic. I can't do this right now."

It's all the answer I need.

I watch him stumble down the stairs and get swallowed whole by the subway, shivering as the adrenaline leaves my body and the chill night air raises goosebumps on my arms.

I walk back to the diner on legs that have forgotten how to move. Mason might've gotten away with a broken nose and a black eye, but I still have to face Killian... Without the backup of Mr. Biking-leathers-Murray.

The crowd has dispersed outside the diner. I'm about to head inside when I hear the roar of a motorcycle from across the street. I turn around to find Caleb Murray fastening a helmet strap beneath his chin and pulling a black visor over his eyes, but not before he looks directly at me, his gaze holding mine a beat too long.

My heart freezes before slamming into my ribcage in its haste to catch up with the beats it missed, and pulse racing, I follow the matte-black Harley with my eyes until it disappears before heading inside to face the wrath of my boss's bruised ego.

"Get that bitch out of here!" I can hear him from the front entrance where Roy has placed my belongings onto a cleared table to stop me from going any further.

"Sorry, kid." Roy stands between me and Killian. "He's been watching Mason for a while now. He's been coming in on Specials' nights, swiping tips off tables, and dipping his hand in the register when you're not looking." He lowers his voice. "You're lucky he didn't call the cops."

Lucky? I can't afford to lose this job.

"Can I just talk to him?"

Roy shakes his head. "You're wasting your breath, kid."

Of course, I am. I just jumped onto Killian's back to stop him from killing my brother. A vision of my interview with Killian springs to mind, practically begging him to take me on because, without me, our little family would fall apart. I literally did everything but tell him we'd end up on the streets, so he's never going to believe that I wasn't tipping Mason off about the best nights to come in and swipe some cash.

Killian owes me two weeks' money, but I don't ask for it. I gather my stuff and walk outside with my head held high—no way the fucker is going to make me beg for my money. I'll just have to find another job. Pronto.

When I get home, Mason is nursing his injuries on the sofa, head tipped backwards over the side, and a packet of frozen broccoli over his swollen eye.

On the subway, I had it all worked out. I was going to yell at him, vent my anger and frustration at losing another job because his itchy fingers and gambling debts follow me around like a lost puppy, but what's the point? Besides, I'm done in.

Mason raises the packet of broccoli and peers at me with his one open eye. "I was going to pay you both back."

He sounds defeated, and I should want to kill him to for dragging me into his problems again, but I just wish he would stay the fuck out of the casinos and do what's right for all of us for once.

"Have you checked on Abigail?"

"No, he didn't, but she's fine." Sienna walks out of the bedroom, glares at Mason, who is already checking out of the conversation. "What happened?"

"Long story." I lower my voice; I don't want to wake Abigail. Getting a cranky five-year-old back to sleep isn't easy, and I'm not mentally prepared for another battle.

"You got fired, didn't you?"

"I can still hear you," Mason murmurs from beneath the slowly thawing packet on his face.

I usher Sienna into the kitchen and dump my purse on the counter. I don't want her to worry about us, but I know that's another battle I won't win.

The burn scars on her neck and jawline are already turning livid, and she instinctively tugs the neckline of her sweater up to cover them. Sienna suffered third degree burns in a road traffic incident in the early hours of New Year's Day five years ago. The driver, some guy she met in the same nightclub where I met Danny Zuko, climbed out of the wreckage and left her for dead; she only survived because I'd alerted the emergency services when I saw the missed calls on my cell phone.

Sienna's version of events is that I saved her life, and I'm stuck with her. Which is why she's here now, babysitting while I work, and Mason does whatever Mason does when he needs money to clear his debts.

My version is that I should never have left her in the nightclub that night to lose my virginity to Danny Zuko, the hottest man alive. The hottest man alive who must've been swallowed whole by a crack in the ground after I left him because I've never seen him again since.

I've looked. Believe me, I've looked.

That night changed everything, for both of us, and I'll never stop trying to make it up to my best friend for as long as I live. Sienna wants to open her own art gallery, and one day, I'm going to make it happen. Even if I'm currently unemployed.

"What are you going to do, Vic?"

Sienna has offered to let me and Abigail, move in with her until we get straight, but I can't leave Mason to fend for himself. What Killian did to him tonight would be nothing compared to the kind of mess my brother would get into if left to his own devices.

"I have a few favors I can call in." I force a smile and fill the kettle to make coffee. "You look tired, Si. Stay over. We can make popcorn and watch a movie." I hate that I only get to see my best friend when she's looking after Abigail.

It's about time both of us caught a break, and I tell myself to stay positive. Perhaps the Universe had that break in mind when it allowed Mason to mess with my job tonight and almost get himself killed.

"I can't." Sienna leans in and kisses my cheek. "Get some rest, Vic, and tell Mason that next time he fucks up your life, I'll do more than bust up his eye."

Sienna sees herself out. I don't even drink my coffee when it's made. By the time I've showered and warned Mason that he's taking Abigail to kindergarten in the morning, I can barely keep my eyes open.

Next thing I know, my alarm is going off, and I'm asleep next to Abigail on top of my comforter with a damp towel still wrapped around my hair.

I kiss her forehead and smooth her hair, the same color as mine, away from her rosy face. It's the third time this week I've come home from work and left again without seeing her awake, and it hurts my heart. But being unemployed will only make our lives a hundred times worse because whose bed would she be sleeping in then?

Thirty minutes later, I'm walking into the lobby of the Wraith, feeling seriously underdressed in black slacks and a white shirt. Interview outfit. Minus the 'lucky' prefix. I'm a hard worker, but even though there are almost nine million people in New York, Mason's reputation clings to us both like Velcro.

My flat pumps click dully across the black marble floor. I've been here a couple times, and it still takes my breath away. Heavy chandeliers hang from the atrium ceiling reflecting a million tiny black stars across the floor and the glass façade, creating the kind of spectacular three-sixty image that wouldn't look out of place in a Broadway show. Even the reception desk is sleek black with gold trimming, the woman sitting behind the desk dressed in an emerald and gold pantsuit.

I try tiptoeing, but it's too late, the security guard has already spotted me and is heading my way.

"I'm here to see Denise Cartwright," I blurt out before he can flash me a look that says I'm in the wrong place and I should turn myself around and march straight back outside where I belong.

"Vicky!"

Denise hurries over to me, taking control by encasing my hand in both of hers and leading me through a black archway that shimmers with gold and into the restaurant where she works as manager. Denise manages every food outlet connected to the Wraith and Caleb Murray's ever-expanding empire.

She was also my mom's best friend and her first NA sponsor when she was trying to get clean. It was Denise who introduced my mom to Quincy, her new husband, too. It won't be the first time she has bailed me out of a situation created by Mason because she feels responsible for us, and I don't like taking advantage of her, but needs must.

Inside the restaurant's entrance, I breathe in the aroma of expensive coffee and chocolate and ignore my stomach growling back at me. Several tables are occupied by guests taking an early breakfast, and it would almost feel cozy if every item of gold-trimmed furniture didn't cost more than I can earn in a year.

Deep breath. "Sorry, Denise, but I need a favor."

Denise's expression doesn't alter. "Let me guess, Mason."

Tears well in my eyes, and I blink them away furiously. "It's an emergency. You know I wouldn't ask if I wasn't desperate. I just need a gig to hold me over until I sort something long-term."

Her mouth twists, and I already know what the answer is going to be.

"Please, Denise, I'll take whatever you've got."

"I don't have any server positions at any of the Murray venues right now." She furrows her brow. "I'm sifting through applications to fill the Exec Concierge position though. If you want to temp it, I can—"

"I'll take it." Jeez, I hate sounding so desperate and try to hide it behind a smile.

"It's a tough gig, Vic."

"I don't care. What do I have to do?"

Denise sighs loudly as if already regretting this. "Whatever Mr. Murray wants, you make sure he gets it. You'll liaise with his personal assistant, Lauren. Call her Miss Ingram, please. She's a power-hungry queen who likes to think that the Wraith is her ship, but she's got her finger on every button, and when she tells Mr. Murray she doesn't like something, it's goodnight before you can blink."

"Got it." My pulse is racing, and it isn't with gratitude that Denise has bailed me out. Again.

"You'll be taking a big job off my hands while I run the restaurant." Denise looks at me from beneath lowered brows like she hasn't quite stressed how important this is.

I nod. "When do I start?"

"Meet me here at one-thirty. I can get you fitted with a uniform and show you around before the shift starts."

One-thirty. I imprint the time on my brain as I thank Denise and step back out into the real world where smoke pours out of the drains and people don't apologize for barging into you while they're too busy talking on their phones to see what's right in front of them.

Mr. Murray. I'm going to be working for Caleb Murray, albeit temporarily, and I can't help remembering the touch of his hands on my arms when he stopped me from getting hurt outside the diner.

2

CALEB

I eat at my desk as usual. I barely taste the food most evenings. The chef knows what I like, and I leave it to him to prepare whatever he wants. I could be a diva about it, but I've got bigger things to worry about.

Like my brother Cash's nightclub getting raided again. Third time since the holidays, and no fucker can tell me it's a coincidence.

My phone vibrates. Another message from Olivia Dragonetti.

Tonight's the night, Caleb.

"Fuck!"

Olivia and I dated for a while back when the Wraith was first built, and I believed that a connection with her family would get me up the ladder without climbing the rungs in the middle.

It was fine for the first few months. Olivia Dragonetti has the kind of looks that got Elizabeth Taylor where she wanted to be. Raven-black hair, dark eyes, high cheekbones, she even has a tiny beauty spot on her upper lip that people mimicked centuries ago with silk patches.

But she's a girl who's used to getting what she wants, no matter how she gets it.

Her unannounced visits to the Wraith started happening more frequently, at all times of the day and night. Olivia would barge into my office, her eyes roaming the room while Lauren glared at her from the doorway, mouthing an apology for not warning me in advance. One morning, she was waiting for me to come down from the penthouse suite, completely naked in my leather chair, legs spread wide and feet on my desk.

"Surprise."

My brother Kyle had already warned me that she'd earned a bit of a bunny-boiler reputation when she followed her ex to his new girlfriend's apartment, waited for him to leave, and then broke in and shredded every item of clothing the woman possessed including the bathrobe she was wearing at the time, and wrote on her butt cheeks with black marker pen: NEXT TIME I WON'T BE SO NICE.

Olivia was seventeen at the time. And Daddy made the situation go away.

I tried ending our relationship the decent way. I told her that I wasn't ready for commitment, that I wanted to focus on my business, that we were both too young. The usual excuses. I even rolled out the typical it-isn't-you-it's-me cop out, although it was one hundred percent fucking her.

I didn't need that shit then.

I still don't need that shit now.

But she wouldn't believe me now even if I promised her that there was no one else. That there'd been no one else for five years, three months, and twelve fucking days, not that I was counting.

No one that lived up to Sandy anyways.

Sure, there'd been other one-night stands—I was only fucking human—but I'd had every private investigator in the city try to find Sandy for me, and every one of them had drawn a blank.

I was drunk that New Year's, but not so steaming that I don't remember every single part of Sandy's body. I can still taste her now. I can still hear her yelling at me, "I want you to let me come," like she'd already accepted that she was mine.

MINE.

And I didn't even realize how mine she was until I saw the specks of blood on the sheet when I woke up the next morning. Alone. I'd felt a surge of emotions that I immediately chalked up to a banging hangover tinged with guilt and something else I've still not managed to label. Suffice it to say though that Sandy made an everlasting impression on me, and I've long since given up trying to fight it.

My cock throbs inside my pants, and I adjust it while I open Olivia's message. That's one sure-fire way to make it grow limp.

Tonight's the night, Caleb.

What does that even fucking mean?

Even if Sandy was a pure figment of my imagination, I'm not stupid enough to date Olivia Dragonetti again. I like my cock exactly where it is and in one piece. I like my life. Contrary to what my brothers believe, I even enjoy eating dinner alone, before I head downstairs to the casino and watch the losers ramping up the zeroes in my bank account.

One day, another Sandy will come along, maybe, and I'll consider settling down and starting a family, but my kids sure-as-fuck are not having a Dragonetti Don as their favorite grandpa.

An email pops into my inbox.

The name Dragonetti makes my grilled lobster sour on my tongue. I guzzle cold water from the glass that arrived with my evening meal, a perfect crescent of lemon twisted onto the rim, before I read it.

The message is simple.

Old man Dragonetti wants a meeting here at the Wraith in an hour.

It isn't optional. Dress code formal. He has a proposal that he thinks will be beneficial to us both.

I sit back and push the sweet pink lobster flesh on my plate around with a silver fork. He's going to make me an offer that I can't refuse because it will mean the Rinse will stop being raided, and my brother's business will continue to flourish so long as I keep the old man happy. I have an hour to figure out my next move and make sure it's at least a couple steps ahead of the Italian family.

The problem is that Don Mateo Dragonetti has the New York City Police Commissioner in his pocket. He has personally funded the private island vacation retreats and country mansions of every member of the Board of Commissioners, and it's no secret that he funded the campaign of the current Mayor of the city.

An alliance between the two families would mean that the Murray brothers are untouchable. It's the best alliance we could ever hope to make, but like all good deals, it comes at a price, and Olivia's message is ringing the kind of alarm bells in my head that no amount of Louis XIII Cognac will erase.

I pick up the crisp white napkin with *Wraith* embroidered in black and gold in one corner to dab my lips, as a slip of Wraith-headed paper tumbles onto the tray. Curious, I pick it up and unfold it. The words 'Thank you' are written in neat cursive.

That's it. *Thank you.*

I turn it over—the back of the note is blank.

Standing, I cross the room and open the door, still holding the slip of paper in one hand. Lauren is seated at her desk outside my office. It's late, but if I'm working, she's working. It makes me feel like a prick sometimes, but Lauren is a bit of a control freak, and she doesn't trust anyone else to look after me if she isn't around. Besides, I pay her well, and I know she appreciates the all-expenses paid Caribbean cruise I send her on every year.

"Mr. Murray?" She's on her feet in an instant. She slides her gold-rimmed glasses back up her nose in a gesture so ingrained she no longer realizes that she's doing it. She's tall, slim, her natural honey-blonde hair now turning gray.

"It's okay, sit down, Lauren." I cover the distance between us in two easy strides and show her the thank-you note. "Any idea who this is from?"

She furrows her brow, her lips almost disappearing into her frown. "Where...? How did you get this?" She turns and peers around the empty office like the culprit might be hiding underneath a desk having somehow escaped the gatekeeper's attention.

"It was tucked inside the napkin on my food tray."

Her face pales, a pink flush spreading up her neck, and I wish I hadn't mentioned it. "I apologize, Mr. Murray. I'll speak to the new Executive Concierge immediately."

I hold out my hand, and she places the note back into my palm. "It's fine. No harm done."

"It absolutely isn't fine," she mutters under her breath as she sits back down. What's next? A party invitation? A request for a private conversation?"

The internal phone is already in her hand as I head back into my office. I scrunch up the note and toss it into the wastepaper basket as I resume my seat and send a curt response to Don Dragonetti.

I'm showered, shaved, and wearing a freshly laundered silver-gray suit, pale green shirt, and emerald-green tie when Lauren announces the don's arrival.

I open the door to greet Don Dragonetti and Olivia with an easy smile and firm handshake.

"Apologies for the short notice," the silver-haired man says without a hint of an apology in his tone.

"Caleb!" Olivia steps out from behind her father and hugs me tightly, kissing both cheeks, and entwining her right hand with mine before I can extricate it. She trails a perfectly manicured fingernail across my tie and settles on the dimple beneath the knot. "This color suits you. It picks out the green in your eyes."

"Olivia." I incline my head and gesture for her to sit with her father in the lounge area of my office. I already had Lauren arrange for the Concierge to bring up a bottle of cognac and some glasses while I was getting ready in my apartment.

I take a seat on the black leather couch across the glass-topped coffee table and pour brandy into three crystal tumblers, adding ice from a black cooler, no soda.

The don sips his cognac and releases a sigh, studying the amber liquid as if only slightly concerned that I might've watered it down or added arsenic to his glass. "Not bad." His lips are permanently turned down at the corners, and a quick glance at his daughter tells me that the expression has been passed down genetically. "You know why I'm here."

Small talk over.

I leave my glass on the table. I need a clear head for this conversation. "My brother's nightclub was raided again."

The don smiles, but it doesn't reach his eyes. Beside him, Olivia's eyes widen as though bewildered that I would even try to lead the discussion. "We have to feed the Commissioner some scraps, you understand."

Fucking scraps?

That's my brother's fucking nightclub he's talking about.

"Of course." Against my better judgement, and to stop my hand from balling into a fist that might just collide with his throat, I swallow a mouthful of cognac and track its journey all the way down. "What can we do to prevent this from happening again?"

Don Dragonetti sets his glass down on the low table and sits forward, elbows resting on his thighs. He has the decency not to rub his hands together like a common fairy tale miser. "I'm certain that we can come to some kind of arrangement, Caleb. One that will benefit both families."

It doesn't escape my attention that Olivia sidles closer to her father, a sly smile curving her mouth upwards as she twists several white-gold rings around her fingers.

"I'm listening."

"The Wraith would not be quite so appealing with the cops making regular visits to the casino on level fifty." There's no threat in the don's voice; he might be discussing plans to install a new chef in my restaurant. "A small monthly transaction should cover the cost of my expenses for seeing that it never happens."

"How small?"

The old man doesn't move. Instead, Olivia slides a silver business card out of her purse and places it on the table between us, face down. It would be far too vulgar to air the figure written on the reverse of the card to the entire room.

I flip over one corner and note the zeroes. I don't pick it up.

This isn't the real reason why they're here. The Dragonetti family has no need of my money, and the cops will never find anything in the Wraith that will give them a reason to shut down the operation. The don is saving the best for last.

I'm all ears.

"I'm sure that we could reach a suitable compromise." I contemplate my brandy and decide against draining the glass. For now.

A flicker of amusement dances across the don's eyes. "On one condition."

And there it is.

I wait for him to elaborate.

"My daughter has expressed a desire to be married. I'm not getting any younger, and I want to be around to play Santa at Christmastime for my grandkids."

Olivia's lips are moist and parted like she's about to seduce a chocolate-coated strawberry.

"Perhaps I'm not making myself clear," the don continues. "My daughter has expressed a desire to marry *you*, and I'm keen to make it happen as soon as possible." He raises his glass in a mock salute to the soon-to-be-betrothed couple and swallows his drink in one mouthful.

Olivia is practically buzzing with childlike anticipation, perched on the edge of the sofa and waiting for me to say, "I do."

"I appreciate the gesture," I say, standing up. "But I'm afraid I can't marry your daughter, Don Dragonetti."

I cross the room and open the door, praying that Lauren has been successful with the little task I sent her earlier before I headed up to the penthouse apartment. She studies me with pursed lips from behind her desk, her spectacles doing little to hide the disapproval in her eyes.

But it's the new Executive Concierge who causes my heart to do something that it hasn't done in a long while, fluttering out of synch and then chasing itself back into its regular rhythm.

Lauren wanted to fire her for the thank-you-note misdemeanor, but I had a better idea. I'd assumed that the woman was thanking me for giving her a job—even though Denise handles that side of the operation—and guessed that she'd jump at the chance to keep me happy if it meant hanging onto a monthly paycheck. But now I realize that I was wrong after overhearing her pleading her case outside my office door. It's the woman whose brother I saved from certain death on the sidewalk last night.

Only now, true to her word, Lauren has clothed her in a shimmering black dress that clings to her in all the right places. The woman in the server's apron has been replaced by someone glamorous, chestnut-brown hair tumbling over her shoulders in soft waves, her mouth curved into a tentative smile.

She has no idea why she's here. But she's about to find out.

I gesture for her to join me. Taking her hand in mine, I murmur, "Keep smiling," in her ear, and lead her into my office.

"Caleb?" Olivia stands up, her cheeks drained of color. "What's going on?"

Ignoring her, I address her father. "The reason I can't marry your daughter, Don Dragonetti, is because I'm already married. To Victoria."

3

VICTORIA

A THANK YOU NOTE.

What kind of asshole fires a member of his staff over something so petty? It was supposed to be a nice gesture, a way of thanking Mr. Murray for rescuing Mason, but then the arrogant asshole goes and ruins it by firing me on my first day on the job.

"Can I at least speak to him?" I ask his hard-faced assistant.

Denise wasn't wrong when she said the woman is a control freak. She stands between me and Mr. Murray's office door like she's half-expecting me to barge inside and call him a prick to his face. Because that would never do. She's obviously given herself the job title of Head of Security as well as Personal-fucking-Assistant.

"No. Mr. Murray is a busy man."

"I only wanted to thank him for last night." Realizing how that sounds, I quickly add, "He helped my brother. Outside the diner where I work. *Worked*." Jeez, how to screw myself over in less than a minute.

She stops trying to turn herself into a human barricade and peers at the tablet glued to her hand. Frown lines appear on her forehead. That must be some email she's reading because her knuckles go white around the edges of the tablet.

Finally, she looks at me as if wishing she'd dismissed me sooner. "Mr. Murray wishes to offer you another role." She might as well have said, "*If I had my way, you'd already be out the door with a signed promise never to return.*"

"Another role?"

"Yes."

Jeez, the woman doesn't make it easy. "What kind of role?"

"Mr. Murray will explain when he's ready, I'm sure. Follow me, and I'll see that you're suitably attired."

"Suitably attired?"

I follow her into a room and through another door into what can only be described as a walk-in closet. This room is lined with clothes, male and female, arranged in color order, with enough pairs of coordinating shoes to fill a shoe store; there are even purses and belts and wallets.

Miss Ingram gestures to a rack filled with little black dresses. "One of these should do. Come and find me when you're ready."

"Wait. Why do I need—"

But she's already gone.

I'm unsure about this. I mean, these dresses are not what I'd expect to wear to work. In fact, I've never owned anything this classy or expensive, and it occurs to me then that perhaps Mr. Murray runs a brothel masquerading as a swanky hotel, and my punishment for sending him a thank-you note is being sold to a client for the night.

Even so, I find a sparkling black dress and literally pour myself into it, studying my reflection in the mirror, and wondering if it's rigged to show a fake glamorous version of the person standing in front of it. I've never looked this good. I barely even recognize the face peering back at me, but I tell myself that Caleb Murray saved Mason, and he wouldn't throw me under the bus instead.

Would he?

Besides, I need the money.

Before I can talk myself out of it, I'm wearing the black dress and talking to Miss Ingram when the door to his office opens, and Caleb Murray is standing there in a suit and tie, gold highlights in his brown hair, and green eyes roaming me from head to toe.

Man, he looks even hotter than he did in a leather jacket. That chest... He for sure works out, and even now I'm imagining him straddling that sleek, black, panther-like Harley with me riding pillion.

So, when he offers me his hand and tells me to keep smiling, I walk into his office with him, heart thumping so crazily, that I think I misheard him when he tells his guests that we're married.

Wait! What the actual fuck just happened here?

As if sensing my reluctance to play along with whatever crazy game this is, Caleb squeezes my hand. My heart obliges by galloping away from me, my lips instinctively smiling at the silver fox and the stunning supermodel who are staring at me from the sofa like I've grown a second head. And ... is that a beauty spot on her upper lip?

Smile, I tell myself. This will all be over soon, and then you can go home and pretend it never happened.

Only Caleb is standing a little too close for comfort, and he smells so good, like freaking cookies, and the supermodel looks as if she wants to throttle me with her bare hands. Not so beautiful now that her expression is twisted into a warped sneer, her cruel intentions toward me manifesting themselves into features more suited to the wicked queen than the innocent princess.

"No." The supermodel shakes her head. "I don't believe you. I'd have heard about it if you were married."

"It was a small private wedding back home," Caleb says.

Okay, so he's still running with the fake-marriage story.

I keep smiling.

"No press involved. Just how we wanted it to be." He squeezes my hand again, and I nod along like one of those marionettes with the painted-on expressions that always freak me out.

Her eyes narrow, and she turns on Caleb. "You're lying. He's fucking lying, Dad." This is aimed at the silver fox. "Who even is she?" Her face contorts again like I'm nobody because I've managed to fly under her glossy-magazine radar.

My hackles are instantly up. Who does this woman think she is? Whatever has gone on between her and Caleb in the past doesn't give her the right to look at me as if I'm not worthy of his attention.

Jutting my chin, I toss my curls over my shoulder and lean so close to Caleb that my left breast rubs against his arm sending a shiver down my spine that I force myself to ignore. "I'm his wife, Victoria Murray." I almost choke on the absurdity of the statement, but my gaze remains fixed on hers.

"Show me the ring!"

I'm momentarily reminded of Abigail stomping her foot, dark curls bouncing around her face when she demands to stay up past bedtime and read more books.

"Olivia." The silver fox places a hand on his daughter's arm to placate her, but she shrugs it off.

Her face crumples then, and her eyes grow large with tears. "Caleb, tell me this isn't true." Okay, so this is how she's going to play it, now that throwing a tantrum isn't getting her anywhere. "Please, babe."

Babe? Ugh!

"I'm sorry, Olivia. I don't know what you wanted to hear tonight, but Victoria and I are very much married, and very much in love."

To prove it, Caleb leans over and kisses me on the lips.

It sends my heart hurtling over the precipice, and my brain cells reeling. No one else has ever kissed me that way, well, no one apart from Danny Zuko, and he only exists in my dreams these days. This situation, Caleb Murray pretending we're married, the beautiful guests with their suspicious eyes and angry hearts, Miss Ingram and her walk-in closet... It all vanishes when I feel his tongue sliding between my lips.

Olivia lets out a low animal-like groan.

Caleb releases me, and it's all I can do to remain standing.

"What about us, Caleb?" she whines.

"Olivia, there is no us." He slides an arm around my waist, and yep, his chest is every bit as solid as I thought it was.

"But I thought... We've always been so good together."

Somehow, even with the whining voice, Caleb remains calm. "We dated for six months, Olivia, and that was ten years ago."

"Okay." The silver fox stands up and raises both hands in a gesture of mock surrender. "I can see that we're done here. Thank you for your time, Caleb. It is unfortunate that we were unable to settle our business proposal as I'd hoped." He takes my left hand in his and raises it to his lips, his eyes noting the absence of a wedding ring. "A pleasure to meet you, Victoria."

The sound of my name on his tongue makes me shiver. I don't know why, but I'm left with the overwhelming sensation that I'd be happier if he didn't know who I was, but it's already too late for that.

He guides a tearful Olivia out the door, and I'm left standing in Caleb Murray's office with his hand around my waist.

When the door closes behind them, he pulls away and watches me with a curious expression on his face. He has green eyes I realize now with a stab of loss that makes my breath catch in my throat.

Stupid, I remind myself. *Stupid!* It was one night, nothing more was ever going to come of it. One amazing, passion-filled, night of the kind of sex most people only ever read about in books. It wasn't real life.

So, why do my eyes fill with tears when Caleb Murray says, "Thank you, Victoria. I should've warned you, but I didn't think you'd go through with it if you knew what I was going to do."

Damn fucking right I wouldn't have gone through with it!

"I'll return the dress," I find myself saying.

"Keep it."

His eyes roam the dress and then he grabs a glass from the coffee table and fills it with amber liquid from an expensive-looking bottle. Of course it's expensive like everything else in Caleb Murray's life.

"It suits you."

"What about the money?" Because, you know, this isn't my reality. I'm not married to Caleb Murray, and he fired me earlier over a dumb gesture that anyone else would've accepted with a smile of appreciation.

"I'll see that you get paid." He's still watching me as if he's only just realizing that he used me—a real live human being—to get a goddamned supermodel off his case. "I'll need you to sign an NDA with Lauren."

And that's what tips me over the edge. He'll send me on my way with a month's wages and a declaration of silence, and I'll still have no job, and rent to pay, while he sits here knocking back cognac with his tight-assed assistant playing havoc with people's lives.

"He knows we're not married."

That gets his attention. His gaze flickers from my face to the dress and back again. "Why do you say that?"

I raise my left hand and flash my naked ring finger. "No ring." I don't know who that guy was, and I don't care to know either, but he sure as hell means something to Caleb Murray.

It is unfortunate that we were unable to settle our business proposal as I'd hoped.

Caleb refills his glass without offering me a drink. "I'll buy you a ring."

"Why? We're not married."

"I need him to believe that we are."

"Why don't you just tell him that you don't want to marry his daughter?"

He looks at me then and shakes his head as if I'm a child who has been listening in on an adult conversation. "It isn't that simple."

"He can't force you to marry someone you don't love."

Now, I know I've said the wrong thing when he pinches the skin between his eyebrows and closes his eyes briefly. When he opens them again and speaks, his voice has become clipped, professional, back in control.

"I'll get my brother to draw up a legal marriage certificate. He can backdate it, and leak something to the press before Olivia gets to them.

"Whoa, hold on." How did this go from a private conversation to full-blown legal documents tying my name to that of Caleb Murray. "I'm not marrying you for real."

"It's just a document. It can be annulled once this blows over."

But I'm not listening. "It might just be a document to you, but to me, marriage is something I only want to do once in my life. When I meet a man and fall in love, I want it to be special."

"And I'm sure it will be." Caleb downs a second drink, grimacing as the burn hits. Man, I could do with one of those, but I'm fucked if I'm going to beg him for a drink. "This changes nothing, Victoria."

The way he says my name stops me in my tracks, like I've heard him say it before.

He holds his phone to his ear, and I'm jolted back to reality.

"Wait!" I pace the room, back and forth, avoiding eye contact with him because I bet that he always gets exactly what he wants with his sexy green eyes, and this girl is not going to be bullied into marrying a stranger. "It changes everything for me." I stop pacing and face him, keeping my eyes on his polished black shoes. "I can't do it. I'm sorry."

I head for the door, and he stops me with a warm hand on my arm, forcing me to look into his eyes. "Name your price, Victoria. All I want is a signature on the bottom of the marriage certificate."

Fuck! Why am I such a sucker for green eyes? I blame Danny Zuko.

"That's all?"

I'm thinking I'll maybe get enough out of him to cover my rent for the next few months until I can get another job and get my life back on track, and perhaps a little extra for Sienna. His hair has copper and gold highlights when it catches the light I notice now; the Universe dealt him a great hand when he was born. It must've taken one look at him and thought this one's going to shine like a goddamned star.

"I might need you to attend a couple events with me, to make it look convincing."

Ohhh... There are worse things a gal could do for money, I guess.

"Can I think about it?"

"Sure. Give me your answer in the morning." Then he hands me a goddamned business card.

Sienna is waiting for me when I get home.

"Where's Mason?" I shrug off my coat, dump my purse onto the table, and toe off my shoes.

"I don't know." Sienna eyes up the black dress, her gaze finally meeting mine. "Don't freak out, Vic, but the school called me when they couldn't get hold of you or Mason. Abigail had locked herself in the restroom because she took a projector apart and they told her it was a stupid thing to do. I had to coax her out with a promise to take her to the Museum of Modern Art this weekend."

Sienna can't help chuckling, and before long, we're both laughing out loud. Abigail is intelligent beyond her years, and this isn't the first time she's gotten into trouble at school, and she's only in kindergarten.

"What kind of teacher tells a kid they're being stupid?" It's a sobering thought, and I'll need to take it up with the head teacher.

"What's with the dress?" Sienna asks.

I smile. "I got married tonight."

4

CALEB

I sleep on it.

Or rather, I alternate between the kind of dreams that wake me up with a rock-hard cock grinding into my abdomen and long periods of staring at the sunken ceiling lights, with what happened in my office earlier in the evening playing on repeat inside my head.

The dreams... I thought I'd had them under control, but now, Sandy is back inside my head with a vengeance. I dreamed that she was bent over my desk, naked ass raised to reveal her wide-open wet pussy, while I spread her thighs and inserted the whole length of my tongue inside her from behind.

But then, after she came and I flipped her over to stick my cock in her mouth, Sandy was Victoria, her chestnut curls framing her flushed face.

I woke up face-down in my bed, drenched in sweat, my cock throbbing underneath me. What is it about Victoria that has resurrected the goddamned dreams? She looked fucking hot in that dress, hot enough to pour into a pair of black latex pants just in time for me to drag them down over her hips... I tried to imagine Victoria in a blonde curly wig begging me to let her come, and my cock started knock-knocking against the mattress all over again.

By six a.m. I'm showered and dressed in a dark-gray suit teemed with a pale-pink shirt and violet-colored tie. I stare at my reflection in the mirror. I'd enjoyed the jet-black Danny Zuko look, felt comfortable in the white T-shirt and leather jacket, had even practiced my 'Grease Lightning' moves before heading out on New Year's five years ago, incognito.

Just for one night, I'd wanted to ditch the Murray mask and trappings and live a little. It was my brother Kyle's idea. "Let's experience life from the other side of the table," he'd said. "Let our hair down without Lauren breathing down our necks."

It was so out-of-character for Kyle that I couldn't refuse. He was a year out of a serious relationship with a woman who broke his heart by cheating on him with a cop, and in that basement nightclub, I saw him smile again for the first time in what felt like forever. He went all out, dyed his hair a couple of shades darker blonde and donned turn-up jeans, a black leather bomber jacket and black shades. He danced like I'd never seen him dance before.

And then our lives changed in the blink of an eye...

The restaurant manager brings breakfast to my office. I don't know why, but I'm disappointed to find that it isn't Victoria wearing that little black dress that revealed nothing and yet promised everything.

My cock twitches in my pants and I inadvertently glance at Denise as she reaches the door. She hesitates. Turns around to face me, a question mark hanging over her.

"What is it, Denise?"

"The temp Exec Concierge..." She chews her bottom lip. "I apologize for whatever she did wrong yesterday, but would you reconsider letting her go?"

When it comes to managing the restaurants, I trust Denise to run them to the standards I demand, but in fifteen years of working for the family, this is the first time she has ever questioned a decision. Why? Or is she simply a sucker for a sob story?

I'm still waiting for Victoria to agree to the fake marriage proposal, but I have no doubts that she will. In which case, she no longer needs the job.

"No."

I see the flicker of frustration in her eyes before Denise thanks me and closes the door behind her as she leaves. I see it, and I do nothing about it. I have more pressing concerns right now, like what to do about the Dragonetti family.

Kyle's office is on the same level of the Wraith as mine, a mirror version of my own office with a mahogany desk instead of the black and chrome desk of my choice. The remnants of a bowl of oatmeal and fruit remain on the coffee table, and I'm greeted by the aroma of freshly brewed coffee from the machine on the counter against the wall.

"The marriage certificate is already drawn up," Kyle says from behind his desk.

"More coffee?" I go straight to the coffee machine.

This is my third cup of the day, and it's barely cutting through the fuzziness in my head. It's doing nothing for the throbbing ache inside my pants either.

"Sure." Kyle slides his cup across his desk. He waits for me to return with two steaming espressos before sitting back in his seat and watching me with hazel eyes that are not quite as green as Sandy's were. "So, Don Dragonetti…"

I smile. "…Wanted me to marry Olivia as a condition of the alliance."

Kyle immediately sits forward. "He knows she's a liability and wants someone to take her off his hands."

"Not someone. *Me*."

He sips his coffee and grimaces. I gave up years ago asking him why he insists on drinking coffee when he can't stand the taste of it, and his response was that drinking soda in board meetings undermined his status and gave clients the wrong impression of him.

"How did he take it?" he asks.

"As expected. Olivia, on the other hand…" I shrug.

"So, you handled the situation by telling them that you were already married."

He isn't judging me. Okay, maybe he is judging me a little, but Kyle knows me better than anyone else, including our mother, which means that he will understand that I had my reasons. Namely, Olivia Dragonetti.

"I couldn't think of another reason to not marry his daughter that Don Dragonetti wouldn't magic away with the snap of his fingers."

Kyle's nose twitches from side to side while he considers this. "You don't think that he'll pay your 'wife' to disappear?"

"I don't doubt that he'll try. We just need to give her a reason to stay."

"We?" Kyle's eyebrows slide into his hairline.

I smile. "Fair enough. *I* need to give her a reason to stay."

"What did you promise her?" Kyle slips easily into lawyer mode.

"Anything she wanted."

"*Anything*?" He scratches his left ear. "What did you say to her specifically?"

"Specifically, I believe I said, 'Name your price, Victoria'."

"To which she responded…?"

"'Can I think about it?'"

Kyle's fingers are tapping across his keyboard. "Okay, we need to draw up a prenup agreement. Set a limit, financially. We don't want her claiming fifty percent of the Wraith when you decide that Olivia has taken the hint and backed off."

When Kyle puts it like that, I suddenly see the whole fake proposal situation in a whole new light. It has been ten years since I dated Olivia. Our relationship barely lasted six months, and she still believes that I'll marry her someday.

What happens if she never backs off? There will be no alliance if Olivia continues to make it personal, but more importantly, what happens to Victoria, worst-case scenario?

"We'll offer her reasonable compensation." Kyle's words

barely penetrate my thought process. "What's her background?"

I think of the sidewalk brawl where I first set eyes on Victoria. "Her brother's a loser."

"Great."

"She ended up temping here. I think there's a connection to Denise Cartwright."

"Okay, I'll look into it." Kyle talks while he types. "A year's salary would be fair."

A year's salary sounds like a fucking kick in the teeth, even to me. I don't even know why I care. The woman obviously has baggage in the form of her loser brother, and she clearly can't hold down a job. But she stepped in when I needed her, no questions asked and didn't even demand on-the-spot compensation.

That's what it is, I tell myself. It has fuck all to do with how hot she looks in a little black dress, or the dream where she was bent over my desk while I fucked her from behind.

Nothing at all to do with that…

My phone rings. My brother Cassius, or Cash for short.

"Caleb, we have a problem."

I glance at Kyle. His fingers stop tap dancing across the keyboard when he spots my lowered brows. "Shoot."

"Olivia just waltzed in with an entourage."

Fuck! I thought it would take a little longer than twelve hours for her to start kicking off. "Keep her there." I end the call.

"Olivia is at the Titan." I stand up and stare at my phone as if I could draw out a message from Victoria through sight alone.

"Alone?"

"Sounds as if she brought back-up."

Kyle rolls his seat away from the desk and hands me an official document. "Basic prenup. I've kept compensation deliberately low. Gives us room to barter."

I glance at the figure Kyle has included in the document. I'll remind him to add a couple of zeroes when I'm finished with Olivia. Leaving the agreement on the desk, I walk to the door, Kyle behind me, his limp only noticeable these days because I know it's there.

"Caleb, don't do anything rash. We want the Dragonetti family on our side."

I don't ask him if that includes Olivia.

Cash's casino and Titan resort sits just outside the city, unmissable from Newark airport, as the name suggests. It's a goliath of a building and a blueprint for the kind of Vegas-worthy resort that offers visitors everything they could possibly want under one roof and subsequently ensures that their cash remains in-house.

Where the Wraith is sleek and black and sexy, the Titan was designed with Hollywood glamor in mind. The fifty-story hotel was constructed with specially created blocks that provide a golden sheen even when the sun is hiding, the rooftop sign is the largest in the entire country. Cash's brief for the architects was bold and brash, and they delivered.

When my driver pulls up outside the entrance, it's easy to pick out the folks visiting the Titan for the first time. They generally have their heads tilted toward the sky, phones raised to capture the golden building in all its morning glory.

Terry, my stepfather, is waiting for me at the entrance. Now in his early sixties, he still wears his trademark outfit of black tailored suit and black jersey sweater and could easily pass for a man fifteen years his junior. He's a formidable figure, and he knows it.

He could've handed over the reins to the empire he built from scratch to his stepsons, walked away, and lived out his days on one long sunny vacation with my mom, but pride in what we've all achieved, and an ingrained mistrust of anyone who isn't family, keeps him rocking up every day as Head of Security. He tours all three resorts based in and around the city, making sure that his team are well-dressed, well-mannered, and well-armed. He spots a smudge on a suit lapel, and the guilty party is sent away with a final warning not to let him down again or suffer the consequences. To date, I've never known anyone receive a second warning from Terry ... and live to tell the tale.

He greets me with a nod. "She's in the exec casino. We've cleared the area."

I can't help smiling. Terry knows how long we've been waiting to form an alliance with the Dragonettis, but he won't take any crap from anyone, not on his turf.

He walks with me, and I'm the one matching his stride. He could walk through this building with his eyes shut and probably still recall every punter at every table. The main floor, a glitzy, gaudy area with blood-red carpets and the obligatory gold accessories, that still manages to pull off looking classy, is filled with people who have no doubt been seated around the same tables all night. They're oblivious to the drama unfolding in the executive area. Drama prevents them from spending money, and we're not in business for the sheer fun of it.

When I enter, Olivia looks up from the roulette table with wide eyes that say I-knew-you'd-come. Her 'entourage' as Cash put it, stands and surrounds her, giving her the appearance of a queen and her army.

Terry waits outside. He'll step in if required, but he understands that I want to deal with this discreetly.

"Caleb." Olivia pouts glossed bottom lip rolling out in her best Shirley Temple expression. "Why so serious?"

I make eye contact with the men in dark suits and black turtleneck shirts as I approach the table; I'm surprised they didn't complete the ensemble with reflective wraparound Ray-Bans. They might be employed by Don Dragonetti, but they won't aim first and risk bringing the wrath of the old Don down on their heads. No matter what Olivia believes.

"Why are you here, Olivia?"

Her perfectly shaped eyebrows lower and her eyes darken. When we dated, it only ever took a mistimed comment or a glance at another woman for the transformation from angel to demon to take place. Because of the Dragonetti name, I overlooked it to begin with, telling myself that I was imagining it, that all Olivia needed was attention to keep her emotionally stable.

I was wrong.

"No law against chancing my luck on the roulette table, is there?"

"None whatsoever." I keep my voice level. "So long as you have the funds to begin with."

Her glossy crimson lips stretch into a dazzling smile. I've seen her use it in the past to get what she wants because it always worked on Daddy. "Caleb, you know I'm good for the money." Her voice drips honey.

I reciprocate the smile. "So, why did you demand 100k markers on my account, Olivia?"

The smile stretches into something no longer pleasant, something altogether more sinister, before she tips her head back and laughs. "What's 100k between lovers, huh?"

"We're not lovers. I'm married. I told you this last night, Olivia."

Olivia sashays towards me, her silk pants swishing between her legs and the matching jacket revealing that she's wearing nothing underneath. On anyone else, it would look sexy, the swell of her breasts between the white lapels, but on Olivia, it's an instant red flag—she does nothing unless it benefits Olivia Dragonetti in some way.

When she's standing in front of me, she traces my jawline with a scarlet fingernail decorated with tiny diamantes. "And I told you that I don't believe you." Our mouths are so close that she pokes out her tongue and licks my lips.

I take her hands and hold her at arm's length. The honey vanishes, replaced by narrowed eyes filled with venom. "You'd better get used to the idea, Olivia. I'm in love with Victoria, and this—" I gesture to the men standing behind her "—isn't going to change anything. It's time to move on."

"I'm not giving you up without a fight, Caleb!" Her voice becomes shrill, and she raises a hand to slap my face.

But Terry is there before her palm can connect with my cheek. "Okay, fun time is over. Time to leave."

He escorts her towards the door, Olivia yelling at him, "Get your fucking hands off me. Wait till my father hears about this."

"Enough, Olivia." I flank her on the other side, while Terry keeps right on moving as if he never even heard the threat.

"Caleb, please," she whines, switching on a pin. "Don't do this. Can we talk about it somewhere private?"

"There's nothing left to say, Olivia."

She struggles to free herself from Terry's iron grip, with no success. "You'll fucking regret this, Caleb. My father will never forgive you for this…"

The men in black follow her outside, and I close the door behind them.

I know this isn't the end of it, but Olivia Dragonetti isn't going to win.

5

VICTORIA

I sleep heavily and wake up feeling groggy and lethargic. The events of the evening before feel like a movie scene that I watched with one foot in that hazy dream-world between sleep and being awake. I only know that it was real when I spot the shimmering black dress draped over the chair in front of my dressing table.

Caleb Murray wants me to pretend to be his wife.

Caleb Murray.

I squeeze my eyes shut and clench my fists like a child waking up on Christmas Day excited to see what Santa left under the tree. I mean, he's one of New York's most eligible bachelors. He's a billionaire. *A fucking billionaire*. And of all the women in the city he could've chosen to fake-wed, he chose me.

"What's wrong?" a small voice asks. "Are you sick?"

"No, sweetie." I roll over and stroke the hair away from Abigail's flushed face, still smiling.

"Are you angry with me for breaking the projector?" Her bottom lip rolls out, and her eyes grow large with tears.

I pull her into me, and hold her tightly, relishing the warmth of her small body next to mine. "No, Abigail, I'm not angry with you. You didn't mean to break the projector, did you?"

"No. It was already broken. I was trying to fix it, but Mrs. Lawrence said I shouldn't have touched it, and it was my fault it wouldn't work."

I have to push Caleb Murray out of my head until this is resolved. Abigail is more important than a silly projector, and it occurs to me then that I could ask Caleb Murray to replace the kindergarten equipment for me. He wouldn't even miss the money. It would be like candy money to someone like him.

But firstly, I need to find Mason and speak to Mrs. Lawrence about getting Abigail reinstated back in kindergarten. She can't have this on her record all through her education. She's a bright kid, brighter than most kids her age, and it isn't her fault that the teachers don't know how to handle her. But most importantly, I need to address the use of the word 'stupid' when addressing a five-year-old child.

I scramble eggs for our breakfast, while singing along to old pop songs on the radio channel. It surprises me that Abigail seems to know all the lyrics to songs that were released in the last century. Where does she even learn this stuff?

"Auntie Sienna likes this song," she says when Cher starts belting out 'Believe'.

That's where she learns this stuff.

I try calling Mason, but the call goes straight through to his voicemail. I don't leave a message; I don't want Abigail to hear the panic I know I won't be able to keep from my voice.

Where is he? I can't believe that he left Abigail alone in the apartment last night. Sure, she was asleep, but anything could've happened to her—my pulse races just at the thought of all the terrible things that you read about in the news. I'm just grateful that she's alright.

Locking Mason away in the same corner-cupboard of my mind as Caleb Murray, I get Abigail dressed and we take the subway to the school.

I'm nervous about meeting Mrs. Lawrence. She's a stout woman who wears her hair pulled back into a severe bun, no makeup, and ugly practical shoes with patterned socks. It's my bad that she always reminds me of Miss Trunchbull from *Matilda*.

Abigail has no such anxiety. She keeps up a steady stream of chatter all the way there, hardly pausing to breathe. She doesn't even need me to respond, which is just as well as my mind keeps wandering to the feel of Caleb Murray's tongue in my mouth.

Mrs. Lawrence greets me with a limp handshake, not quite what I expected. It does nothing to ease my nerves though. Mason still hasn't called me back, and I should've given my decision to Caleb already.

"Abigail." Mrs. Lawrence peers at us from behind her desk, pudgy fingers entwined. "Do you have anything that you would like to say?"

"She didn't break the projector—" I begin until the head teacher cuts me off with a look that would splinter glass.

"I would like Abigail to answer the question."

Okay...

"I was trying to fix it," Abigail says, and my heart melts at the confidence with which she addresses the older woman. I decide on the spot that I will kill anyone who tries to bully this confidence out of her. "Because it was broken."

"Hmm." Mrs. Lawrence turns her attention back to me. "You understand that this was an expensive piece of equipment that the school will now have to replace."

"I think I can help with that." I *hope* I can help with that, if only one of the wealthiest men in the city doesn't go back on his promise.

Mrs. Lawrence's mouth quirks to one side like she seriously doubts I have that kind of money to hand over.

I'm so sick of being the person who works hard and never gets anywhere that my fingers automatically flex, and adrenaline pumps through my veins.

"I want to talk about Abigail being told that she was doing something stupid." I clear my throat; this is no time to sound feeble and puny. "What she did wasn't stupid. She has this knack of fixing things around the home, like toys and plugs and..." Stop rambling and get to the point, I admonish myself. "And even if it was a stupid thing to do, it isn't acceptable for a teacher to use that word in front of a child."

Mrs. Lawrence's expression doesn't falter. "Are you quite finished, Miss Callahan?"

I nod, having already run out of steam.

"In cases like Abigail's, in my experience at least, regular elementary schools have neither the funding nor the resources to challenge the child and help them to grow. The child subsequently gets bored, and then, in time, gets labelled a troublemaker."

Wait, it almost sounds like she's on our side.

"Despite what you might believe, I have Abigail's best interests at heart," she continues.

"You do?"

"I've taken the liberty of gathering some information for the Lutheran Preparatory Academy." She slides some leaflets across the desk towards me, and I pick them up moving on autopilot. "The school will be more suited to Abigail's advanced needs." Pause. "Unfortunately, it is not government funded."

My stomach twists as I study the images of young children with smiling faces on the leaflets in my hand. What Mrs. Lawrence is saying is that this is going to cost me more money that I don't have.

Yet.

By the time Abigail and I are standing on the sidewalk outside the school, I've already made up my mind.

We wander into Central Park, find a bench and sit down. While Abigail feeds the birds with a bag of crumbs that I brought with us, I slide the business card from my pocket and message Caleb Murray.

Okay, I'll do it.

His reply comes straight back to me.

How soon can you get here?

Shit!

I try calling Mason, but his calls are still going straight through to voicemail. I text him: *Call me back. It's urgent!* Nothing.

I try Sienna next. As bad as I feel for always falling back on my best friend, Sienna is like a second mom to Abigail, and I trust Sienna with her more than I trust Mason. But she isn't picking up either. Then I remember that she has a meeting with an art gallery that might want to showcase one of her paintings. I quickly type out another message and hit send:

Good luck!

I scroll through my list of contacts which mostly consists of ex-employers and people I've worked with and fallen out of touch with. It doesn't usually bother me that I'm not like other women who have a vast friendship group, people they meet up with once a week and chat with on the phone every day. But right now, with Abigail suspended from kindergarten, it means that I'm stuck for someone to look after her.

Unless... I wonder if Denise will watch Abigail for half an hour if I take her with me to the Wraith. She can sit at a quiet table with a bowl of ice cream and a reading book, and she'll be fine.

I type out a message to Denise—*Sorry, I need another favor*—and then delete it. I've already pushed my luck too far, and I didn't even get a chance to explain to Denise why I got fired, so I figure it will be best to rock up with Abigail and talk to her face to face.

"How do you fancy going to a posh hotel for ice cream?" Okay, so I'm assuming that ice cream will be on the menu, but I'm not lying about the posh hotel bit.

"What flavor ice cream?" Abigail studies me intently.

She'll recall this conversation word-for-word when we arrive, and if it doesn't pan out just like I said, it will throw her all out of synch, which will make it harder for me to settle her down at bedtime. But what choice do I have?

"What flavor do you want?"

Her mouth scrunches up to one side while she ponders her favorite ice cream. "Pistachio."

Pistachio?

"Sure. It's a fancy hotel. They'll have every flavor ice cream you can think of." Please, God, I thin,k let them have fucking pistachio or at least let them have a chef who can whip some up in five minutes.

"What flavor do *you* want?" The question takes me by surprise.

"Sweetie, I have to go to a meeting with the man who owns the hotel, so I won't be getting ice cream."

"Is it a meeting about a job?" She jumps off the bench and waits for me to do the same.

Tears sting my eyes. Abigail doesn't miss a thing. "Yes, it is. So, I'll need you to be extra-good for my friend Denise."

"Who's Denise?"

She slips her hand into mine and we walk through the park heading towards Manhattan. "A nice lady I've known all my life."

"How come I've never met her before?"

"Because she's very busy."

This seems to satisfy her, and I try to quell my racing pulse the closer we get to the gleaming black spear of a hotel looming above the skyline.

"You're not wearing your interview clothes," she says when FAO Schwarz comes into view.

I peer down at my faded jeans and puffer jacket. She's right. But I don't have the time or the energy to go home and come back again; I'm afraid that I'll talk myself out of what I'm about to do, and Abigail needs this. Sienna needs this.

We all do.

Because now that Caleb Murray has offered me a lifeline out of this way of life, I can't imagine an alternative future without it, much to my own chagrin. But you know what, he chose me for a reason and, like the poker player bluffing his way through a round, I'm going to play it for all I'm worth.

"This is a different kind of interview." I grip her hand more tightly. "I can... I can wear whatever I want." Abigail isn't the typical five-year-old who will buy into any story I tell her; it has to be believable.

Fifteen minutes later, we stand outside the Wraith, and she tilts her head back to stare at the top. "Why is it black?"

"I guess the owner wanted it to look different than all the other buildings."

Abigail looks all around and shrugs. "They should've made it smaller then."

I can't argue with that kind of reasoning.

My heart is racing when we step inside. The young woman behind the reception desk takes one look at Abigail and her eyes widen as if she's already imagining fingerprints on every surface.

I approach her with a chin-jutting confidence that I don't feel and hope that Abigail doesn't mention ice cream. I don't want to freak the woman out any more than she already is.

"I'm here to see Denise Cartwright." I smile like this is a regular occurrence. Nothing to worry about at all.

She scans her computer screen, deliberately avoiding eye contact with either of us. "Ms. Cartwright isn't on site today."

"She isn't? Where is she?"

She turns gray-blue eyes my way. No smile. "She's at the Titan until six p.m." It's obvious from her tone that she thinks it's none of my business.

"Okay." My mind is galloping at an even faster pace than my heart.

What do I do now? Turn around, walk away, and hope that Caleb Murray doesn't find someone else to replace me? There must be hundreds of women better suited to the role of a billionaire's wife than I am, and he probably knows all of them. But I can't do that.

One glance at Abigail's huge brown eyes peering up at me, and I know that isn't an option. This is her future at stake here too.

I have no choice. "I have a meeting arranged with Caleb Murray."

The woman opens her mouth and closes it again, swallowing whatever it was that she was going to say. Her eyes slide back to the screen in front of her. "There's nothing in Mr. Murray's diary."

I doubt that, but I keep this observation to myself. Spine straight. Try to look like I have as much right as anyone else to be here. "Can you please tell him that Victoria is here to see him?"

"I..." Her eyes settle on the top of Abigail's head briefly. "I don't think—"

"Victoria *Murray*." I emphasize the last name. It gets the reaction I was hoping for.

She raises the phone to her ear, turns away, and says, "Miss Ingram, there's a Victoria Murray here to see Mr. Murray."

I can imagine Miss Ingram's face right now. But she must be expecting me too, because the receptionist tells me to take a seat and Mr. Murray's personal assistant will be down shortly.

Less than a minute later, the elevator door opens, and Miss Ingram steps out, eyes hard as stones and lips forming a narrow line. She falters when she spots Abigail standing beside me, her hand in mine.

"What's this?"

I knew there was a reason why I didn't like Miss Ingram.

"This is Abigail." I force a smile. "My niece."

"Can we get pistachio ice cream now?" Abigail asks, choosing her moment.

6

CALEB

My smile fades when I see the kid with Victoria.

They look as if they've spent the day on the streets in puffer jackets and jeans, rosy-cheeked, and hair mussed up by the late-winter breeze. Victoria watches me wide-eyed, clearly uncertain how I'll react to the news that she has a kid. Would I have signed up for this if I'd known in advance? The way my cock is aching at the sight of her, I think I already have my answer.

But this ... changes things. The world of a mafia boss isn't exactly the kind of world you want to bring a kid into. I want kids one day. One day when I'm ready to walk away from this life.

"I'm sorry, Mr. Murray." Miss Ingram grabs my attention, and I can't help smiling to myself. I can picture her face when she saw the dark-haired kid with the woman she fired yesterday. "If I'd known in advance... I'll speak to Roxanne at the reception desk."

"It's fine, Lauren."

I don't take my eyes off Victoria. Something about the way she's looking at me makes me want to do things to her that would traumatize the kid for life, not to mention get me arrested.

Victoria waits for the door to close behind Lauren before she says, "I'm so sorry. I didn't have anyone to watch Abigail. Her dad has gone AWOL, and my best friend has an important meeting with an art gallery today that I couldn't ask her to cancel because she's waited so long for this opportunity and, well, I didn't want to keep you waiting." Her voice dips at the end like she's burnt herself out getting this all off her chest.

But I'm still dwelling on the words *her dad has gone AWOL*.

What the actual fuck.

What kind of asshole does that to their woman and kid? You don't impregnate a woman and then continue to live like a bachelor, especially a woman like Victoria. She deserves better. So does the kid.

"What's his name?" My voice sounds husky even to my own ears. I clear my throat, grateful that at least my cock has responded badly to the news also.

"What?" Victoria furrows her brow. "Who?"

"Her dad." My gaze flickers to the child who has Victoria's hair and eyes and already promises to be a beauty when she's older. "You said he's gone AWOL."

Victoria sucks on her bottom lip, and I have the overwhelming urge to take it between my teeth and stick my tongue in her mouth.

"Mason Callahan."

I press the button on the landline handset, and Lauren answers before it even rings on her desk. "Are they ready to leave, Mr. Murray?"

"No, Lauren. I want you to find a guy called Mason Callahan for me."

"Where is he?"

"If I knew the answer, I wouldn't ask you to look for him."

I end the call and walk around the desk to face Victoria. Before I can speak, her shoulders slump, and tears collect on her bottom lashes. "Thank you. I'm worried that he's gotten himself into serious trouble."

The prick doesn't deserve her worry, but I keep this to myself. When I find him, I'll pay him to disappear until this is all over. I can't have him making this difficult for us, and it's too late to start over, not when Olivia will go out of her way to prove that I'm not legally married.

"Does he know about us?"

She blinks back the tears like she doesn't understand the question. "Us?"

"Us, Victoria. You and me. Our contract that you agreed to earlier. Are you still together?"

"Together?"

How else can I put it? "Do you live together? Is he going to sell his story to the press and try to swindle me for a couple million bucks?"

"I..." She shakes her head. "Mason wouldn't do anything like that."

"You're sure about that, are you?" It comes across way harsher than I intended, and I instantly regret it when she backs away from me.

"It's fine. I get it."

Her tone is cold, and I want warm Victoria back. I want the woman in the black dress who kissed me with her eyes closed. The woman who appeared in my dream with her legs spread wide and her butt in the air, ripe and wet, just waiting for me to fuck her.

"You've changed your mind because you don't want any trouble." She swallows hard. "Maybe you should've thought about that before you got involved with Olivia Dragon-face and dragged me into it. I thought that you were a man of your word, Caleb Murray. I guess we were both wrong."

The disappointment in her voice cuts straight through my chest and slices me open. No one ever questions my authenticity—I say I'm going to do something, I do it, no matter the consequences because I'm generally three steps ahead of everyone else, and the consequences are what I make them.

She goes to walk away, and I grab her arm, but she flinches away from me as if stung, staring at her arm still clad in the puffer jacket. "Wait. Look, I wasn't expecting you to show up with a kid. I don't want her to be involved in this. It's, well, let's just say that this is no environment for a kid."

"Too late, Caleb. She just got kicked out of kindergarten, and I need the money to send her to a different school."

"She got kicked out of kindergarten?" I'm waiting for the punchline that doesn't come. "How is that even possible?"

"Why do you care?" She sucks in a deep breath and releases it slowly. "Don't worry about it. It's not your problem."

She's right, it isn't my problem, so, why am I so reluctant to let her go?

"I want to help," I find myself saying.

I'm so close to her that I can smell the sweet lime and coconut scent of her shampoo. Without realizing what I'm doing, I take a lock of her hair and rub it between my fingers, stopping myself before I raise it to my nose like some kind of pervert with a hair fetish.

"How much do you need?" My voice is husky again.

"I don't need anything from you, Mr. Murray."

She straightens her spine, and I catch a glimpse of the fighter in her. Not the woman who jumped into a fight to save her loser brother, but the woman who is determined to succeed no matter what life throws at her. And it's obvious it's throwing some stinking shit her way right now, shit that I have no intentions of adding to.

"I'll find another way to fund Abigail's education."

She tries to sidestep around me, and I block her path, backing her up against the wall.

Instinct kicks in, and I place my hands on the wall on either side of her head, my face so close to hers that I can feel her warm breath on my cheek. She doesn't fight it. Instead, her eyes lock onto mine, and I'm reminded again of Sandy's eyes with the green and amber flecks sparking out from dilated pupils.

Sandy...

The name is on the tip of my tongue, and I swallow it before it can escape. I don't know why, but I don't want Victoria to know about Sandy. She's already met Olivia, and I've already slid a few feet down the slippery slope in her estimation without calling her by another woman's name.

"Stay." My lips caress hers.

"Why?"

"Because we have an agreement."

She lowers her eyes, and I realize that I'm losing her.

"And because I want you to stay."

She peers directly into my eyes again. "Even with Abigail," she whispers.

"Even with Abigail."

I must be crazy, but my lips are on hers, and she's kissing me back. I pin her to the wall with my body, raising her arms above her head with one hand, and unzipping the coat with the other.

"Stop." She twists her mouth away from me. "Abigail."

Fuck! I'd gotten so carried away that I'd forgotten all about the kid.

I pull away, my pants stretching over the bulge in my boxers which, thankfully, is covered by my jacket.

When I turn around, I find the kid, Abigail, sitting on one of the sofas with my tablet in her lap, the glare of the screen reflecting off her cheeks. "What are you doing?" I cross the room in three strides, panic coursing through my veins. The damage she could do if she hit the wrong key...

"Abigail?" I can hear the horror in Victoria's voice even though she's behind me, and I can't see her. "Where did you find the tablet?"

"On the desk." The kid glances at my desk like I'd left it sitting there so she could play with it. "I'm playing Solitaire."

Fucking Solitaire? How does she even know what Solitaire is? What do they teach kids at kindergarten these days?

Victoria reaches the sofa before I do. Sitting beside Abigail, she studies the screen, a smile lighting up her face. "Are you winning?"

"Sure. I win every time."

"You do, huh?" Victoria peers up at me. "She's only playing a game. No harm done."

"Did you touch anything else?" I ask Abigail.

"Nope."

Then it dawns on me that the tablet was locked when she picked it up. It's always locked. "How did you unlock it?"

"I figured out your pin while you were kissing." She barely even glances up from the screen.

Victoria sucks hard on her bottom lip to suppress the chuckle threatening to explode.

"How did you figure out my pin, Abigail?" She's like a mini version of Victoria sitting beside her, too young to even know how to switch on a tablet.

"Easy. It's the street number of the hotel."

"You worked that out all by yourself?"

Victoria's head moves from side to side following the conversation as though she's watching a tennis match.

"Yes." Abigail doesn't even glance up from the game she's playing.

Something about the kid has piqued my curiosity. She's been kicked out of kindergarten, I assumed for being naughty, and here she is playing Solitaire on my tablet which she hacked into while I was thinking about bending her mom over and screwing her from behind. "Can I see?"

I skirt around the sofas and sit on the other side of her so that she's squashed between me and Victoria. She's already close to completing the game, but a quick glance tells me that she has missed a card.

"There." I point to the eight of hearts. "This card can be moved."

"Not yet." Abigail continues to flick through the deck on the screen until she comes across the card she's obviously been waiting for. One move, and I can see that the game is wide open for her to clear up.

"How did you do that?"

"I watch the cards."

"You watch the cards?"

If she's telling the truth, the kid is a genius. The kind of client we look out for in the casinos and try to curb before they clean out the banker. The kind of person we could always use on our side.

"Did you know she could do this?" I lean forward and address Victoria while Abigail starts another game.

"Abigail is very bright." Victoria keeps her voice low and her eyes on the tablet. "She was suspended from kindergarten for dismantling an expensive projector."

"It was broken," Abigail interjects.

"The head teacher suggested that the Lutheran Prep Academy would be better suited to her ... talents."

"How old is she?" I ask.

"I'm five." Abigail peers up at me, and I get the feeling that she's sizing me up and deciding whether to trust me or not.

"I'm impressed, Abigail. Who taught you to hack into computer equipment?"

"No one. I taught myself."

"She watches YouTube videos," Victoria says.

"I'll pay for her to get into the Academy." I'm not just doing this for Victoria now. With the right tuition, the kid would be an asset to the Murray family business when she's older, and there are way too many shysters out there who would exploit her if they knew what she could do. "A talent like this needs nurturing."

"Whoa." Victoria is on her feet in an instant. "What's going on here?"

"Nothing." I stand up; it's a tough habit to break, needing to be the one doing the intimidating. "The kid—*Abigail*," I correct myself, "needs someone looking out for her."

"You think I don't know that?"

"That's not what I said."

"It's how it sounded." Victoria's hands are balled into fists. "When we walked in here, you were worried about Mason ruining your scheme to get your ex off your back, and now you're acting all protective like we haven't done alright without you so far."

"What's wrong with wanting to protect you?" I don't understand how Victoria is twisting this around and acting like I'm the monster here when the kid's dad has vanished like a genie in a bottle as soon as the going gets tough. "I take care of what's mine, Victoria."

"Why?" Her cheeks are flushed, and it isn't just because she's still wearing her coat. She lowers her voice and turns away from Abigail so that she can't hear what's being said. "Why do you want to protect her? What's in it for you, huh?" She doesn't add that Abigail isn't mine—she doesn't need to.

"I get my ex off my back as you so rightly pointed out."

Victoria shakes her head. "There's more to it than you're letting on." She glances at Abigail, and her expression immediately softens. "She has me to look out for her. The deal is off. Come on, Abigail. We're leaving." She holds out her hand for the kid to take.

"Can we get ice cream now?"

"Don't leave, Victoria." What am I doing? There must be an easier way to stop Olivia, but short of forcing her upon one of my brothers, I can't think of anything else right now. "Look, don't get me wrong, her talents in a casino... Hell, I could make a fuck-load of money out of her. But that's not what's going on here."

"You cussed," Abigail pipes up. "You need to put money in the cussing jar."

"The cussing jar?" I can't help smiling even if it isn't reciprocated by Victoria. "Please don't back out now. I want to help you. Both of you."

"You think you can get Abigail into the Academy?"

"I know I can." Say it with confidence; it works every time.

"And you'll find my brother too?"

"Your brother?" It's my turn to be confused.

"Mason. Abigail's dad."

Mason Callahan. I was so taken aback when Victoria walked in with Abigail that I didn't even register the name when she said it. The brother who got into a sidewalk brawl is Abigail's father. I don't know how that happened, or where her mom is, but I'm guessing Victoria is the one who cares for her much of the time as well as working God knows how many jobs to pay the bills.

And suddenly, I realize that I'm not even fazed by the kid's presence in this relationship. *Fake* relationship I remind myself.

"Yes, I'll find Mason. Now, who wants ice cream?"

7

VICTORIA

We sit at a table in the restaurant that I'm guessing is usually reserved for Caleb and his guests. He sits facing the other tables with an unobstructed view of the entrance, while Abigail and I sit with our back to the room. No one comes over to greet him—perhaps the staff are under orders to ensure that he isn't interrupted—but I sense that he knows every time a customer moves, exactly what each table ordered, and how much their bill came to.

All while paying attention to me and Abigail.

For a short time, he makes me feel like we're the only people who exist in the entire world, ordering a second helping of pistachio ice cream for Abigail when she proudly declares that her first dish is empty.

"Victoria and I need to discuss something important."

He looks her directly in the eye when he speaks, and I find myself wondering if he has nieces and nephews too. For a billionaire businessman, he seems to know how to be on her level so that she trusts him, and my heart does that funny, fluttery thing that only belongs in romance novels and rom coms.

"Is it Auntie Vicky's new job?" Abigail scrapes the bottom of the dish with a silver spoon and only peers at him when she's quite satisfied that the only way she'll get any more is by licking the bowl.

Caleb smiles and sets my heart off all over again. Perfect green eyes, perfect hair, perfect smile; did anything even remotely flawed ever land in his lap?

Yeah, me. The thought pops into my head unbidden, and I hide my face behind my perfect glass of iced water.

"Yes, it is." A server appears at the table even though I never saw Caleb gesture for her to come. "Would you like to go with Frankie and bake cookies?"

"Where?"

It's something I've noticed more and more frequently with Abigail as she gets older, she likes to know the order of events so that she knows what to expect. Caleb has saved the day by giving her the pistachio ice cream I promised her earlier, but she won't forget that I told her she'd meet Denise at the hotel. I'll have to deal with that one later.

"In the kitchen." Caleb lowers his head so that he's on a level with her and points at the swinging doors through which another server is backing into the restaurant balancing a tray of food on one shoulder. "Just through there. Our cookie chef makes the best cookies in the world."

"How do you know they're the best?"

"Because I've tried all the other cookies, and believe me,

they're not as good." He pauses, shoots me a look to ask if he's doing okay, and I nod. "Would you like that?"

"Can I eat the cookies I make?"

"Sure, so long as you save some for me and Victoria."

Abigail frowns at him. "Why do you call her Victoria?"

"Because that's her name." He sits back in his seat.

"Everyone else calls her Vicky or Vic."

Caleb smiles at me. "What do you think I should call her then?"

Abigail ponders the question for several moments. "Vicky." She stands up and walks around the table to the server. "My name is Abigail. Pleased to meet you, Frankie."

My heart melts as it always does whenever Abigail uses her manners. I watch her follow Frankie through the swinging doors to the kitchen and almost hit the ceiling when Caleb's hand covers mine.

"Sorry." He moves his hand. "I didn't mean to make you jump. She's a great kid."

"Even when she isn't counting cards and hacking into your computer equipment." Maybe I should rein it in a little until he has transferred the money into my bank account for Abigail's education, but my mouth has this habit of speaking before it engages with my brain. Perhaps Abigail is more like me than I realized."

But Caleb laughs, and for one fleeting moment, I can hear it again. Danny Zuko appearing in front of me, that goofy smile on his face when he spots the blond wig and the painted-on pants. "*Sandy?*"

What is it about him that has dragged that memory kicking and screaming back to the surface and is now refusing to let it go?

"She's a credit to you." He holds my gaze, and I'm transfixed by those green eyes.

"What did you want to talk about?" I ask eventually.

"My brother has drawn up the marriage contract."

Now, I understand why this table is reserved for him—the tables nearest to ours are all empty so that no one can listen in on his conversations.

"He has also drawn up a prenup agreement." His fingers sneak back across the table towards mine, and this time, I don't pull away. "I meant what I said yesterday, Victoria. Vicky." He pauses, getting a feel for the name on his tongue, and I can't help smiling because I like the way it sounds when he says it. "I want you to name your price. Whatever you need, tell me."

Tears sting my eyes, and I turn my face from him, trying to blink them away before he notices. Too late. He catches one on his fingertip and tilts my chin towards him.

"Why are you crying?"

"Because it doesn't feel real. I keep thinking that any moment now you're going to tell me that you've changed your mind and then..."

"And then you'll remember that you've still got to pay the rent, and find your brother, and a new job, and Abigail will still have no school to go to."

I sniff loudly; not my finest look, but Caleb doesn't even flinch. "This kind of thing doesn't happen to people like me."

"People like you." He holds my gaze, and I feel myself melting into those eyes. "Who are you, Vicky? Who is Victoria Callahan?"

Where do I start? I almost screwed this deal by bringing Abigail with me; just wait till he hears about my addict mom and how she left me and Mason to fend for ourselves while she was out of it in some dingy basement filled with other addicts, used needles, and battered tin pots.

I shrug and force a smile. "I'm just the kind of gal who never gets to go to the ball." *Sandy?* "Well hardly ever, anyways."

He watches me closely as if he can see right through me and knows exactly what's going on inside my head. So, I force my thoughts away from Danny Zuko and back to the present. "You don't need to worry about contacting the Academy. I know the head teacher there."

"You do?" Why am I surprised? I bet Caleb Murray has contacts all around the city and even in the strangest places.

It occurs to me then that we've spoken about money—I've yet to mention the money I need to help Sienna; I'm building up to it—but we haven't even scraped the surface of what this pretend married life is going to mean to both of us in practical terms. Heat floods my cheeks when my mind instinctively spirals down a rabbit hole in which Caleb and I are sharing his super king-size bed and we're both naked...

"What happens once I've signed the contract, Caleb?"

"I'll get a wedding ring made for you. You'll need an engagement ring too. Have you ever thought about the kind of diamond you would like?"

I almost choke on my water, and I'm pretty certain some comes out of my nose as I splutter liquid back into the glass. A server appears from nowhere, whisking the offending glass away from me and replacing it with a spanking clean one.

"Um, no, not really."

"It's fine." He dismisses the question with a wave of his hand. "We'll go to Tiffany's tomorrow. Discreetly. I don't want anyone finding out until we've scheduled the press release." The efficient businesslike tone is back.

But my mind is still stuck on Tiffany's. Does he have any idea how expensive that place is? My brain catches up and I remind myself that, of course he does. He's Caleb Murray.

"Press release?" I squeak. "With photos?"

"Yes. I'll arrange for you to speak to my personal shopper. You can use the salon here in the Wraith any time you like. I'll get Lauren to let them know to expect you. Perhaps we should arrange a wedding reception. We can hold it here in the ballroom. Or at the Titan."

He must notice the dizziness taking hold behind my eyes because he hesitates then, trying to gauge which part of these arrangements I'm unsure of.

"We can hold the reception somewhere else if you'd prefer. I'll leave it to you, Vict—Vicky."

I dig my fingernails into the palm of my hand. Finally, something I can use to ground myself before I get carried away on a rollercoaster ride of diamond rings, personal shoppers, and exclusive salons.

"Why would you leave it to me?" My voice has chosen now to desert me. "What if I choose a venue that you don't like?"

He spreads his hands wide. "I'll choose somewhere better." He laughs, but it fades when he realizes that I'm still a little shell shocked. "Don't all brides want to plan their own weddings? Haven't you been thinking about this since you were a little girl?"

I don't tell him that I never had time to think about weddings because I was too busy looking after Mason. And besides, I'm not a bride, I'm just a fake wife.

"Fuck," he mutters to himself. "I'm sorry you don't get to do the whole white wedding thing. Look, if you want to scrap the reception, we'll figure out another way to introduce you to everyone we know."

Put like that, I don't know which is worse, meeting everyone individually or being on show at my own wedding reception like it's a beauty pageant.

"No, I'd like to organize it myself," I manage, my head still reeling from the whirlwind I've found myself in. "I'd like to be an event planner someday."

Caleb sits back in his seat, catching the condensation on the outside of his glass with his thumb. "Think of this as a starting point then."

I nod, thinking about Sienna and her meeting at the gallery today. "You said I could ask for anything." Deep breath. "My friend, Sienna. She's always been there for me, and the one time she needed me most, I let her down."

I can't tell him why; I just have to pray that he believes me.

"Five years ago, on New Year's, she was involved in a car wreck. The asshole she was with left her for dead and saved himself. She suffered burns all over her body. She still needs cosmetic surgery on some of the scars, and she doesn't like taking money from me, but well, I promised myself that one day, I'll help her to open her own gallery."

I wait for him to tell me that he isn't going to be that generous. Not art-gallery generous. But instead, he says hoarsely, "Whatever you want, Vicky. I'll keep my word."

I smile, but I sense that he's no longer paying attention, and there's still so much more to discuss. "Where will we live, you know, once everyone knows that we're married?"

"I haven't thought about it." He dabs his mouth with a pristine white napkin. "If you'll excuse me, Vicky, I have a meeting to attend. I'll have Lauren email the contract to you."

He stands, lingering beside the table as if he has forgotten something important. "I'll have Frankie bring Abigail back out when the cookies are ready."

Then he walks away, and I'm left wondering what the hell I've gotten myself into.

8

CALEB

I head back to my office before the meeting with my brothers. I need time to think.

Kyle was involved in a road traffic incident on New Year's five years ago. Cash and Bash pulled him out. They got him to the ER, got his leg patched up, fabricated a whole story about an accident on a motorcycle, made sure it didn't reach the press while I was fucking Sandy in a friend's apartment, too busy to check the messages on my phone. They said the woman he was with was dead.

Fuck! I knew I should've checked it out for myself. You want something done, you've always got to do it yourself.

I ignore Lauren trying to catch my attention from her desk. Inside my office, I half-fill a glass with brandy and down it in one, disappointed when the burn vanishes almost immediately.

Same accident? What are the chances…?

Kyle and Sienna? I wrack my brain trying to recall the name of the woman Kyle left the party with, or the costume she was wearing, something to erase this crazy story from my head and stop me from jumping to any more conclusions. Because already I'm thinking there's a tiny possibility that if Sienna was at the same party as me and Kyle, she might know Sandy.

Might.

A powerful word with a gigantic question mark attached to it.

But still... Can I afford to let it go? The best PIs in the city haven't even come close to finding her, and here's Victoria walking into my life with a best friend who might just happen to be the missing link.

Fate?

Perhaps. Do I believe in fate and chance and coincidences? Nah. We make our choices and we shape our lives into what we want them to be.

And what do I do about Kyle? Ruthless mafia boss—I'll take on the likes of Don Dragonetti and his nutjob daughter any day of the week. But when it comes to my family, I will literally do whatever it takes to protect them.

Kyle might be my big brother, but I've always been his protector. His mentor. His wing man and buddy. He had asthma as a little kid, and it used to melt my heart seeing him reach for his inhalers whenever our father started kicking off at our mom for his dinner not being ready when he came home, or for leaving toys lying around the house, or giving one of his own sons the last cookie in the jar.

Our dad's anger issues affected Kyle more than it affected the rest of us. Cash and Bash were too young to understand. Mom would bundle them into their bedroom and close the door, telling them it was a game of sleeping lions and the first one to make a sound was the loser. I was too busy shielding Kyle to let anxiety take hold. But when he hurt Mom real bad, I stood guard over Kyle, a bread knife in my hand, and waited for the paramedics to arrive, muttering the entire time, "Touch my brother and I'll kill you."

It was an easy role to step into. It's almost like it's what I was born to do.

Kyle withdrew into a shell. For a while there, when Mom was out of the hospital and struggling to keep a roof over our heads, his asthma got worse. I'd sit up at night watching him breathe, waiting for his chest to go concave with the effort of filling his lungs, knowing that was the time to get him medical help. At school, the other kids would pick on him because he didn't fight back, and that made me see red. Literally.

The teachers told Mom I had anger management issues, and I know now that she was scared I had too much of my dad in me. I got into fights every day, until the bigger kids realized that they always came off worse. I got a rep in middle school for being a scrapper. But kids started treating me with respect, keeping their distance, trying to be my friend, and backing off when they understood that it was me and my brothers, and no one else was welcome.

Then, when Mom met Terry, he recognized in me the same qualities his own parents had seen in him. Terry, despite being a mafia mobster, took me under his wing. He nurtured me, gave the anger an outlet, something to focus on, a direction, and it became the unspoken legacy that someday, I would take over from him.

Which is why it still grips my heart and squeezes until I can hardly breathe, that the one time Kyle needed me, I wasn't there for him.

After, he was obsessed with finding out what had happened to the girl in the car with him. Almost as obsessed as I was about finding Sandy. I scoured the media for the story of the dead woman pulled from a burning car wreck, and when I found nothing, I assumed it had been a cover up. That was the world we lived in—that kind of shit happened all the time.

But what if Sienna was that woman, and I just happened to have fake-married her best friend? How would Kyle feel about it? Should I tell him now or get all the information about Sienna first?

Kyle's mental health is stable now. Two years of therapy has taught him to deal with his obsessive survivor guilt—do I really want to undo all that hard work and plunge him straight back into all those scary emotions? Kyle with asthma is one thing, but Kyle locked inside his own head is quite another.

I've answered my own question.

And then there's Victoria. *Vicky*. She believes that the guy Sienna was with that night was an asshole who saved his own skin and left her to die. She has lived with that belief for five years; I'm not going to change her mind overnight. Probably best to let her meet Kyle, find out for herself that he's one of life's nice guys without any external influence before trying to convince her that he's not the asshole she thinks he is.

Besides, this is only temporary. We pretend to be in love until we get Don Dragonetti and his psycho daughter off our backs, and then life goes back to normal. With or without Sandy.

So why can I still feel Victoria's body pressed up against mine?

The swell of her breasts squashed up against my chest. Her hair in my fist. Her breath on my cheek.

I go to my desk and buzz through to Lauren. "Any update on Mason Callahan?"

Pause. I can almost hear her counting to three rapidly in her head and pasting a small smile onto her face before she responds. "Nothing yet."

"Double the resources. Triple them if you have to. I want him found."

Cash, Bash—short for Bastien—and Terry join me and Kyle in my brother's boardroom on the floor below my office in the Wraith.

Cash and Bash are identical twins—they have the same sandy hair, same gray-blue eyes, same features, but stand them next to one another in identical black suits, and the differences are immediately obvious. Cash's aura is dark where Bash's is light. Cash is the kind of guy you wouldn't want to meet in a dark alley in the Bronx at night. His eyes are constantly seeking danger, a creature of the night, a feral animal on the prowl. While Bash's eyes are bright and honest, his smile is just casually there for everyone he meets.

Demon and angel.

Two halves of one whole.

Many people have made the mistake of underestimating Bash's ruthlessness when it comes to business, while others have steered clear of Cash, assuming incorrectly, that he's the last person they should get involved with.

"This contract needs to be watertight," Kyle says. "If the don gets a hint of this being anything less than all-singing, all-dancing, prince charming and fucking Cinderella happy-ever-after, you know what will happen."

"Why don't we just set Olivia up with someone who'll keep her in her place?" Cash downs a shot of whisky and refills his glass. My brother has liquor in his veins instead of blood.

"Got any suggestions?" Kyle sips his own iced water.

"Sure." Cash shrugs. "Ivan Petrov. He was dating the model whose ex tried to set fire to her. He's been lying low since he obliterated the slimeball ex from the face of the earth. There were tenuous links to the fucking president, and the family turned him into a shadow to prevent world war fucking three, but he's back now. No way Olivia Dragonetti would mess with him."

"I can arrange an introduction," Bash offers.

"Sounds good to me." Cash downs a second drink and goes to stand up.

"Okay, boys." Terry waves a hand in a downward motion to settle them down. "You've had your fun. Don Dragonetti links this back to us when it all goes horribly wrong and we might as well pack up now, last one to leave the building, switch off the lights."

I smile. Terry might not be as hands-on as he used to be, but he has his finger on the pulse of every mafia movement of every family in the city.

Cash shrugs and pours himself another drink. Kyle eyes him up, no doubt wondering how much booze it would take to floor his little brother. I could save him the bother and tell him that I've never seen it happen yet.

"So, you're down with the whole fake-marriage scheme?" Cash asks Terry.

"It wouldn't have been my game plan, which makes it as good as anything I'd have come up with." Terry winks at me. "If we can pull it off."

Not pulling it off isn't an option. He knows this. We all do.

"Which brings me back to making sure this is authentic." Kyle straightens an already immaculate folder on the polished table in front of him. "I've drawn up a marriage contract and prenup. We don't want Victoria taking the Murrays to the cleaners when her best friend suggests she can make a few extra bucks out of us."

"Fuck, Caleb," Bash says, wincing dramatically. "Victoria who? I mean, how well do you know this gal? Is she out there now flexing her talons and chatting to the press? Or—"

"Or is she locked up in your office, cuffed and gagged, with Ingram on guard duty?" Cash butts in.

An infectious chuckle passes between the twins. At least they have the same sense of humor.

"She won't talk." I sip my brandy.

The marriage isn't up for debate—they knew this before they were called in for the meeting—but I value their opinions. Every single one of them. It's why we've almost cleared up on the New York City casino scene—we each play to our relevant strengths, and as a team, we're pretty fucking formidable.

With Don Dragonetti on our side, no one would touch us. Without him... Cash will be indicted for a list of organized crimes as long as my arm, and it'll take some major palm-crossing to keep him out of jail.

"How can you be so sure?" Bash asks. "How long have you known her?"

"Twenty-four hours give or take."

"Jeez." Cash rubs his jaw with the palm of his hand. "What did you do, pull her in off the street?"

"Something like that." I swallow a mouthful of brandy. It's hitting the sides now, just like I needed it to because I haven't dealt them the punchline yet. "She won't talk because there's a kid involved."

"What the fuck?" Cash puffs up his cheeks and releases his breath slowly.

Bash wrinkles his nose.

Kyle is already manipulating the prenup to include a kid who might come back to demand a share of the family fortune in ten years' time.

"Her kid?" Terry asks.

"Her brother's kid. But Victoria is basically bringing her up."

Terry sniffs, his tell when he's trying to keep three steps ahead of the game. "Father on the scene?"

"AWOL. I've tasked Lauren with finding him."

"You worried he might blow things up?" Terry asks.

"He's a low-life loser so I wouldn't put it past him."

"Leave it with me." Terry nods at Kyle whose fingers are flying across his laptop keyboard. "I'll make sure he keeps schtum." He unlocks his phone, locates the number he's looking for, and fires out a message.

"And if he doesn't, he'll soon wish he had." Cash laughs.

"Okay, we need a fallback plan." Kyle peers at each of us in turn.

"I still vote Ivan Petrov," Cash says.

"Meanwhile, we need to keep Victoria and the child safe." I'm trying to keep the meeting on track.

Protecting Victoria and Abigail must be our priority because Olivia Dragonetti is used to getting what she wants, and she wants to marry me. Not for love or an alliance between families that would be beneficial for all, but for no other reason than no one walks away from her and lives to tell the tale.

They all watch me closely, eyes narrowed like I just bit the head off a bat, Ozzy Osbourne style.

"Okay," Cash says, "I hate to point out the obvious, but you live in a fucking penthouse apartment that hasn't seen a fingerprint since the day you moved in. Where are you planning on hiding this kid? Assuming that keeping it authentic means you'll be fucking her auntie's brains out every night."

I don't like Cash's tone. I know I came close to fucking Victoria's brains out in front of Abigail earlier, but the way he says it lowers it to screwing-an-escort-in-an-elevator level. And Victoria isn't that kind of woman. That isn't what this is.

I mean, I don't know how I know this, but my cock is telling me that screwing her from behind while she is bent over my desk isn't going to be a one-off. If she tastes the way I think she will, I'm going to want to fuck her on every available surface in every available room inside the Wraith, and then some. Because without me even realizing, Victoria is sneaking under my skin the way Sandy did five years ago.

"It's the least I can do for her," I say. *Focus, Caleb.* "Getting tossed into the ocean in a pair of cement boots isn't part of the deal. She's got a kid to think about. And Abigail is special."

Cash is still being vocal. "Okay, so who are you, and what have you done with my brother Caleb?"

"Define special," Bash joins in like they're some kind of comedy act. Bing Crosby and Danny Kaye, anyone? Any moment now, they'll get up and perform a tap dance across the table.

"She's gifted. Abigail hacked into my tablet and sat there playing Solitaire. She's been kicked out of kindergarten for dismantling a fucking projector. The kid is five years old."

For once my twin brothers are silent.

"Solitaire?" Kyle arches an eyebrow.

"She knew how to clean up the game in one move."

Okay, so maybe it's an exaggeration, but it's how I recall the conversation going. I don't know much about kids. Scratch that—I know zero about kids—so maybe all five-year-olds can play Solitaire. But I don't believe that's the case.

Going by the smirks on the twins' faces, I'm starting to think that maybe I was wrong, and Abigail isn't a genius.

Kyle's tone is serious. "You mustn't lose sight of the fact that this is a temporary situation, Caleb. We get the Dragonettis off our back, form an alliance, and Victoria and Abigail both walk off into the sunset."

"I know." I drain the liquid in my glass. I can't think about that right now.

"Her future isn't with the Murray family," Kyle reiterates like he isn't sure that I heard him the first time around.

Before I can think up a suitable response to prove that I understand the situation, Terry puts his phone down on the table quietly, and says, "No sign of Callahan. Not even a lingering whiff of his cheap aftershave, which could be a problem for us."

If Terry thinks this is a problem, it is a problem.

"You want my advice," he continues, knowing that his advice is our bible, "Victoria and Abigail should stay with you." He pauses. "And I'm not going to be the one who breaks it to your mom."

9

VICTORIA

"Oh my God, I'm so happy for you!"

I throw my arms around Sienna and squeeze her tightly. There are tears in my eyes. No one deserves recognition for their work more than she does. No one deserves happiness more than Sienna does after what she's been through with the relentless skin grafts and medication and pain.

"I have a good feeling about this one, Vic. This is only the beginning."

I pull away from her and hold her at arm's length. I wish I could promise her that this is the year I'll make all her dreams come true, but I don't know Caleb Murray well enough to believe that he'll be true to his word. Not yet anyway.

"It is." I nod. "Soon everyone in New York will know how amazing your work is. Just think, this time next year you'll be famous."

"I don't want to be famous." Sienna picks Abigail up and

nuzzles her nose. "Do I, Abi? Auntie Sienna just wants to make enough money from her artwork to live, huh?"

"It's okay," Abigail says as Sienna sets her back down on the sidewalk and leads us inside her favorite café. "Caleb Murray is going to give Auntie Vicky money to buy you a gallery."

Sienna stops so suddenly that a woman in an expensive cashmere coat walking along behind us almost headbutts her. She clucks her tongue loudly and sidesteps us shaking her head.

"Vic?" Sienna asks, oblivious to the other woman's discomfort. "What's she talking about?"

Heat inexplicably floods my cheeks at the thought of Caleb Murray. It all happened so fast I'm still not convinced that I didn't imagine the whole thing.

"His lawyer has drawn up a prenup. He's going to pay for Abigail to attend the Lutheran Academy. He's going to give me more money than I could make in a lifetime of waiting tables, Si. So, I told him that I want to help you start up your own gallery."

I wince. I think I know exactly how this is going to go. There's no way that Sienna will accept that kind of money from me even if it is Caleb Murray's money really.

"It's pocket money to a man like him, Si. He won't even miss it. He'll write it off against his tax return or whatever people like him do. I bet he'll even find a way to make money out of it." I'm running out of steam at Sienna's lowered eyebrows and open-mouthed expression of suspicion.

"Prenup?" she says eventually. "You're actually going through with this?"

I shuffle closer to the café window to make way for the other pedestrians before we cause a traffic jam. "Can we go inside and talk about this?"

"Okay." Sienna holds my gaze. "But I want to know everything."

I smile. I don't even know what everything is yet, but I've never kept a secret from Sienna, and I don't know what I'll do if she tries to talk me out of it.

I mean, my head is telling me how crazy this whole situation is —billionaire bachelors like Caleb Murray don't marry ordinary women like me. They marry supermodels and actresses and daughters of billionaire businessmen like Mr. Dragonetti. But fake-marrying Caleb Murray will change all our lives. Literally. Abigail will have a chance at a decent future. Sienna will get her gallery. And I'll be able to clear Mason's debts and start over in a decent apartment, maybe even start up my own interior design business that I've always dreamed of.

How can I turn it down now that I've had a glimpse of a better life for us all?

Then there's what my heart is telling me... Only one other person has ever made my knees tremble the way Caleb Murray does, and Danny doesn't exist in the real world. He was a magical one-night stand. An apparition. A figment of my imagination.

We find a table in a quiet corner of the café and order hot chocolates all round with extra cream and marshmallows for Abigail.

While Abigail is spooning whipped cream into her mouth, I

tell Sienna about the marriage contract and prenup. "He wants to help us, Si."

"Why?" She hasn't touched her drink. "What's so wrong with him that he has to arrange a fake marriage?"

I hadn't thought of it this way, and I find myself instantly on the defensive. "There's nothing wrong with him. He just needs to get his psycho ex off his back."

Sienna twists her mouth to one side. "So, he's going to use you to do that, and then what? What's in this for you?"

"We all get out of this rut. I won't have to wait tables anymore. You won't have to struggle to work three jobs in between painting, and Mason and Abigail will have a fresh start."

"What does Mason think about this?"

"Daddy is AWOL," Abigail chimes in, popping a soggy marshmallow into her mouth.

Sienna grins at her, the smile fading when she turns her attention back to me. "AWOL?"

"Caleb has people looking for him. His phone is switched off, and he didn't come home last night. I'm worried about him, Si."

Her eyebrows disappear beneath her bangs. She doesn't need to remind me that I'm always worried about Mason. "You know that he'll try to squeeze this situation for every cent that he can get."

I shake my head. "He won't be able to. That's the whole point of the contract."

"What about when he sells your story to the press?"

"Caleb won't let him do that either."

"Won't let him?"

I know that Sienna is simply being practical and looking out for me, but I feel guilty for ruining her good news with my own. She doesn't like it, and I wonder if I would react the same way if our roles were reversed.

"He'll probably pay him to keep quiet." I peer around the café at all the people going about their regular day. My life is never going to be regular again thanks to Caleb Murray. Everything about this situation is so surreal, I keep thinking that at any moment now, I'll wake up and realize that I'm late for work at the diner.

"Where will you live?" Sienna raises her hot chocolate to her lips and inhales the sweet aroma. "You know, while you're fake married. Are you moving in with him, or will he give you a room at the Wraith? He wants this to look real, right, so the psycho ex leaves him alone. Will you go and run errands together? Will you split the chores and the cooking or, let me guess, he has staff to do all this stuff for him?"

"We haven't discussed details." I swallow a mouthful of hot chocolate, disappointed that it's already starting to cool. Sienna is thinking about practical living arrangements and all I can think about is sleeping in Caleb's bed.

Sienna inhales deeply. "Sorry, I know I sound cynical, but I don't want you to get hurt, Vic."

"I won't get hurt." I'm just happy that my best friend hasn't warned me I'm making the biggest mistake of my life. Yet.

"What's the timescale for this fake marriage?" Sienna sits back in her seat.

"I don't know."

"What happens after? You just pack your bags and move out while he signs the goodbye check?"

I shrug. "I haven't thought that far ahead."

"Okay." Sienna finally tastes her drink and spreads her hands wide. "What happens if you catch feelings for him?" Before I can protest, she adds, "Hear me out, Vic. Remember Danny?"

My face grows hot, and I keep my eyes on Abigail who is dunking marshmallows in her drink with a long-handled spoon. "How could I forget?"

"That was one night—one slightly inebriated lust-filled night, I grant you—but look how obsessed you were with finding him after."

"This is different."

"Is it?" Sienna reaches across the table and squeezes my hand. "Look me in the eye and tell me that you don't find him attractive."

"I..." I swallow hard. "He is attractive."

That's the biggest understatement of the year. Caleb Murray is fucking hot. Potentially as hot as Danny, or at least the images in my head of Danny eating me up against the wall of his apartment then fucking me in his bed.

"Auntie Vicky kissed Caleb." Abigail chooses this moment to let it slip that she saw what happened in his office.

Sienna blinks ferociously and tilts her head to one side, waiting for me to elaborate.

"It isn't what you think," I blurt out. "We didn't kiss."

"I saw you." Abigail slurps the last of her hot chocolate.

"You took Abigail with you?" Sienna whispers even though Abigail is sitting right next to her.

"You were busy, and Mason..." I shake my head. I don't want to keep reminding Abigail that her dad has gone missing. "I thought Denise would watch her for half an hour, but she was at the Titan."

"The Titan?" Sienna's mouth quirks up at one corner.

"A hotel owned by the Murrays." At her half-smile, I ask, "What? What did I say?"

"Nothing. I just don't think you realize what you're getting into, Vic. I'm worried that—"

Before she can finish, my phone vibrates, and my heart skips erratically when Caleb's name appears on my screen. Fingers trembling, I unlock my phone and read the message:

Where are you? I'll send a car to collect you and Abigail. You're moving into the Wraith.

"What is it?" Sienna asks, and I turn my phone around to face her. She reads the message, her eyebrows practically disappearing. She has something to say, and I don't think I'm going to like it. "What if you don't want to move into the Wraith?"

"We need to make it look real." I peer down at my hot chocolate, the melted cream creating an oily patch on the surface. "It's only temporary."

Sienna nods slowly. "Why does he want you to bring Abigail?"

"She has nowhere else to go while Mason is..." Doing whatever Mason does when he's on a downward spiral. I don't know why but I don't want to tell Sienna about Abigail hacking into Caleb's tablet either.

"Vic," Sienna says softly, "just be careful. I mean, what do you know about the psycho ex? What if she decides to cause trouble for you both? It's not fair oto Abigail to drag her into this too."

"Caleb wouldn't let anything happen to us." I glance at Abigail who is sitting upright in her seat and following the conversation, her eyes bright and wide. I would protect her with my life, and something tells me that Caleb Murray would do the same.

Sienna releases a heavy sigh. "I only hope you're right."

Abigail sits on every seat in the back of the stretch limo that Caleb sends to my apartment to collect us. She talks the entire time, peering out of the tinted windows at the people and buildings we pass, and sipping orange juice with lots of ice cubes from the mini bar in the back.

Lauren greets us when we step out of the elevator and into Caleb's penthouse apartment. Miss Ingram's lips are pinched together like this situation is highly irregular, and she's only going along with it for Caleb's sake.

I stare, open-mouthed, at the living room which is like something out of *Gossip Girl*. It's huge, bigger than my entire apartment, and filled with large squashy sofas strategically arranged around glass-topped coffee tables the size of a king-sized bed. The paintings on the walls are huge and vibrant, splashes of tangerine and violet and cerulean bringing life to the understated, carefully chosen furniture. The rugs look as if I could bury my feet in them. But the focal point is the feature window wall with an unobstructed view of the city.

Abigail pulls away from me and, ignoring Lauren who gives off unmistakable don't-touch-me vibes, runs past her to Caleb who appears from somewhere within his cavernous penthouse apartment. In one fluid movement, she jumps up, wraps her arms around his neck, and expects him to hold her. And he does.

I don't know what I expected, but it wasn't for him to walk closer to the window with Abigail in his arms and point out various buildings on the New York skyline.

Miss Ingram discreetly backs away and into the elevator, leaving me standing in the entrance feeling like the antelope who wandered into the lion's den.

"Auntie Vicky, come and look," Abigail squeals.

Sometimes I think that Abigail must be an old soul with all the information that she astounds me with every day, but I've never seen her attach herself to Mason the way she has instinctively done with Caleb. Does she sense that he can offer her stability, security, and protection also? Or has she been missing a strong father figure from her life, an alpha male, a label that would never stick to Mason even though I love him dearly?

I feel a fresh stab of guilt in my chest. Should I have done more to knock Mason into the kind of father that Abigail needs rather than following him around and clearing up his mess? Sienna would remind me that Mason isn't my responsibility, but still, I can't help feeling that I've been too passive when it comes to my little brother.

I navigate my way around the furniture, breathing in the showroom-smell of new carpets and furniture polish, and my stomach twists at the vision in my head of how this room would look after twenty-four hours of me and Abigail living here.

"There's the Empire State Building." Abigail points at the window.

I smile. "It's okay, you can put her down now," I address Caleb. "She's just excited after the limo."

Caleb lowers her to the polished wooden floor gently, and I pray that the soles of her boots are clean. I meet his gaze, and my cheeks start burning. He's even more beautiful outside of his office if that's possible.

"Will you show us to our room so that we can unpack our stuff?"

The limo driver offered to get our bags sent up, and as I can't see them, I assume that they've already been sent to whichever hotel room Caleb has allocated to us.

He nods. "This way."

It feels awkward now that we're here, even though this was his idea, and I feel swallowed whole by the enormity of what we're doing. I don't belong here. I'm not this person; I don't know how it feels to not worry about paying the rent, or not to have to search the bargain counter in the grocery store, or to relax on a couch that looks as if no one's butt has ever touched the cushions.

We're pretending to be married like little kids who are role playing in their parents' wedding outfits, but this is real life, and we're not kids. Will he want to spend time with me, or will I only be his wife for social engagements? Will I have to ask permission to leave the room, or will I be free to come and go as I please? How can we pretend to be in love if we know nothing about each other?

We haven't even scratched the surface of what this means to both of us in practical terms, and now that I'm here, I'm worried that I've bitten off way more than I can chew. Or swallow. However the saying goes, my mind instinctively drifts to stroking my hands across Caleb's naked chest as I follow him along a hallway as wide as my living room.

He opens a door and stands aside. "Main bathroom."

Main bathroom? Where the hell does he hide the other bathrooms?

I peek inside from the doorway and allow my eyes to roam around the room that's as large as a swimming pool. The tiles are marble—I'm guessing, not that I've ever seen real marble tiles—in shades of blue that make it feel as if I'm underwater. Abigail runs inside, squealing, and I swear the tiles actually ripple.

"The bath is a swimming pool, Auntie Vicky."

"Not quite." Caleb inclines his head. "It's a jacuzzi. There's a sauna through the door at the end,"

Jacuzzi... Sauna... *O-kay.*

The strange thing is that he isn't gloating. He's just showing us around before he takes us to our room; maybe he's going to test me on his apartment later before he introduces me to his acquaintances. I'd best stop gaping and start paying attention.

Further along the hallway, he opens another door—why are the doors all shut? –and says, "Your room."

My room?

I poke my head around the doorway and take it all in, vaguely aware that my mouth is still open, and that I'm acting like a child who just discovered the real Santa in the magical North Pole.

It's huge—I'm already starting to realize that everything in this apartment is huge, including the bed in the center of the room —painted in delicate shades of green. A potted plant in the corner touches the ceiling, its branches draping gracefully towards the floor like a willow. The silk comforter on the bed is a dark mossy green. The mountain of silk cushions is emerald trimmed with silver to coordinate with the lampshades dotted around the room.

I step inside. There are no wardrobes, no furniture at all other than the bed and nightstands complete with a stack of books in various genres.

"I've always wanted to have a bed in the middle of the room." I turn around to face Caleb who is watching me with a curious expression on his face.

He comes in, crosses the room, and opens another door that I hadn't even noticed since I'd been so excited about being able to walk all the way around the bed. "Dressing room."

"No freaking way."

I don't even realize I said the words out loud until he laughs.

Abigail is already inside the dressing room, running her hand across racks of clothes and picking up shoes with heels that I'd break my neck in if I ever tried to walk in them. "Look at this bag, Auntie Vicky." She spins around to show me a pink bag with BALENCIAGA printed across the front in bold black font.

"Abigail put the bag down." I hold my breath, praying that her hands are clean. I can't even begin to imagine how much that bag would cost, and I can't afford to replace it.

"There are other bags if you don't like that one," Caleb says. "I think the clothes are your size." His eyes roam my body, and goosebumps immediately pop on my skin.

"I..." I shake my head. "I brought my own clothes."

"Victoria, I need you to look like Mrs. Caleb Murray." The soft expression is gone; professional Caleb is back.

My heart is still racing at our forced proximity, but I remind myself that I need to keep a clear head. Sienna is right, I can't afford to let him get under my skin.

I nod once, not trusting myself to speak.

"Abigail's room is next door." He keeps his green eyes on me, and I hate that I already know how difficult this is going to be.

"I've got my own room?" Abigail sets the bag back down on a polished shelf and runs after Caleb.

I find her in a room that's almost as big as mine, spread eagled across a pink sleigh bed, surrounded by soft toys. An easel has been set up in one corner. There's a huge flatscreen TV on one wall, a Barbie dollhouse as tall as Abigail, and a desk complete with a laptop and various other devices that I'm certain no child should be allowed in control of.

"Caleb, I..." Jeez, where do I even begin? "Who does this stuff belong to?"

Because it's so ingrained in me that we don't live like we just bought out FAO Schwarz, that I can't bear to think of Abigail's disappointment when we have to walk away from this life.

Caleb furrows his brow. "It belongs to Abigail."

"You bought it for her? How?" He only met Abigail a few hours ago. Unless he's lying to me, and he has a secret child somewhere.

A shudder travels down my spine. I don't know anything about him, and yet I've introduced Abigail into a world that doesn't exist in real life, at least not for people like us, and who knows the kind of trauma she'll be left with when this is over.

"I don't think that she should…" Deep breath. "The computer equipment…"

"Is child restricted." Caleb arches an eyebrow as if offended that I think he's clueless about children.

"What else can I see?" Abigail is standing between us, and I didn't even hear her move.

"There's a rooftop garden." Caleb watches me carefully like he's waiting for my reaction.

"You have trees on the roof?" Abigail wrinkles her nose. "How do they grow?"

"They grow in pots." Caleb answers Abigail's questions with more patience than I'd have given him credit for. "There's a swimming pool on the roof, and a sundeck."

"Can I go see?" Abigial turns to me. "Auntie Vicky, can we go swimming on the roof?"

"I'm sorry, sweetie, but I didn't pack your bathing suit."

I don't want to be the one to rain on her parade, not when she's already looking at Caleb like he's some kind of demi-god, but this is one of those occasions when being practical has to reign supreme.

"There are bathing suits in the walk-in closet." Caleb eyes me coolly. "But swimming will have to wait. We have an appointment at the Lutheran Academy."

10

CALEB

Victoria—I've realized that I can't think of her as Vicky; it just doesn't fit with what I see when I look at her—meets me in my office wearing a wine-red woolen dress that clings to her in all the right places.

"Is this okay?" She spreads her arms wide so that I can check out the outfit, and all I can see is the swell of her breasts through the material, and the curve of her hips.

"It's fine." I have to look away before the bulge in my pants starts telling a different story.

In the car, Abigail sits between us, chatting the entire journey about one of her kindergarten teachers who would bring books into school for her to practice reading in a quiet room, and give her scraps of plastic and wood and allow her to construct whatever she wanted. The kid is bright, but I'm not really paying attention. Each time I look at her, my eyes drift to Victoria's flushed cheeks and long, dark eyelashes. She isn't wearing makeup, although the dressing room is stocked with everything that she might need, but her skin is flawless, her hair thick and glossy, and her lips…

I force myself to stare out the window until we arrive. *Focus, Caleb, jeez.* Other than the brief introduction to Don Dragonetti and Olivia, this is the first time that we will be seen together outside of the Wraith, and even though Brailand Voth, the head teacher, is discreet, other people like to gossip.

So, I'm taken aback when the new head teacher greets us in the modern reception area.

"Catherine Montgomery." Her handshake is firm, her voice clipped. She has honey-blonde hair rolling in fat waves over her shoulders, clear blue eyes, and classic features, but she pales beside Victoria's warmth, like a white lily overshadowed by a vibrant gerbera. "The new head teacher," she adds with a glint of amusement in her eyes.

I had no idea that Brailand Voth had been replaced. Lauren didn't even mention it when she made the appointment and added it to my diary, and I make a mental note to speak to her when I'm back in the office.

It isn't until we're seated around the desk in Catherine Montgomery's office that she acknowledges Abigail. After introducing herself, she says, "Abigail, do you understand why your parents want you to attend the Lutheran Academy?"

I sense rather than hear Victoria's gasp when the head teacher uses the word parents. It doesn't go unnoticed by Ms. Montgomery either.

"Because I can't go back to kindergarten," Abigail says.

"Do you want to go back to kindergarten?"

"Is that important?" I interject, and Ms. Montgomery shoots me down with an icy look.

"No." Abigail swings her legs back and forth under the seat, and I'm reminded that she might be intelligent beyond her years, but she's still just a little kid.

"Why not?" The head teacher watches her closely.

"Because they said I broke the projector, but they're lying. I was trying to fix it."

"Abigail is good with electronic equipment." Victoria spins a narrow silver band around her finger. An anxiety tell. "She fixes things at home. She knows her way around a laptop too." Her voice trails off like she has offered too much information already.

"What do you think we can offer her here that she won't get from kindergarten?" Ms. Montgomery aims the question at Victoria.

"I-*we* hope that you'll encourage her to explore what she's good at. To challenge her strengths." Victoria swallows, a faint flush creeping up her cheeks.

Ms. Montgomery remains silent, and Victoria squirms in her seat.

Finally, obliged to fill the uncomfortable silence, Victoria says, "Abigail is exceptionally bright, and I don't want her to be held back."

"From experience, children find their own way." The head teacher's tone is neutral.

"Yes, but they need the right encouragement." Victoria glances at me as though looking for validation.

"Does she get the support she needs at home?" Ms. Montgomery asks, her focus is still on Victoria.

"Ye-es."

I wince at the hesitation in Victoria's voice. Doesn't she realize that Ms. Montgomery is deliberately trying to intimidate her? She's picking on her rather than me because she has picked up on Victoria's vulnerability, but she should know that she's better than this. My hands ball into fists at the thought that life has knocked her down so many times that she's forgotten how tall she can stand.

"How soon can she be enrolled?" I wait for Ms. Montgomery to slide her attention my way.

"Assuming that she passes the entry requirements, it will take four to six weeks."

"The entry requirements?"

"Abigail will need to complete the entry exam. Then, provided her results are suitable, she will be invited to attend an interview with her parents. I must advise you that we wouldn't normally consider students with unfavorable reports from previous educational institutions."

"Abigail's report won't be unfavorable," Victoria blurts out. "They'll tell you how bright she is."

"I don't doubt that she is bright," Ms. Montgomery says coolly.

"I'll pay the admission fee now," I join in. "The Murrays will be happy to sponsor the Academy for whatever it needs."

The head teacher's eyes narrow briefly, a faint smile twitching at the corners of her mouth. "This isn't about money, Mr. Murray. It's about Abigail's suitability to attend the Academy.

I must determine whether I feel that she will benefit from being educated here."

"Surely Abigail will thrive with the appropriate nurturing." Victoria has stopped spinning the ring around her finger, and I can hear the fight back in her voice.

Good.

The woman sitting behind the desk has no God-given right to determine whether a child is or isn't good enough to be educated here. It's like playing the lottery with kids' futures, and I have no intention of leaving Abigail's education to chance.

"I agree that she will thrive in the right environment," Ms. Montgomery continues, "but whether the Academy is that environment remains to be seen."

I stand abruptly and offer the head teacher my hand. "Thank you for your time. We'll take Abigail elsewhere."

"Caleb?" Victoria's eyes are wide with panic as she rises. "What are you—"

"We've heard enough. As you pointed out, Abigail will thrive in the right environment, and this isn't it."

"But we... How do you—"

"I'm sorry you feel that way, Mr. Murray." The head teacher talks over Victoria, confirming that I've made the right decision. "Abigail may still sit the exam if you would like."

"It won't be necessary."

"Caleb please..." Victoria's eyes are pleading with me not to ruin this opportunity for Abigail, but I need her to understand that there are other schools, other ways of getting her niece the education that she needs.

Ms. Montgomery is on her feet behind her desk. "Perhaps you both need some time to discuss this in private." The dig isn't lost on me. She's insinuating that we should've discussed our options prior to this appointment.

"Not at all." I smile. "We'll see ourselves out."

"Where are we going?" Abigail jumps to her feet and slides her hand in mine.

My chest swells with the knowledge that I can help this kid, I can give her the chance that her loser father will never be able to provide. I crouch in front of her so that our eyes are level. "Staten Island."

One call to Lauren is all it takes to secure the public open hours at the software lab on Staten Island for our own personal use. I want to see what Abigail can do. I don't want to hear it from Victoria, I need to see it for myself before I can consider the way forward. My knowledge of kids is limited, but this isn't about knowledge. This is about doing what's right for an innocent kid whose birthright has handed her an empty plate while mine is overflowing.

Victoria is quiet in the car, forehead pressed against the passenger window. I'm no expert on women either, but I know she's trying to figure out how to convince Catherine Montgomery to let Abigail take the entrance exam. She thinks I've let them down. She thinks I've ruined Abigail's life for some kind of power trip, and this makes me angry.

I've told her that I take care of what's mine, so the sooner she learns to accept that, the easier it will be for us to get along.

And the kid is even brighter than anyone has given her credit for. The technician, a young woman with black hair in a tight ponytail and wearing black-rimmed glasses shows Abigail how to program a basic piece of software, and Abigail not only gets it the first time, but asks the right questions to move onto the next stage.

The technician is suitably impressed. She pushes Abigail, encourages her with technical words that wash over Victoria's head and leave her open-mouthed, the technician's excitement demonstrated by the squeal in her voice and the way she beckons her colleagues over to watch.

I call Lauren and ask her to get Brailand Voth on the phone; if he has moved on to another school in the city, he'll accept Abigail, no questions asked.

I'm not expecting Lauren to tell me that he's uncontactable.

I walk outside of the lab, phone pressed to my ear. "What does that mean?"

"His personal number has changed, and his PA has been dismissed."

"So, find another way to reach him. No one is unreachable, Lauren, not even from outer space."

Brailand Voth is flying under the radar. I don't know why this gives me such a sense of uneasiness. He isn't part of a 'family'; he isn't a gambler; the IRS isn't hunting him down for a million-dollar tax bill he's been avoiding. He was born into wealth—unlike the Murrays—but we became best friends at high school when we both made the football team and have remained close ever since.

Until now.

He is still on my mind when we exit the penthouse elevator of the Wraith and find my mom on one of my sofas, a freshly brewed coffee in one hand.

Her face lights up when she sees me with Victoria, her brown eyes quickly appraising the woman by my side and settling on Abigail. Surprise registers momentarily in her eyes and vanishes just as quickly.

"Caleb!" She sets the cup down on the coffee table and is on her feet in an instant, crossing the room to take Victoria's hands in hers. She kisses Victoria's cheeks, and my chest floods with relief at the gleam in her eyes.

My mom likes her. I know this isn't real, but her approval is important to me. My mom is the bravest, gentlest person I know. When she likes someone, she'll give them the world if it's within her grasp, but if someone crosses her, they'll soon wish they'd walked in the opposite direction when they first saw her coming. She has an unfailing instinct when it comes to people.

Apart from when it came to my dad. Or maybe their violent relationship taught her to trust her gut. Either way, she takes no crap from anyone. Not even Terry. Especially Terry.

"I'm Moira, Caleb's mom." She arches an eyebrow my way. "When were you going to introduce us?"

I smile. I should've known Terry wouldn't be able to keep his mouth shut. I wonder how much he told her though.

"Soon, Mom." My arm instinctively slides around Victoria's waist, and I pull her close to my side. My mom notices, of course she does. "This is Victoria. And this—" I take Abigail's hand and pull her in front of us "—is Abigail, Victoria's niece."

Her lips twitch upward at the corners. "Lovely to meet you both. Anyone who can drag my son away from his office is more than welcome in the family. Where have you been today?" She means, where have we been since Terry attended the crisis meeting this morning.

"Staten Island," Abigail says. "I built a computer."

Mom smiles. "You'll have to show me sometime. I don't know the first thing about computers." This isn't true. Terry doesn't call her The Chef for no good reason. No one can cook the books as well as my mom can.

"We tried to get her into the Lutheran Prep Academy," Victoria says, perhaps sensing an ally in my mom.

"But?" Mom's gaze flits between the two of us. "Couldn't Brailand help?"

"He's gone AWOL."

It isn't until I say the words out loud that uneasiness solidifies in my stomach. Mason has gone AWOL too. Is there a connection? If so, it doesn't take rocket science to figure out the common denominator—I'm the one who is searching for them both.

"Anything I can do to help, you just let me know," Mom says, oblivious.

"Thank you," Victoria says, extricating herself from my side, and it's like a draft of cool air from an open window suddenly hitting me. She fits next to me like we were tailor-made for each other, and I have to remind myself that this kind of stuff only happens in the movies. Or at New Year's costume parties. "It's very kind of you."

Mom must sense the note of despair in Victoria's voice. "Hey, there's no such thing as a problem that can't be solved. Isn't that right, Caleb?" She glances my way, but her attention is all on Victoria.

She knows something is going on, but she doesn't know what. If she did, she wouldn't be quite so subtle.

"Victoria and I have agreed to be married, Mom."

Wow! That sounded way worse than I intended, but how else can I word it? If I said that we're married, Mom would automatically assume that we're in love and that this is the happy-ever-after she would wish on all her kids. When it is nothing more than an agreement. On both sides.

She isn't saying anything.

"It's just until I get Olivia Dragonetti off my back." Like a cop in an interview room, Mom has this knack of remaining silent and forcing her kids to keep talking. It's quite a skill. "Don Dragonetti offered to form an alliance with the Murrays, with marriage to his daughter as a condition."

Still nothing. It would be easier if she yelled at me that I was making a huge mistake and messing with people's lives, but yelling isn't Mom's style.

"I'm assuming you've made this official." Mom's tone is neutral; she isn't judging my decision, she's already a few steps ahead, working out the practicalities of a fake marriage.

"Kyle drew up the marriage contract and prenup."

She nods once. She'll go through the prenup herself when she's finished with me—if there's a loophole to be found on

Victoria's side (which there won't be), she'll fill it in with cement and grow daisies on top so that the Murrays come out the other side looking squeaky clean and smelling of roses.

"And how about you, Victoria?" Mom takes Victoria's hands like they're about to dance. "How do you feel about this?"

At least she didn't ask what's in it for her. She'll make sure that Victoria is suitably compensated for playing the role of Mrs. Caleb Murray if she doesn't believe that I've been generous enough. Mom will step into her own role of the compassionate mother-in-law with ease, but her priority will always be to protect her family.

"I..." Victoria glances at me, and I have the overwhelming urge to catch the teardrops forming on her bottom lashes and kiss every inch of her. "I'm doing this for Abigail." She sucks on her bottom lip, and she literally has no idea how fucking sexy it is.

"They kissed," Abigail chimes in.

Mom's smile comes easy to her. "That's what people do when they're in love, Abigail. What's your favorite fairytale?"

"*Beauty and the Beast.*"

"Good choice." Mom crouches in front of her. "I'll let you in on a secret: that was my favorite fairytale too when I was a little girl. And I was quite disappointed when the beast turned back into a prince."

Victoria chuckles. "We prefer the beast too, don't we, Abigail?"

"We like him when he's happy." For a moment, Abigail sounds like a regular five-year-old, and a surge of protective energy flushes through me. If anyone dares touch her, I swear I'll cut off their fingers myself.

Mom straightens. She's still holding Victoria's hand, and I watch her gaze settle on the empty ring finger. Without warning, she slides her engagement ring from her own finger and slips it over Victoria's finger.

"What?" Victoria shakes her head, her eyes wide with panic. "No. No, I couldn't possibly wear your ring." She tries to tug it over her knuckle, but Mom stops her.

"You want folks to believe that you're in love, you gotta do this properly."

"But..." Victoria turns her gaze to me, imploring me to give the ring back. "This is your ring, Moira."

It's the first time I've ever looked at the ring Terry gave Mom when he proposed to her. *Really looked at it.* It's a huge emerald surrounded by diamonds on a fine platinum band, and, when Victoria holds it up to the light streaming through the windows, it sends shimmering green and gold patterns pirouetting across the living room.

"It's no secret that my engagement ring would go to my eldest son's future wife, Victoria. But as Caleb has beaten Kyle to it, no one would question you wearing the ring. In fact, if you weren't wearing it, they would question why not. Such is the way of the world, and if we're doing this, we're doing this properly."

I smile. "Thanks, Mom."

She dismisses the thank you with a wave of her hand. "Is Victoria going with you tomorrow evening?"

Tomorrow evening? Don Dragonetti's birthday dinner. Kyle and I both received invitations, and it's common knowledge that the police commissioner and mayor are also on the guest list, along with Dmitri Petrov, Sen Jozen—head of the Japanese mob—and Brandon Weiss.

"Tomorrow evening?" Victoria's question echoes my own thoughts.

"Sure, why not?"

"Caleb, I don't know about—"

"You have nothing to worry about, Victoria." Mom takes over, leading Victoria towards the coffee maker in the kitchen. "I'll tell you all you need to know."

I watch my mom operating the coffee machine and pulling cups out of the cabinet, chatting away as if they'd known each other all their lives, and I realize that perhaps this is what my mom has been waiting for, her sons to settle down so that she can welcome daughters-in-law and grandchildren into her life.

And I have to go and ruin it for her with a fake marriage and no wedding.

11

VICTORIA

There's so much to take in.

You don't think about other people's lives until you're thrown into the middle of them. Sure, I was aware that Caleb Murray was wealthy—I mean, you only have to walk past the Wraith at night and see the prestige vehicles being parked up by the valets, and the guests in their expensive suits and diamonds to understand the kind of wealth associated with the Murrays—but I never considered what that meant in everyday terms.

Until Moira filled me in over several cups of coffee—rich and chocolatey, not the cheap granules I usually pick up from the grocery store—and some wafer-thin biscuits covered in thick dark chocolate.

She spoke about actors, socialites, and celebrities the way Sienna and I would speak about our mobile hairdresser and the woman at the cash register in the grocery store. She dropped names like Meg Ryan and Lady Gaga into the conversation without even realizing. I found out which celebrities were dating—information that wasn't readily available on social media—who was having an affair with whose husband or wife, and Moira's predictions for celebrity marriages and babies for the coming twelve months.

By the end of the conversation, my head was spinning.

"You'll be fine, Victoria." Moira smiled. "Look, I know that you must have your reasons for agreeing to help Caleb, and I'm not going to pry," she quickly added when I opened my mouth to speak, "but I want you to know that you can trust my son."

Tears pricked my eyes. Perhaps it was the overwhelming amount of information she'd offloaded onto me and the fear that, within twenty-four hours, I would be stepping into my role as Caleb's wife in public. But my emotions had been swinging violently between emotional wreck and sugar-rush excitement ever since.

This morning, Abigail and I went up to the rooftop where we found inflatables in the pool, and our own chef who prepared snacks and cocktails—mocktails for Abigail—behind the bar. The sun came out, and for a couple hours, I forgot about the impending dinner at the Michelin-star restaurant Cesar with Caleb's acquaintances. I forgot about Olivia Dragonetti, and our fake marriage contract, and the heavy emerald-and-diamond-ring on my finger.

I almost forgot that it had been two days since I'd heard from Mason.

Moira collects Abigail from Caleb's apartment shortly after lunchtime. She offered to babysit, and although I was uncertain about leaving Abigail with a stranger and didn't want to impose on Moira's time, Abigail is excited to go to Moira's house. She slips her hand into the older woman's palm with a fluffy unicorn tucked under her other arm and kisses me goodbye like Moira is her favorite grandma.

Standing in the middle of Caleb's apartment, I suddenly feel lost. I've practically raised Mason and Abigail singlehandedly, and now, I realize with a sharp pang of disappointment, that I don't know what to do when I'm alone.

After my one-night stand with Danny five years ago, my monthly cycle was late. I'm never late. I experienced twenty-four hours of sheer, hair-pulling, ugly-crying panic. Abigail was a few months old, and it was already obvious that her mom was going to hand her over to Mason, which meant that the responsibility would fall onto my shoulders.

But once the panic subsided, I realized that being a mom was all I'd ever wanted. A child of my own—Danny's child—filled me with such immense joy that I already knew what maternal love was.

Then, when my cycle regulated itself a week later, I went from a floating sense of euphoria to crushing grief. It was almost as if I'd held our baby in my arms and had it snatched away again. A baby would've been a reminder of what happened that night. A tiny piece of Danny to keep close to my heart forever, as difficult as it would've been struggling on my own with a young child.

Maybe that pregnancy scare is the reason why I still feel scarred by that night of passion. I needed to know that there was a reason why Danny came into my life. But I'm still searching for it, because I refuse to believe that it was a one-night-only thing.

Anyway, I have six hours to kill before Caleb and I are going out.

It usually takes me thirty minutes max to get ready for a night out, but I'm in the penthouse apartment of the Wraith, I remind myself, and Caleb is still working.

What's the point of a fake marriage if I don't take advantage of my husband's assets?

Chuckling to myself at the image of Caleb Murray straddling a sleek black Harley, I wander into the main bathroom. I fill the tub with steaming hot water and expensive coconut-and-lime-scented bubbles from the selection provided on the glass shelf, undress, and slide in. I sit back and close my eyes.

If anyone had told me a week ago that I'd be soaking in Caleb Murray's bathtub with his mom's engagement ring on my finger, and a meal planned at Cesar, I'd have thought they were living in la-la-land. But here I am. Is this what the universe planned for me all along?

If so, it's hard to imagine why.

I change position, and my fingers brush a jet under the water. Caleb said this was a jacuzzi. Opening my eyes, I locate the button and press it, steady streams of bubbles massaging my back. Oh my God, this is bliss.

I remain in the tub until my fingers are pink and wrinkled. Then, I moisturize, wind my damp hair around soft, fat curlers, and wander back to my bedroom with a fluffy, white towel wrapped around me.

What to wear tonight?

Moira warned me that the police commissioner and mayor and their wives would be there, along with various other high-ranking members of the community. I'm assuming that Olivia Dragon-face will be there too, and if our last meeting is anything to go by, she'll be dressed to impress.

Dressed to impress Caleb, anyway.

I check out the clothes in my dressing room. When I arrived with Abigail yesterday, I felt stung that Caleb had filled an entire room with clothes for me, knowing that my wardrobe wouldn't contain the kind of outfits his wife would wear. Mainly because I'd never blow six months wages on a dress. But now, the thought of wearing my shabby best dress in Olivia's company makes my stomach twist with ... jealousy?

Why?

Caleb Murray would never have noticed me if I hadn't been trying to stop Killian from killing my brother. I was his concierge for a whole four hours, during which time he didn't set eyes on me once, and he certainly wouldn't pick me out in a restaurant if I spilled red-wine on his pristine silk shirt. So, why do I want him to look at me instead of Olivia Dragonetti?

Is it pride? I'm his wife; we've only just gotten married in a fictitious Irish ceremony, so he should theoretically only have eyes for me. Shouldn't he?

The more I think about Olivia Dragonetti fawning over Caleb in his office the more determined I am to upstage her. But when I enter the dressing room, the sheer volume of clothes hanging neatly on the rails immediately drowns my resolve. It has been so long since I've been shopping with enough money in my bank account to buy clothes for myself that I no longer remember what suits me. The lack of price tags, instead of helping, is making it even harder. The choice!

Avoiding the clothes, for now, I do my makeup first, seated in front of a mirror surrounded by theater lamps. Every item is still sealed. Immaculate. A million miles away from the bedraggled brushes and almost empty pots in my own faded makeup bag.

"Get a grip, Victoria." I peer at my reflection in the mirror. "You're a female. You know what needs to be done here."

I stick to neutral colors, keeping it subtle. Dragon-face—yes, I've already ditched the Olivia—is bound to go OTT, and no one likes a showoff peacock. At least, that's what I repeat like a mantra in my head.

Oh man, what a difference expensive makeup makes. When I'm finished, I turn my head this way and that in front of the mirror and a frisson of pleasure rushes through me.

Do I really look like this?

Will Caleb even notice?

Dragging myself away from the mirror, I stand in front of the rail filled with runway-worthy dresses and stare. What color should I wear? Should I stick to the reliable little black dress or be adventurous and wear Barbie pink or lilac or sunflower-yellow?

"No." I shake my head at the yellow. Not for tonight.

I pull out a pink dress with a plunging neckline and hold it in front of me. Maybe...

But when I try it on, I know it isn't right. I'm way too nervous to pull it off tonight in front of Caleb and Dragon-face, and the mayor of New York City.

I tug it back over my head, careful not to smudge my makeup and hang it back up, a little askew, but my heart is racing erratically, and my mouth is too dry for me to fuss over it. It feels, irrationally, as if the rest of my life is riding on tonight.

Next, I try on a sparkling gold dress which looks dazzling on the hanger and makes me resemble a Christmas tree angel standing in front of the mirror.

Nope!

Tossing adventure to the wind, I resort to a safe black dress. Too dowdy. The silver dress is only marginally less Christmassy than the gold, the blue is boring, and the green is ... not the right shade. The white pantsuit is stunning, but when an image of me spilling red wine on it pops into my head, I quickly undress and add it to the growing mountain of clothes on the floor.

I lose track of time. How can choosing an outfit be this difficult? I bet Blake Lively doesn't have this problem, but then she probably has a whole team of people choosing her designer outfits for her.

I'm so hot that sweat is beading on my upper lip, and I'm worried that I'm going to need to shower again before I go out. When I hear the elevator ping and Caleb's footsteps crossing the living room, I'm back in the first little black dress I tried on before outfit-mountain became a thing.

I freeze. Should I go and speak to him in the living room or wait until it's time to leave? Will he want to see what I'm wearing, or should I surprise him? I know so little about the man I'm supposed to be in love with that I can't even figure out something as simple as getting ready for an evening on the town.

Heart thumping, I listen for the sounds of movement around the apartment. Silence. Then water running. He's taking a shower.

Now I wish I wasn't so indecisive because it's almost time to leave.

I wait for his clipped footsteps across the hallway floor before I tentatively open my bedroom door and step outside. Caleb is standing there, staring at the doorway, and our eyes meet, my cheeks growing even hotter. Damn! At this rate, I'll have to redo my makeup before we leave.

"Is-is this okay?" I chew my bottom lip while Caleb's eyes roam my body, making me feel naked.

He doesn't speak.

"I didn't know what to wear." I find myself instinctively filling the silence.

Caleb looks me directly in the eye and says, "Come with me." Then he takes my hand and leads me back inside my bedroom, past the bed taking center-stage and into the dressing room.

My heart is racing sickeningly. Why is it that whenever Caleb touches me, my mind immediately sends images of Danny Zuko into my head?

Come with me.

It's what Danny said when he took my hand outside the restrooms in the nightclub, and my heart has latched onto it and is sending all sorts of crazy signals down to my sex. Jeez, I need to get a grip.

Caleb takes a hanger from the rail and holds it out for me. It's a red dress with a Bardot neckline, cinched waist, and floor-length hem that would drag across the floor like a wedding gown train on me. "Try this."

"I..." I swallow. "It's red." It's so red that I never even looked at it because it isn't my color.

Caleb smiles, and I realize that he's still holding the dress.

I take it from him and stand there like I'm waiting for him to give me instructions. When it's blatantly obvious that he isn't going anywhere until I try on the dress, I murmur, "Will you turn around?"

He full-on smiles at me but turns around anyway.

I shrug off the black dress, step out of it so that I'm standing in front of the mirror in my bra and panties, and remove the red gown from the hanger. It feels heavy. Expensively heavy. But when I pull it over my hips and arms and study my reflection, I get a glimpse of what Caleb must've seen when he bought it.

It's stunning. My breath catches in my throat as I hold the low-cut neckline to my chest and reach around with one hand to fasten the zipper.

"Here, let me." Caleb's warm fingers brush mine as he tugs the zipper slowly up the back of the dress.

Heat floods my neck and face when I realize that he must've seen me in my underwear in the mirror behind me. I don't know why this makes me feel like a giggling teenager, but I lower my eyes from his gaze and focus on the dress.

"This will have to come off." Caleb deftly unhooks my bra and slides it over my shoulders, adding it to the pile of discarded outfits on the floor. My nipples immediately harden, visible through the gorgeous fabric when he finishes zipping me up.

Caleb's breath is warm on my bare shoulders and the back of my neck, and I can smell cookies again, or vanilla, it's hard to differentiate when his face is this close to mine. My pulse races, and my pussy is tingling and ... wet. I can hardly breathe, and when he whispers, "Stay right there," I follow him with my eyes, panting, as he slides open a drawer inside one of the closets.

He doesn't meet my eyes when he comes back holding a fine silver chain with a red stone pendant set in it. A ruby?

Standing behind me, he sweeps my hair forward over my shoulders and fastens it at the back of my neck.

He doesn't move. Our eyes meet in the mirror as his lips drop to my exposed shoulder. I instinctively tilt my head to one side, offering him my neck, and his tongue travels across my skin to my earlobe, his teeth nibbling gently.

"You want this, Victoria."

I let out an involuntary groan. It isn't a question, but Christ alive, isn't it obvious? "I want this," I breathe, my cheeks glowing.

His tongue slides into my ear. He murmurs, "M'áilleacht," and oh my fucking God, if it isn't the sexiest thing I've ever heard. I never knew it could feel so good. A hand slides around me and inside the neckline of the dress, his fingers seeking out my erect nipple. I turn my face towards him, our lips coming together, while his fingers tease my nipple, pinching and squeezing, forcing the air from my lungs as I gasp against him.

Then, without warning, he pulls away, his hand sliding back out of the dress, his lips still reaching for mine. "We should go," his voice is husky.

I lick my lips, relishing the taste of him, and straighten the dress over my chest. My pussy is throbbing. My heart is beating frantically. I didn't want him to stop, and that frightens me because this isn't real, and I know that I can't have him.

I follow Caleb out of the Wraith on autopilot and into the waiting Hummer limo.

My body is still in the dressing room, tingling at Caleb's touch, at his warm breath on the back of my neck, and his fingers squeezing my nipples. My heart is still galloping around inside my chest at the raging emotions tearing through my body. And as if this isn't already the worst way to start an evening as his fake-wife, his brother is waiting for us inside the car with a supermodel sitting on his right sipping champagne from a flute.

"Oh." It comes out before I can stop the disappointment from permeating the air in the back of the vehicle.

Without realizing, I'd hoped that Caleb and I would be alone. No, more than that, I'd hoped there might be a repeat performance of what happened in my dressing room. Because I was doing it again. I was falling hard for the hottest man on earth; second hottest if I believed that Danny Zuko really did exist.

Caleb's brother's eyes linger on the dress a beat too long and then meet mine. He smiles and shakes my hand. "Kyle Murray. Caleb's brother. I bet he's told you nothing about me."

I can't help smiling in return, grateful to have something normal to focus on. I shake my head. "Nothing."

"Typical." Kyle raises an eyebrow in his brother's direction. "This is Suki."

Suki. The name sounds as exotic as she looks. She's wearing a short, glitzy gold dress, revealing long legs that appear to have been glossed to within an inch of their lives. Her lips are glossy too, her eyes smoky beneath jet-black bangs that she can barely see out of.

"Suki, this is my brother Caleb and his wife Victoria."

Suki leans forward and kisses Caleb's cheek before brushing her lips against my face and sitting back in her seat.

I sit beside Caleb and accept the glass of bubbly that Kyle hands to me. I can feel Caleb's thigh pressing against mine; I can smell his cologne and hear the faint rustle of his pale pink shirt against his black suit jacket. On anyone else, black would look formal, austere, but on Caleb, I can still picture him on the back of his Harley.

I don't pay attention to the conversation in the car. I don't know what they think of me. Obviously, Kyle knows about our arrangement, he drew up the marriage contract, but Suki has barely looked at me, and I know I shouldn't take it personally, but I can't shake the feeling that I don't belong in this world.

And we're not even at the restaurant yet.

So, a thrill travels down my spine when we pull up outside Cesar and Caleb takes my hand to help me out of the car. Caleb won't let me get this wrong, I tell myself. This is his life, after all.

A light flashes, blinding me momentarily. *Paparazzi?*

Caleb squeezes my hand. He leans in close and whispers in my ear, "Don't worry. You're with me, remember."

How could I forget?

The restaurant is sleek, modern, low lights casting shimmers across the golden accessories. The maître d' ushers us away from the main dining area and into the salon, a room where large parties can eat in privacy. The seats here are black, coordinating with the black lamps placed along the center of the long table which is already set with white plates, pristine napkins, and a variety of glassware.

Several people are seated around the table, but I don't recognize Mr. Dragonetti. Olivia isn't here yet either; of course she isn't. She'll no doubt be the last to arrive, wafting in on a fine mist of Chanel No. 5 and demanding everyone's attention.

Ugh. I don't like that I've allowed this woman to rattle me when I don't even know her. This isn't me. I generally steer clear of gossip and drama because who has the time, right? But something about Dragon-face has rubbed me the wrong way, and I don't even think this is all about Caleb.

The woman is trouble, and like a cat sensing danger, my hackles are up.

Caleb introduces me to the mayor and his wife, a beautiful woman with clear dark skin, gloriously thick black hair, and high cheekbones. I sit between her and Caleb, and she immediately turns around and says, "Where did you get your dress, honey? It's stunning."

My shoulders relax a little. You see these people on the news and see their photographs over the tabloids and social media, and your mind automatically sets them apart from the rest of the world, like they're a different species.

But as the seats fill, and the conversations are like those at any regular dinner party: the latest Marvel movie, basketball teams, the upcoming Met Gala ball, I realize that they're just people. Sure, they have wealth, and powerful jobs, and designer labels tucked inside their outfits, but strip that away, and they're just like anyone else walking around New York City.

My stomach lurches though when Olivia Dragonetti, wearing a billowing black and silver gown, arrives with her father and makes a beeline for Suki. They know each other. I don't know why this makes me feel hot and uncomfortable, but even when they're air-kissing each other's cheeks, Olivia's eyes are on me, reminding me that I'm not like them.

"Ignore her." Caleb's lips brush my ear, and my nipples instantly harden as a blush creeps up my neck. "She's trying to get a reaction."

Mr. Dragonetti shakes the men's hands around the table and bends over me to kiss my cheek. His gaze lands on Moira's ring, and I flex my fingers without thinking. I catch Kyle's eye across the table, and he winks at me.

Maybe I'm not as bad at this as I think I am.

I catch Rose Weiss's eye several times between courses. She seems the most genuine out of the women, but her husband Brandon, like Caleb, keeps her close to his side, and we don't get an opportunity to chat.

Between the main course and dessert, the conversation transitions to business matters. The talk seems to instinctively bypass the women like a bad smell, and I can't tell if they choose to ignore the topic or if the men warn them in advance to listen but refrain from speaking.

I had no such warning from Caleb.

I don't fully understand what's going on, but it seems to me that Mr. Dragonetti still wants to form a business alliance with Caleb despite his rejection of the older man's daughter. I also get the impression—and this is where it becomes a little bit foggy—that the mayor and police commissioner are here to offer their stamp of approval. Or not. The birthday party is simply a distraction, the glue bringing all the players together.

What I don't understand is why. What does this have to do with the mayor and police commissioner? Unless they stand to reap some financial benefits from the coalition. A bribe perhaps to overlook some dodgy financial transactions?

Caleb is perfectly at ease, one hand casually resting on my thigh. He's the doting new husband, refilling my wine glass whenever he notices it empty, murmuring into my ear to check that I'm okay, entwining his fingers with mine between courses. The only thing he doesn't do is invite me to join in the conversation.

By the end of the evening, my head is thumping from too much wine and from being in a permanent state of alert so that Caleb and I don't drop our façade.

I excuse myself and go to the restroom where I'm surprised to find my heart racing loudly when I'm surrounded by silence. Exiting the cubicle, I'm caught off-guard to find Olivia Dragonetti touching up her lip gloss in the gold-edged mirror behind the basins. I didn't hear her come in.

It occurs to me that she was deliberately silent when she came into the restroom, so I take a deep breath and force a smile. I run the cold faucet and splash my face, dabbing it dry carefully with paper towels.

I want to be the first to speak; I'd take some small glory from being the bigger person after our first meeting, but I can't think of anything to say that wouldn't sound like I'm the geeky high school teenager trying to befriend the most popular girl in town.

She beats me to it. "I know what you're doing." She doesn't even have the decency to face me squarely, but instead peers at me via the mirror while she sprays her neck with perfume.

I meet and hold her gaze. "What am I doing?"

"You only want Caleb for his money. Your brother has a whole catalog of debts he'll never be able to repay, and you're using Caleb to bail him out."

My determination to not let her get to me crumbles at the mention of Mason. "How do you—"

She laughs; it isn't a sound that other people would want to join in with. "What, you think I don't have connections? Caleb would never marry someone like you, a waitress from a backstreet café. I don't know how you trapped him, but I sure as fuck am going to make sure you don't get away with it."

Tears prickle my eyes, and I tell myself not to cry in front of her. Anywhere else, but not in front of this woman.

I pick up my purse and turn to face her. "You're wrong. Caleb and I love each other. We're married whether you choose to believe it or not."

An ugly grin spreads across her face. "That's why his car is waiting for me outside, is it?"

"H-his car?" Don't bite. If I let her get to me, she's already won.

But still reeling from Caleb's rejection in the dressing room, my self-esteem must be at an all-time low because I head blindly towards the door of the restroom, and instead of making my way back to the salon, I stumble past the maître d' and straight towards the exit.

"Victoria?" I hear Caleb calling me, but I don't stop.

I don't even think about where I'm going until I'm outside and the chilly night air brushes my arms.

That's when I hear a pop that sounds remarkably like a gunshot.

12

CALEB

I knew something was wrong when Olivia left the salon shortly after Victoria excused herself to go to the restroom. I wanted to follow her, but Don Dragonetti was trying to convince the police commissioner that the Rinse would run smoothly with an alliance between mafia families, and I couldn't let them iron out the details without my input. This is my brother's business they're toying with.

Mom warned me not to let Olivia out of my sight. She even quoted the old English idiom, *hell hath no fury like a woman scorned*, until I reminded her that Olivia isn't scorned, she's simply spoiled. "All the more reason to keep Victoria safe," she'd said.

My mom's words are still playing out behind my eyelids when I spot Victoria bolting towards the exit. "Victoria!" I call out her name, but she either doesn't hear me, or she doesn't want to be with me.

Then I spot Olivia skulking near the chrome counter in the main dining area, with a twisted smile on her face.

I'm only half a dozen steps behind Victoria, but it's enough to make me run when I hear the gunshots. My heart is hammering to get out of my chest when I find her standing just outside the restaurant. Frozen. Her back to me.

Somewhere nearby, glass shatters. Someone screams, I think it's coming from outside. Voices behind me. Panic fills the air. And still Victoria is rooted to the spot.

I run to her, shrugging my suit jacket off my shoulders, and throwing it over her head without thinking. Survival instinct kicks in. I coax her into a crouching position and cover her with my body. Shielding her from whatever is going on.

Through my jacket, she feels as frail as a bird. Her heart is racing wildly. I scan the sidewalk and spot someone lying on the ground a few feet away, blood oozing from a shoulder wound. A man.

Don Dragonetti!

Other pedestrians are lying on the ground with their arms covering their heads. The traffic has stopped. I hear sirens in the distance; maybe they're heading our way, maybe they're not. It's a regular night in New York City.

What this isn't, is a regular night in the life of Caleb Murray.

A hand lands on my shoulder. I glance around to find Kyle kneeling beside me, his face pale in the glow of the streetlamps. The lights inside the restaurant have been dimmed. No one is moving.

"See to Don Dragonetti." I gesture with a nod in the don's direction. He's motionless, but there isn't enough blood for the shoulder wound to prove fatal.

Thank fuck.

I can't even begin to think about what this will mean to our already tenuous relationship. If he tries to pin this on the Murrays, it will ignite the war we've been trying to avoid. But right now, I need to move Victoria to safety.

As Kyle crawls over to the don, I fire a message through to Terry. He'll want to handle this one personally.

Sliding my phone back inside my pants pocket, I raise the collar of my jacket and peer underneath it at Victoria. She's trembling violently. "It's okay, I'm getting you out of here."

She blinks, forcing tears to spill over her bottom lashes. "Abigail..." she whispers.

"Abigail is fine."

She just almost got killed, and her first thought is for her niece. Her scumbag piece of shit brother doesn't deserve these women in his life, and once this is over, I'm going to make sure he knows it.

Victoria nods. "I want to go home."

She means home-home, but this isn't the right time to tell her that I can't take her home. That she's safer with me even though I'm probably the last person she wants to be with right now.

"I'm taking you home. The car will be here any minute." I shift my legs around her, so that I'm shielding her from the view of Don Dragonetti when I notice blood on her arm.

Shit.

"Victoria, are you hurt?"

She shakes her head, her eyes dark and wide. She's in shock. It will sting like fuck once the adrenaline starts to fade.

I have two choices: I can take her to the ER, or I can take her home and look after her myself. Okay, scratch that. I only have one choice. Too many questions will be asked at the hospital, and this isn't the way I'd planned on announcing my marriage to the rest of the world.

A final glance at Kyle and the mafia boss, who is now sitting upright on the sidewalk, blood seeping through his shirt sleeve, and I know what I must do.

When the car pulls up on the curb, I nod for Terry and his man to get out and help Kyle move Don Dragonetti into the back seat. It's the least we can do: get him away from the crime scene until his own men can move him to a safe house.

A second car pulls up behind Terry. The sirens are getting closer, but my stepdad probably made it as difficult as possible for the emergency services to get here, buying himself a few precious minutes to scope out the damage first.

Two men in black suits climb out. One opens the back door while the other tries to help me move Victoria, but I scoop her up into my arms, her head still covered by my jacket and resting against my chest and cross the sidewalk in three easy strides. Inside the car, I pull Victoria onto my lap and hold her close until we're moving away from the restaurant. Her shivering subsides a little, but I don't relax my hold on her.

The car pulls into the Wraith's basement lot and my secure parking area.

"We're home now." I smooth Victoria's hair away from her face like she's a child. "I want you to stay under the jacket until we're inside, okay?"

The trembling resumes, and she grabs my sleeve. "No, Caleb. What's happening? I need to get Abigail and take her home."

"Abigail is safe, I promise you." I lower my voice to a whisper. "Do you trust me?"

She peers into my eyes in the stark overhead lights of the parking lot, and despite the fear in her dilated pupils, she nods.

The bodyguards shield me from the rest of the lot as I climb out of the car with Victoria in my arms. Two strides, and we're in the penthouse elevator. Victoria's heart is still thudding, but now her heartbeats are more in sync with mine, and I feel her relax against me as I carry her through my apartment and into my bedroom.

I set her down on top of the burgundy silk comforter, and unwrap my jacket from around her shoulders, plumping up the pillows underneath her head. I allow my eyes to close briefly with relief when I realize that the wound on her upper arm is little more than a graze.

This isn't the world I want to bring my wife and kids into, but what's worse in Victoria's case is that I never elaborated on what she was signing up for. Selfishly, I bribed her with financial gain, and never once indicated that she was stepping out of a humdrum life and into a world where danger and glamor walk hand in hand. I never really gave her the choice. She had to accept because, thanks to me, the alternative was unemployment and the bread line.

"Caleb?" The fear is back in her shrinking voice. "What is it?"

"Don't panic, Victoria." I sit on the side of the bed and place my arms on either side of her head, forcing her to look at me. Only at me. "I'm going to fix you some brandy, and you're going to drink it for me like a good girl."

"No." Her eyes flicker to the wound on her right arm, but I intercept her gaze before she can see it. It's probably starting to smart about now, but it'll hurt a lot worse without the brandy.

"I need you to trust me."

While I'm talking, I reach for the brandy decanter on the nightstand and half fill a heavy crystal tumbler. Supporting her head, I raise the glass to her lips and wait for her to swallow the amber liquid. She grimaces as it goes down.

"It burns, huh?"

Victoria nods, and I lay her head back down on the pillow. "Stay right there." Her eyes widen briefly before she inhales deeply and closes them again.

I fetch the medical kit from my ensuite. When I sit back down beside her, her eyes flicker open, and she smiles lazily at me. "Caleb..." It's the brandy taking effect.

"Close your eyes." I open a sterile antiseptic wipe to clean the graze. "This might sting a little."

Victoria wriggles on the pillow trying to get comfortable, her hair fanning out around her. She releases a sigh, and I clean the wound gently, my gaze dipping back and forth to be sure that I'm not hurting her. She hardly stirs. When I've cleaned the blood from her skin, I inspect the wound more closely before I cover it with a dressing. The bullet must've grazed her. She got lucky, this time.

She doesn't need stitches, but I still need to convince her to keep quiet about the incident. And why should she? She got a whole lot more than she bargained for when she signed that marriage contract and buying her off won't quite cut it anymore.

I watch her sleeping.

There's a vulnerability about her that's quite addictive. It's not a weakness, if anything it's her strength, but she just doesn't know it yet. It set her apart from the other women at the table tonight, made her seem real when everyone else was masquerading as the people they're expected to be. Ironic really.

I brush her cheek with my fingers, and she rolls towards me, nuzzling my hand, and tucking my arm between her breasts. It's a subconscious move, and my dick immediately responds inside my pants. I came too close to fucking her earlier; I can't let her get under my skin because at some point, when this is all over, I need to let her go.

But this is way fucking harder than I thought it would be.

I can see the swell of her breasts through the red fabric, the mound of her pussy where the dress has gotten caught up between her legs. I could rip the dress off her and stick my tongue between her legs—it would be one way to wake her up, but that isn't my style. I like my women conscious and willing.

"Caleb?"

The whisper barely pushes through my thoughts, and I realize that my fingers have found one of her nipples beneath the soft fabric. It automatically stiffens to my touch. "That's it, come to me, baby."

Maybe I drank too much in the restaurant, or maybe the adrenaline rush of protecting Victoria outside the restaurant has erased the voice of reason inside my head because, without thinking, I lean forward, so close our lips are touching. "Open up and let me in, Victoria."

She does as she's told and parts her lips to let me in. She tastes of the sweet wine we drank with dessert, and there's something so heady about it, that I fill her mouth with my tongue, my fingers squeezing and flicking her nipple. Her hands slide around my neck, holding me close, her fingers dragging through my hair, and I know we shouldn't be doing this, but I can't for the life of me think why when it feels this goddamned good.

"The dress is coming off."

I pull away from her long enough to unzip it at the back and drag it down over her hips, exposing her breasts, her pinkish-brown nipples, and black lace panties. I devour her with my eyes. There's something about Victoria that is so sensual, so familiar, that it's impossible for me to keep my hands off her.

"I could look at you all night," I murmur, and she lets out a groan of pleasure. It's almost like she was made for me, like I've been searching for her all my life without even realizing. "You're so fucking gorgeous, mo stoirín." My words sound husky even to me.

A smile tugs at the corners of her lips. "Say that again."

I lower my face to hers and kiss the corners of her mouth. "You're so..." I nibble her bottom lip between my front teeth. "... fucking..." I lick her lips, my hand stroking her neck. "... gorgeous..."

"And the rest." Her eyes are glittering.

"Mo stoirín."

Victoria arches her back, pressing her lips against mine like she can't get enough of me, and it's all the prompting I need to push me across the line of no return.

My hand is inside her panties, and I insert a finger into her pussy before I can stop myself. She's warm and wet and tight, and I have a hazy vision of Sandy sprawled across the bed while I push myself into her.

Victoria groans against me, eyes closed.

I insert a second finger. "So fucking tight." I feel her swallowing my fingers whole, and I resist the urge to open her up so that I can stick my tongue in her. Not yet. My cock is ready for her, but I want to take my time. She's like a blank canvas just waiting for me to fill her with color.

I leave my fingers inside her while her pussy constricts and throbs around them. I suck on her nipple, nibbling and tugging until it's pink and swollen, and Victoria responds with wetness between her legs, allowing me to push a third finger inside her. "You're so wet." Her body writhes and wriggles, and I hush her groans by filling her mouth with my tongue. "Are you always this wet, Victoria?"

"No," she gasps.

Dragging my hand down her throat and between her ripe breasts, I follow it with my tongue, sucking on the underside of her breast until a faint red mark appears.

My mark.

It's like a red rag to a bull. I want to claim her, take her in every way possible so that she knows she belongs to me. I want to leave my mark all over her so that every time I see her naked body, I'm reminded that she's totally and irrevocably mine.

I suck on the underside of her other breast so that she has matching marks.

Victoria must realize what I'm doing because she raises her upper body onto her elbows and watches me. "Caleb, no..." She shakes her head.

I go back and kiss her, squeezing her throat gently with my free hand. Her eyes widen but not with fear. "You can't stop me, Victoria. You trust me, don't you?"

"But I—"

I grip her neck a little harder and smother her mouth with mine. "Do you trust me?"

She nods. "Yes." It's little more than a whisper.

"Stay there." I kiss the tip of her nose.

Her trust makes my cock throb inside my pants. She could spread her legs wide, suck me dry, and then ride me like a bucking bronco, but nothing will ever compare to knowing that she is offering her body to me with complete and utter trust.

She is mine to do with as I please, and fuck me, do I have plans for her tonight.

Still fully clothed, I slide my fingers from Victoria's sex with a satisfying sucking sound. Standing at the end of the bed, I drink up the view of her lying on top of my comforter wearing only her panties. I pull them off her slowly, smiling to myself when I see her pussy convulsing.

I spread her legs wide and kneel between them, opening her up gently and licking the outside of her pussy, tasting her wetness. I insert my right index finger, then my left, and tease her open just wide enough to push my tongue through the middle.

"Ready?" I ask her, and she nods, her breathing shallow. "I can't hear you. Are you ready?"

"Yes," she pants. "No. I don't know."

"Too late. I'm going in."

I push my tongue all the way in, licking her taste off my fingers, and probing with the tip. She tries to move her hips out from under me, but I grip her thighs more tightly and lick until my tongue aches, and she is throbbing against my fingers. Then, I slowly slide my fingers out and hit the spot with my tongue.

This time, Victoria cries out loud. She arches her spine, gripping the pillow beneath her head with both hands like she's clinging to a life belt.

I lick until she's almost there, her breathing shallow, her wetness dripping from her, and then I pull out and suck on her clit until the groans are replaced by whimpers somewhere between excitement and tears. "Want me to stop?" When she pants in response, I ask again, "Do. You. Want. Me. To. Stop?"

"No," she manages.

I keep sucking until her body convulses with the power of her orgasm. Whipping my cock out of my pants, I close her legs, straddle them so that she can't move, and slide my erection inside her. She's wet and tight and warm, the tightness increased by the feel of my balls sitting on her closed thighs, and I want to fuck her all night like this.

I lay on top of her, supporting my upper body weight with my elbows, and stroke her hair away from her face. I kiss her, and she blinks at her own taste, but then she wraps her arms around my neck and licks her wetness from my lips like an affectionate puppy.

I allow her to have her moment before I grind my cock inside her. She gasps. Her eyes lock onto mine, and she pulls my face closer. "Caleb…"

Her kisses grow hungrier, more demanding, the harder I slam into her, and I feel my own precum mingling with her wetness. I'm not ready to come yet. "Say it."

She blinks. "Say what?" she whispers.

"Fuck me, Caleb."

She hesitates like she has to think about it, and I stop pounding her. I'm holding her to ransom until she tells me what I want to hear.

"Fuck me, Caleb."

I pull out, and in one fluid movement, kneel over Victoria and flip her over, dragging her hips towards me, and pushing her head and shoulders into the pillows. With her butt in the air, I spread her pussy wide and lick her from behind, probing with one finger to bring her to a second orgasm. While she's coming, gripping the pillows tightly with both fists, her face smothered by her hair, I rim her, keeping the orgasm flowing with my wet fingers.

Then I thrust my cock inside her sex, all the way. My balls slap wetly against her pelvis, and I slow it down. I'm still not ready to come.

Sliding my cock all the way out, I tease her pussy and butthole with the head, rubbing it around her, and pulling her hips onto me, before sliding it all the way back in. In and out. When she starts to feel dry, I lick her from behind, her pussy swollen, her orgasm still lingering like an itch that won't be satisfied.

"Tell me you want me, Victoria." I ram my cock back inside her, holding her hips against me so that she has to take it.

"I ... want ... you..."

"Louder." I stop grinding. Hold her still so that she can feel me throbbing inside her.

"I want you."

"You'll have to do better than that, Victoria. Tell me you want me like you mean it."

A gurgle of laughter escapes her lips. "I want you, Caleb. *I freaking want you.*"

I lean over her, cupping her breasts with both hands and twisting her nipples while I ram into her from behind. She grinds her hips against me, and that's when I allow myself to come, my entire body shuddering against her until we both collapse in a heap on the pillows.

13

VICTORIA

Maybe we fall asleep for a couple of hours. Or maybe I simply lay there in Caleb's bed, his arm flung across my chest, his face close to mine, watching him sleep.

It is still dark when he stirs. I'm naked, he is still wearing his suit pants and shirt from the evening before. I breathe his oxygen, and it feels so right that I don't want the night to end.

He opens his eyes and smiles.

I smile back. I still feel the pang of letting Danny Zuko slip through my grasp, but I understand now that this ache has become a habit that I've clung to the way a child clings to their favorite blanket. A crutch of sorts. A fond memory to keep me warm at night and whenever I'm feeling lonely and undesirable.

His fingers locate my nipple, and he leans over me to suck on it. "Ready for round two?" My pussy, although sore and swollen, immediately responds by tingling, and the crushing tiredness I felt before evaporates like warm breath on a cold window.

Pulling the comforter over his head, Caleb disappears. He spreads my legs and licks me so gently that my orgasm explodes almost immediately, my body convulsing, my breathing shallow.

Caleb reappears. "Don't think you're getting away with it that easily."

Slowly, with his eyes locked onto mine, he unbuttons his shirt and tosses it onto the floor. Then he unzips his pants, freeing his engorged cock in one easy movement. He slides them off and adds them to the pile of discarded clothes on the floor along with his boxers.

It's the first time I've seen him naked, and he's every inch how I imagined him to look when I watched him straddling his Harley the night he saved Mason. He obviously works out. He probably has a freaking gym nestled somewhere within his cavernous apartment. His shoulders are wide, his chest smooth, and his six-pack ripped. His torso is covered in Celtic tattoos, intricate crosses, knots, and infinity symbols that I could spend hours trying to unravel.

I allow my eyes to drift slowly down to his defined pelvis and finally settle on the length of his cock.

It takes my breath away. How did it even fit inside me?

"Your turn." He holds the base of his cock and starts rubbing it, and I can't help envying his confidence in his own skin.

It isn't vanity. I mean, he must know how hot he is, he probably has women like Suki telling him he's hot every day of the week, but he isn't arrogant about it. This is all about feeling comfortable with his body, something I've always struggled with, considering my inability to get laid until I met

Danny Zuko. And even he didn't come back for more. There's only so much rejection a gal can take.

I roll onto my knees and inch towards him, his cock growing even larger if that's at all possible. I don't know what he wants me to do. That's a lie; I mean, I know what he wants me to do, but my experience of doing it is still on level zero.

Lowering my head, I wrap my hand around his girth and take the head into my mouth. I can taste me on him, and it sends a thrill down my spine. With him in my mouth, I lick all around the head, sliding the tip of my tongue into the slit and nibbling with my teeth.

"Deeper." His voice is husky.

I open my mouth wider, lower myself onto him until I can feel him touching the back of my throat. The gag reflex is instantaneous, and I pull away, hiding my face because I don't want him to see my eyes watering.

But Caleb removes my hands and cups my face in his. He tilts my head back, grips my chin, and kisses my lips. "You can do it, Victoria."

Does he know what he's doing? Is this all part of his plan to get me to be submissive? Because it works.

I grip him tightly and take him into my mouth, forcing myself not to gag. My hand instinctively starts rubbing, gently to begin with, and growing more forceful as I pump his cock in and out of my mouth. He wraps his fists in my hair and grips me tightly. "Keep going, m'áilleacht."

I lose all sense of time and place. All that exists for me is his cock in my fist and my mouth, and the taste of his precum in the back of my throat. A spear of panic travels through me. Do I swallow when he comes, or do I catch it in my mouth and spit it out? What would he want me to do? What if I can't even make him orgasm?

But I must be doing something right because Caleb releases my hair, unwraps my fingers from around him, pulls out of my mouth, and pushes me back horizontally across the bed.

Grabbing my thighs, he pushes them back so that my knees are on either side of my head, exposing my sex to him. Then, on his knees, he inserts a finger into my pussy, catches my juices and slides it between my lips, forcing me to lick my own taste off him while he rams his length into me. "Do you like tasting yourself, Victoria?"

"Yes." Part of me wants to scream that I love it, but something is still holding me back.

It's a heady combination, his finger in my mouth and his cock pounding me so deeply, I swear I can feel it hitting the base of my spine. I feel my own orgasm erupting as his body judders and he comes inside me.

But he doesn't leave it there. Whipping his cock out of me, he shoves it into my mouth, holding my head with both hands, so that I have no choice but to swallow the last of his cum.

When he is done, Caleb lies beside me, still teasing my erect nipples with his fingers.

As the heat of the moment cools, I can't help wondering what this means for us. The fake marriage is temporary, I get it, and I'm no expert when it comes to sexual relationships, but my gut is telling me that he wants me as badly as I want him.

So, how do we walk away from this when the time comes? Because, I don't know about Caleb, but I can't simply let him vanish too.

Before I can voice my thoughts, his phone vibrates, and he leaves my side, the rush of cool air on my bare skin making me shiver.

He sits on the edge of the bed with his back to me, his cell phone held to his ear, and his voice low, allowing me an unobstructed view of his broad shoulders and toned physique. Before he even ends the call, he is on his feet and heading for the ensuite.

"Where are you going?" I sit up straight, acutely conscious of my nakedness now that I'm alone on the bed.

He halts halfway across the room, his gaze lingering on my breasts before he raises his eyes to meet mine. "I have some business to attend to." He pauses. "I want you to stay in the apartment, Victoria. Anything you need, let Lauren know, and she'll arrange it for you."

"Wait. What?" I'm on my knees, covering my breasts with the comforter. He has seen every part of me, has tasted me inside and out, but I feel vulnerable now that he is back in Caleb-Murray-wealthy-hotel-owner mode. "Why can't I leave? What about Abigail?"

"Abigail is fine."

"So, what, you think I'm in danger?"

I glance at the dressing on my arm which I barely noticed while Caleb was fucking me all through the night. I told myself that the shooting was simply a case of wrong place, wrong time, but his reaction this morning is starting to freak me out. What the fuck have I brought Abigail into?

"It isn't a chance I'm prepared to take. I told you before, I take care of what's mine."

Anger courses through my veins. I refuse to be held prisoner in his apartment even if it is the most luxurious apartment in New York City. I'd rather be at home where nobody knows me apart from Sienna and a couple of neighbors. At least there I'm free to come and go as I please.

"But I'm not yours, am I?"

I wait for him to say something, but when he lowers his eyes to the floor, I realize that I have my answer. I clamber off the bed, still clutching the comforter to cover my nakedness.

"I'm going to get Abigail, and then I'm taking her home."

"Victoria, please." He inhales deeply, oblivious to his own nakedness. "I promise that I won't let any harm come to you or Abigail. I know that I need to make things up to you. This should never have happened, but I just need a little time to resolve it. Please."

The *'please'* gets to me. When he looks at me that way, I can almost convince myself that he feels something for me, that this could be more than just an arrangement to get Olivia Dragonetti off his case.

"Okay, but you can't keep me locked up in here."

He opens his mouth to protest that I'm not locked up but must change his mind. "Get dressed. I'll take you to my mom's."

Moira and Terry live in a huge gray-stone colonial mansion on Staten Island. The center of the property is glass-fronted affording views of the spectacular interior staircase which are even more impressive when we step inside.

The gold-balustraded staircase sweeps up to the next level in a double-sided spiral, giving the entrance atrium the appearance of an exhibition center. It is decorated with heavy chandeliers taller than a grown man, vibrant tribal artwork, and life-sized, bronze lion statues that appear to be guarding the property.

I'm still gaping at the sheer scale of the house when Moira comes to greet us, holding Abigail's hand.

"Auntie Vicky!" Abigail runs to me and jumps into my arms. "You should come and see the swimming pool. There's a treehouse in the garden and a pond with fish in it and a basketball court."

I set her down. "Maybe you can show me around in a little while if Moira doesn't mind." I glance at Caleb's mom, who is smiling at Abigail fondly.

"Of course I don't mind. You're welcome to stay here as long as you like."

"Stay here?" I turn my attention to Caleb. Is this why he agreed to bring me to Abigail, because he wants his mom and stepdad to keep me prisoner instead?

"I just thought you might be more comfortable here." His expression is unreadable, and I wish, not for the first time, that he would tell me how he really feels.

"Where will *you* stay?" Jeez I sound needy, whiny, like a teenager. Or like freaking Dragon-face herself.

A faint smile plays with the corners of his mouth. "I have business to take care of and then I'll be back."

"Caleb, you're not leaving already." The voice belongs to a young woman with blondee mermaid curls and a wide smile who is coming down the stairs. "I never get to spend any time with you these days."

My stomach twists. Another admirer?

She goes to Caleb and gives him a hug which he reciprocates with his arms wrapped around her. Releasing her, he says, "Victoria this is my baby sister, Emily."

"Hey, not so much of the baby sister." She punches his arm playfully.

"Emily, this is my wife, Victoria."

It takes several beats for his words to sink in. She blinks once, twice, three times. "Wife? You got married without telling me?" She faces Moira. "Mom, did you know about this?"

Moira raises both hands in mock surrender, and I suspect that Emily has them all wrapped around her little finger. "I only found out yesterday."

Emily shakes her head at her mom and brother, then smiles at me. "Oh my God, I can't believe you finally tamed my brother. Please don't tell me that you belong to the same motorcycle club. No, you're too beautiful to be a biker."

She comes and takes my hand and leads me and Abigail through the house, talking incessantly.

"This calls for a celebration. I'll get Nikos to fix us a drink and bring it outside to the decking, and you can tell me all about how you two met."

I glance over my shoulder at Caleb who grins and shrugs. He obviously isn't prepared to argue the point with Emily; she has probably done him a favor by keeping me busy so that he can escape and attend to whatever business matter is so urgent.

Nikos must be the gardener. He is a young man with olive skin, thick dark curls, and eyes that are all for Emily. At her request, he goes inside to the kitchen which is larger than my entire apartment to fix us cocktails, while Emily drags me and Abigail to a decking area complete with blazing firepit and woolen blankets.

Emily sits on a sofa and tucks her legs beneath her. When I'm seated with Abigail on my lap and a blanket thrown over us, she says, "Sorry, I should've said congratulations, but I'm still processing the news. Where did you get married? Why weren't we invited? When did this even happen?" She squeals like a child. "I always knew Caleb would do something like this."

Her enthusiasm is infectious, and I can't help laughing.

"Auntie Vicky has a diamond ring," Abigail chimes in.

Emily's gaze drops to the emerald on my finger. "Mom gave you her ring! It looks so beautiful on you Vicky."

She automatically shortens my name, and I think that we could be good friends if this marriage was real. There is something very likeable about Emily, and I find myself wondering if she knows Olivia Dragonetti.

I'm angry with Caleb for leaving it to me to tell his sister the truth. I don't want to be the one to dampen her excitement, but I can't lie to her.

"Emily I—"

Nikos comes outside with our cocktails and a special drink for Abigail complete with cherries, a slice of pineapple and a sparkly streamer, which he sets down on the huge glass-topped table between the sofas.

"Thanks, Nikos." The way Emily looks at him, I can tell that she's smitten too, but it's obvious that neither of them have plucked up the courage to say anything.

She sits back and sips her drink through a straw, waiting for me to spill the beans.

Deep breath. This was Caleb's idea; I'll tell her the truth, and then he can fill in the details when he gets back.

"Emily..." I puff up my cheeks. This is way harder than I thought it would be because, after last night, I wish it wasn't just a marriage contract and a prenup agreement. "I hate to disappoint you, but we're not really married."

She furrows her brow. "So, what, you're just engaged to be married?"

I shake my head while tears sting my eyes.

"I don't understand. You're wearing Mom's ring."

I keep my voice low; Abigail is trying to spear the cherries out of her drink with the cocktail stick streamer, but she hears everything, and I can already see how much she likes Caleb. I don't want to shatter her illusions of him.

"Caleb asked me to pretend to be his wife. Kyle drew up a marriage contract. It's only temporary while Caleb resolves the situation with Olivia Dragonetti."

I catch a glimpse of movement from the corner of my eye and turn around to find Mr. Dragonetti watching us from inside the open kitchen doorway. I don't know how much he overheard, but he turns around and heads back inside the house, and I realize that I've literally destroyed Caleb's plans because I couldn't keep my mouth shut.

14

CALEB

"Word on the street is that Olivia Dragonetti is behind the shooting." Terry comes straight out with it. No messing around.

Now that her name is in the frame, it makes perfect sense. She followed Victoria to the restroom, made certain that she left the restaurant exactly when she needed her to, and then sat back and watched the scene unfold.

"Victoria was the target." My jaw clenches.

The woman is even more dangerous than I gave her credit for. But I swear, if Olivia Dragonetti so much as damages a hair on Victoria's head, I'll kill her myself.

"Not necessarily." Terry's voice is even, steady. The leader of the pack.

We're in the Rinse's boardroom, another family meeting, and yet another of which Olivia Dragonetti is the focal point. If she wanted our attention, she has already succeeded. But she has underestimated the Murrays if she thinks this little charade will intimidate us into backing down.

She clearly doesn't know me at all.

"You and Kyle were there," Terry continues. "There are no prizes for guessing where the don will be looking to place the blame for the bullet in his shoulder."

My gaze drifts to the twins. A faint smile is already twitching at the corners of Cash's lips. Olivia is so hellbent on revenge for my rejection of marriage that she risked her own father's life to take us down.

"She isn't that clever," Cash says. "Precisely how long did it take you to find out that she was behind the shooting? Don Dragonetti will get the same info."

Terry spreads his hands wide above the table. "The don didn't get to where he is today by listening to the footmen. They follow his orders. And his orders will be to retaliate."

"So, we tell him the truth." Kyle looks at each of us in turn.

Where Terry is the practical family member with his ear to the ground and enough inside knowledge to take down every mafia family in the city, Kyle is the voice of reason. The one who knows how to manipulate the law to keep us just on the right side of legal.

"I think we should hold fire." I sip my iced water, buying myself some precious moments to assemble my thoughts.

I can still feel Victoria's mouth wrapped around my dick. I can still taste her, still feel my balls slapping against her ass when I fucked her from behind. I can still smell her on me even though I showered the smell of her sex off me. But I need to focus. I made a promise to protect both her and Abigail, and I aim to keep that promise, no matter what it takes.

"She's careless." I'm thinking out loud. "Reckless. She's learned nothing from her father because she's too preoccupied with blowing up her ex's lives. She can't let anything go, and ultimately, this will be her downfall."

"What are you thinking?" Terry asks.

"First things first, we ramp up security around Victoria and Abigail. Olivia will be rampaging when she discovers that Victoria is neither wounded nor scared."

I glance at Terry who nods once. "Goes without saying. We'll keep them safe."

"Secondly, we provide Olivia Dragonetti with a distraction. We trace her exes, make it worth their while to make a reappearance, no matter how brief, and when she loses her shit, we make fucking certain that her father is around to see it."

Everyone is silent for several moments.

Finally, Bash says, "That will never work. How long has it been since you and she were an item? Whatever you did, bro, you did it good because she's got it firmly fixed inside her pretty little head that you're the one she wants, and no one else is going to have you."

"So, we give her a new distraction." Cash shrugs. "She'll never buy into you wanting her back. Not with Victoria on the scene."

My cock twitches inside my pants at the thought of Victoria's butt in my face. He has a point. I couldn't even pretend to want Olivia Dragonetti right now, not with my balls already filling up for Victoria.

"Ivan Petrov." Cash inclines his head. "Just saying."

"No can do." Terry sits forward, rests his lower arms on the table, and steeples his fingers. "Olivia approached the Petrovs with her harebrained scheme to shoot her father, and they walked away from it."

"Sensible." But I still think this is the only way. "We need to expose her for the loose cannon she is."

"An alliance with the Petrovs?" Kyle suggests.

I shake my head. "Don Dragonetti is still our best potential alliance. His connections far outweigh his daughter's irrational behavior." The glimmer of an idea is taking shape inside my head. "Dragonetti might believe that Cash is behind last night's incident, but he'll side with whoever offers him the best deal."

"So, we offer him a deal that he can't refuse." Terry picks up the thread. "Including a way to get his uncontrollable daughter off his hands."

"Any suggestions?" Kyle arches an eyebrow.

He looks tired. I would trust my older brother with my life—I'd trust him with Victoria and Abigail's lives too—but his place is behind his desk doing what he does best. Keeping us all in line.

"Whatever we do," Terry says, "we need to make it look like it was the don's idea. He's a proud man. He was born into this way of life, and he's acutely aware that his legacy will be passed onto his only daughter. Without Caleb in the mix, he can seek an alliance with any of the other families."

"So, we need to make our offer sing to him." I rub my jaw with my hand. "Kyle, I need you to let me know how far we can go with casino intake. Terry, what are we talking here? Money?"

"Mostly. Old man Dragonetti is struggling financially. His daughter is bleeding him dry, which is saying something when you consider her father's wealth."

"But..." I prompt him.

"But..." Terry inhales deeply. "I think this goes way deeper than zeroes in his bank account. Why do you think he wanted an alliance with us in the first place?"

"Aside from offloading his daughter." I don't smile. Nothing about Olivia Dragonetti is humorous. "Because he trusts us."

Before we took over from Terry, and he stepped back from the business side of the family name, he instilled in us the need for authenticity. He prided himself on his word being worth its weight in gold and insisted that if we ever let him down in that respect, he would take us down himself. He wasn't wielding fear like a baton, he was simply protecting the family. And we would all rather cut off our right hand than destroy the family honor.

"Don Dragonetti needs people around him that he can trust." Terry shrugs, "Sure, he hoped that you would deal with Olivia."

"Probably wanted you to impregnate her," Cash adds, "and give her a mansion in which to play happy families."

He's probably not far from the truth.

"But more than that," Terry continues, "he knew that an alliance with the Murrays would strengthen his own position in the community."

"Which would work both ways." I'm still not sure where Terry is leading with this one.

"We need to make him an offer he can't refuse, so that when we present him with his daughter on a plate, he trusts that we're doing the right thing for both families."

Bash scratches his head and lets out a low whistle. "Not much of an ask."

Now Terry smiles. "Olivia is the gun just waiting to go off. We find a way to control her, and everything else will slot into place."

"She's so self-absorbed she'll eventually shoot herself in her own foot." I think of the graze on Victoria's arm. "But I'm not risking Victoria or Abigail to get her to slip up."

"No one's asking you to." Terry's tone is firm, in control. "We need to steer her away from you and Victoria."

"You're planning a wedding reception, right?" Bash asks. "You know that'll tip Olivia over the edge. She might just be crazy enough to attempt another incident that night."

A glance around the table, and I know that my brothers and Terry agree.

"Too risky." I shake my head.

"We need to go ahead with it though," Terry says. "Fan her jealousy. We just make sure the distraction is in place first. It'll bolster her ego, convince her that she's invincible."

"Especially if we keep the alliance quiet." It could work. I'm already imagining the amount of security we'll need to ensure Victoria and Abigail's safety. "We'll hold it in the Titan's ballroom."

"What about the distraction?" Kyle has been quiet until now, following the conversation, his mind one step ahead of the game.

"I'm up for it," Cash says. "I'll show her what a real man is made of."

Bash snickers. "Best leave it to me then. I'll take one for the team."

Terry shakes his head. "The don sees you, Cash, as collateral damage. You'll still be on his radar for getting him shot, don't forget."

"Hey, I'm still here," Bash says. "Unattached. A hottie even if I do say so myself. A real catch some might say."

I don't like where this is going. "There must be another way. Not palming her off onto one of my brothers is the reason I married Victoria in the first place."

"You're not legally married in the eyes of the church," Kyle says coolly.

I ignore him. "I still don't think this is the way forward."

"I agree that Cash and Bash are risky." Terry raises his steepled fingers to his lips. "She had her sights on you, Caleb, because you're not quite so ... volatile."

Cash laughs. "He's too soft, you mean."

"I'll do it." Kyle's voice breaks through the jesting and brings me down to earth with a jolt.

"No." I think of all the therapy Kyle has been through since the accident. He'll never be able to handle Olivia Dragonetti, and I don't want to see him dragged back down into the black spiral he fought so hard to climb out of. "She'll never buy it."

"Why?" Kyle narrows his eyes. "Because I'm not you?"

"No, because you're the sensible one." I mean it as a compliment even if it sounds derogatory once the word is hanging in the air.

"He's most like you," Terry says.

"You can't possibly think this is a good idea."

Terry shrugs. "Why not? If anyone can pull this off it's Kyle. No offence lads," he addresses the twins.

"She'll do it to make you jealous," Kyle says.

"Can you handle that?"

Kyle grins. "Sure, I can. This is only temporary, right?"

I have to smile. "Only until the wedding reception. We catch her out on the night and let her father take over. Agreed?"

Everyone around the table murmurs their agreement. My gut doesn't like it, but we need to take Olivia out of the equation somehow if the alliance is to succeed, and I've already wasted too much time trying to think of a better option.

"Any sign of Callahan?" I ask Terry.

He sucks in a deep breath. "Not a whisper."

"Someone else has flown off the radar." I tell him about Brailand Voth. "Can you see what you can find out for me?"

I can tell by the distant look in his eyes that he's already mentally searching for the connection.

"Where is Dragonetti now?" I ask as an afterthought as we all stand to leave.

"Where do you think?" Terry smiles. "He's holed up in my best guest room."

My heart skips erratically when I think of Victoria and Abigail. I left them at Moira and Terry's mansion to keep them safe, not so they could play Monopoly with the head of the Italian mafia.

"Why? Why didn't his men relocate him to his own safe house?" What am I missing here?

"He had his reasons." Terry's expression is neutral. He knows what they are, but he isn't letting on. "His men treated his injury in our safe house. It was my idea to move him into the mansion."

My brothers and I have never questioned Terry's decisions, and I'm not about to start now, but mentally I'm en route to Staten Island to collect Victoria and Abigail and take them out of the equation.

"Where better to hide a mafia boss than in plain sight at a rival family's home?" Terry is gauging my reaction.

"You said he suspects Cash."

Terry shakes his head. "I said he'd be looking to direct the blame Cash's way. Look..." He inhales, puffing up his chest. "I know he'll try to find out if we played a part in last night's shenanigans, but it doesn't mean that he won't be looking elsewhere."

Mateo Dragonetti suspects an inside job; it's the only reason I can think of that would keep him at Terry's mansion instead of his own safe house.

But where does that leave Victoria and Abigail?

15

VICTORIA

I ask Emily to stay outside with Abigail and rush into the house to speak to Mr. Dragonetti. I find him alone in what must be the family den. There's a gigantic flat screen TV on the wall, and a sunken sofa littered with cushions that would easily seat ten people. A coffee station takes up one corner of the room, and the floor-to-ceiling windows overlook the landscaped gardens which stretch as far as I can see, surrounded by majestic trees.

Mr. Dragonetti smiles at me when I barge into the room and gestures for me to sit with him.

It feels strange reclining on a sofa in Terry and Moira's house with a man like Mr. Dragonetti after what happened the night before, even more surreal than fake-marrying Caleb. But it isn't until I curl my legs under me and turn to face him that I notice the bulky bandage beneath the sleeve of his sweater.

"Are you... Were you hurt last night?"

He offers me a gentle smile. Close up, and without his daughter's fury dominating the room, I can see that he must've been a handsome man in his youth. His silver hair is still thick with no signs of receding; his eyes are clear brown, and his nose is slender, all the classic features of a twentieth-century Hollywood movie star. But there are deep grooves across his forehead, and heavy pouches beneath his eyes that suggest his lifestyle keeps him awake at night.

"I'll live, Victoria."

I swallow. Now that I'm here, I realize that I can't blurt out the question I need to ask him. If he didn't hear what Emily and I were talking about, I want it to stay that way. I can't ruin this for Caleb, and besides, I'm not ready for this to be over. Not after what happened between us last night.

I expected Mr. Dragonetti to be unapproachable, given the guests at the dinner party and the direction the conversation took, but I realize now that he is nothing like his daughter. "Has this happened to you before?"

His face lights up with his smile. "If you're asking if danger comes with the territory, the answer is yes." He pauses. "But yesterday was quite an unusual occurrence."

"Unusual in what way?"

"So many questions. Did your husband forget to warn you about the kind of life you were getting yourself into?"

Shit! He obviously heard enough.

"I ... just never expected it to happen to me." I'm stalling, and I can see in his eyes that he knows it. My fingers instinctively cover the dressing on my arm under my sleeve.

His eyebrows lower, and the smile fades. This is the man I expected to confront, the formidable man with clenched jaw and dark eyes. "Who took care of you?"

"Caleb. It's nothing. Just a graze."

"And yet here you are with me, wanting to know if I am hurt."

His voice softens, and I understand why Olivia is the way she is. I don't know if Mr. Dragonetti has other children, but I'd bet that she is still treated like his baby. Unlike Emily though, Olivia expects attention from everyone who orbits her existence.

"I... It's scary. You must've been scared too."

Knowing that he was shot and that the bullet probably glanced off him and hit my arm, doesn't make the situation any less frightening. I might not have been the target, but he's right: this is the life I've gotten myself mixed up in by agreeing to fake-marry Caleb Murray.

This time, his smile reveals faintly discolored teeth. "No one has ever asked me this before. In the moment, I thought only of my daughter."

My stomach twists. Of course, his first thought would be to keep his daughter safe—it's parental instinct. He is Olivia's protector. It's just frustrating that the mention of her name can have such a negative effect on me.

"And now?" I ask.

"Now I see before me a brave young woman, and I understand why Caleb chose to marry you."

"Marry me?" I blurt out before I can stop myself. Is he hinting that he knows we're not married, or is he just genuinely a nice guy? I wish I could read him, but my experience of dealing with people like Mr. Dragonetti is severely limited.

"You must forgive my daughter, Victoria." *Must I? Forgive her for what? Trying to steal my husband?* "My wife died when

Olivia was a little girl, and I know I'm guilty of being too lenient with her. I hope that someday you and she can be friends. You see, Olivia needs people like you in her life."

I seriously doubt that we will ever be friends, but I don't voice my opinion out loud. Relief that Mr. Dragonetti hasn't mentioned the fake marriage combined with confusion at the way the conversation has turned leaves me speechless.

He is still a mafia boss, his daughter is still an asshole, and this doesn't change the fact that we both got shot last night.

For the next few hours, while Emily plays with Abigail in what used to be Emily's playroom when she was a little girl, Moira and I start fleshing out plans for the wedding party.

The Titan's ballroom, according to Moira, is already glamorous. She talks about the pale gold décor and the sprung flooring that is perfect for dancing as if she doesn't want me to alter anything. But when I tell her that I'd like it to be Great Gatsby themed, with lowlights, and flapper dresses, and the men in linen suits, she doesn't try to change my mind.

Moira agrees to handle the guest list. She asks me who I would like to invite, but with Mason still missing, and my mom in Florida, the only person I can think of is Sienna.

A thought occurs to me. "My friend is an artist. Maybe I could commission her to create some artwork for us. Maybe pictures of me and Caleb in scenes from *The Great Gatsby*."

"If you think there will be enough time." Moira peers at me from behind spectacles linked to a fine gold chain around her neck. She is on her tablet preparing the guest list.

"We haven't set a date for the party yet."

"The sooner the better, sweetie." Her voice is all honey and lightness, but I get the first glimpse behind it of a strong woman who has carved out her own niche within this male-dominated mafia family. "I was thinking perhaps the week after next. Unless you have any objections."

She wants this whole situation over and done with. She has a mafia don in her house and a woman masquerading as her daughter-in-law, not to mention the ripple effect following last night's shooting incident.

But tears well in my eyes at the thought of walking away from Caleb in two weeks.

I hoped we would have more time together. I hoped, stupidly perhaps, that we could get to know one another, build on the obvious attraction that exists between us. I'd even hoped that Moira might be on my side, but I understand now how wrong I've been. Her allegiance is and always will be to her children, and I can't blame her for that.

"No. No objections," I mutter.

But I have lost enthusiasm for planning the event.

When Caleb said that I could organize our wedding reception, I'd felt the thrill of opportunity coursing through my veins. It's what I've always wanted to do, ever since I was a little girl creating imaginary parties for my dolls. At high school, I would use the computers to check out celebrity balls, storing the glossy images inside my head, and tweaking them in the solace of my bedroom at home, adding my own personal touch to décor and themes and colors. Sienna found her creative outlet through watercolors, but I found mine through glitzy imaginary galas.

Now, my first opportunity to plan an event that will be attended by some of the wealthiest people in New York has been tainted by the palpable taste of losing Caleb Murray.

He was never yours to begin with, my stupid brain yells at me.

So, what was last night all about then, my heart murmurs back.

"Why don't you call your friend now?" Moira suggests.

I know she was kind enough to look after Abigail and welcome me into her home, but now all I can hear is the desperation in her voice to get us out of Caleb's life so that their world can return to normal.

I take my phone out of my pocket and try Sienna's number. It rings and rings and then cuts off. Sienna doesn't like using voicemail, so I wait a few seconds and try again, with the same result.

I type out a message: *Hey, Si, give me a call when you get time. It's regarding wedding plans.* That should grab her attention.

"She must be busy," I say to Moria's enquiring eyebrow.

Caleb walks in then, and my heart performs a triple-somersault. I wish it wouldn't. I'm already trying to mentally prepare myself for when this is all over and we'll never see each other again.

"Ah, there he is." Moira slides from her chrome bar stool at the kitchen island and kisses Caleb's cheek. "We're discussing the wedding reception. The Titan is available two weekends from now."

She busies herself making coffee, and Caleb's eyes lock onto mine. An unfathomable expression dances across his features before he rearranges them into a small smile. "How do you feel about that? Will it give you enough time to plan it the way you would like?"

Is that disappointment I can hear in his voice? Or am I just fooling myself that there's a connection between us? Maybe it was just sex to him. Maybe he makes every woman he fucks feel as special as he made me feel last night.

Sienna is right. I need to stop giving off chilly vibes and live a little; perhaps then I'll stop falling headfirst for every guy who shows me some attention. *Every guy?* Who am I kidding? There's only ever been Danny and Caleb, and I'm acting like a sixteen-year-old schoolgirl all over again.

"It'll be fine," I manage when I realize that he's still waiting for an answer.

I consider telling him that I can't get hold of Sienna, and I'm not attending my own wedding party without my best friend, but I decide against it. It's enough that he's going to give me money to help Sienna, it doesn't mean that he cares about her.

He nods once. "Mom will help you with the guest list."

"Already on it, Caleb." Moira comes back to the island with coffee for her son.

They exchange glances that don't include me, and I wonder if bringing the reception forward was Caleb's idea all along.

Caleb sips his coffee and sets the cup down on the island counter. "Is Dragonetti still here, Mom?"

"He was in the den when I spoke to him this morning," I blurt before Moira can speak.

Caleb's eyes flicker back and forth between us, and now I'm certain that there's something going on that I don't know about. "I'll go and find him." He's gone before I can ask him what's going on.

I don't think it's a conscious reaction, but Caleb has this knack of making me feel like an outsider, when his words tell me that he wants me to slot into his life. And this is one of those moments. Sure, no one knows him as well as his mom does, but if he wants to convince the rest of the world that we're married, shouldn't he be including me in whatever is going on here?

Caleb returns to the kitchen a few minutes later. "He's gone."

16

CALEB

"What did you speak about?"

It sounds harsher than I intended but armed with the information Terry imparted at the meeting, I need to know exactly what's going on. Victoria doesn't know the mafia boss. She doesn't associate with the kind of people I deal with every day. She has no idea what people like Don Dragonetti are capable of.

"Nothing really." I can feel Victoria visibly shrinking away from me and immediately relent.

"Did he ask you about our marriage?" I tone it down. I don't want her to clam up because she's scared of me. Fuck knows, I can be an intimidating bastard when I need to be but now is not one of those moments.

"No."

Something in her tone suggests otherwise, but I'm not going to be a brute about it. I don't like how she's staring at me like

I'm an ogre. I liked it way better when she was telling me how much she freaking wanted me to fuck her last night.

"I-I asked him if he'd been shot before." Her voice is timid, small, thanks to me, but I can't help smiling. "And he said that he'd like me and Olivia to be friends someday."

I hear my mom's sharp intake of breath from the corner of my eye.

"I think you should stay here until the wedding reception."

My cock deflates at the thought of not sharing my bed with Victoria tonight, but a promise is a promise, and the don can't be seen to take a bullet in his arm and take it lying down. He will retaliate. But the big question is how.

Victoria slides from her stool and faces me squarely. She might be a good nine inches shorter than me in her stocking feet, but I can feel the slow-burning rage building up inside her. I guess it's how she's dealt with her scumbag brother all these years.

"No. I'm coming with you, or I'm going home."

Game on. "You know I can't let you go home. I promised to—"

"Protect me?" She arches an eyebrow. "I get it. But protect me from what exactly? *Don* Dragonetti?" She emphasizes the word 'Don' like she only just understood the implications of the title.

"He's a dangerous man, Victoria. I can't protect you, if I don't know where you are."

"So, take me with you then. Isn't that what husbands do?"

"Victoria, Caleb is only thinking of what's best for you and

Abigail," Mom interjects. "You know that Terry and I would love to have you stay here."

"It's very kind of you, Moira, but I can't impose on your hospitality. This is between me and Caleb." Victoria keeps her eyes on me when she speaks.

"It's okay, Mom."

I glance at her and give her the nod that I have the situation under control even though I've never felt less in control in my life. Since Victoria walked into my life, I've felt as if I'm wading through quicksand that keeps shifting out from under my feet. The parameters keep altering. In any other circumstances, I'd deal with Olivia and form an alliance elsewhere, but her and Abigail's presence in my life complicates matters.

I will not see them get caught up in this to save my own reputation. Because that's what this boils down to. An alliance with the Dragonetti family will give me the security to step down at some point in the future and raise a family, peacefully, and without the constant threat of danger or destruction.

"You said you didn't want to be trapped inside my apartment," I reason. "I'm offering you an alternative where I know that you will be safe."

"I'm not scared of Don Dragonetti." She opens her mouth to say more, and closes it again, the words left unspoken.

"Well, maybe you should be."

My fists instinctively clench at the thought of Olivia trying to hurt Victoria. How can she be so naïve? She shared a few words with the man and now she thinks that he has her best interests at heart.

"Whoa, what's going on?" Emily appears from the decking end of the kitchen, Abigail by her side. "I can feel the heat from outside."

"I'm just trying to convince Victoria to stay here for a while." From the way Emily's eyes slide towards Victoria and back again, I can guess that she knows the truth about our agreement too.

"And I'm trying to tell him that we should stay together." Victoria's tone is defiant.

"I like it here," Abigail says, and Victoria flashes me a look that says we should leave Abigail out of it.

Emily grins. "Now, now children, anyone would think that you're an old married couple."

Yep. She knows.

"I don't see what the problem is. Why can't she stay wherever she wants?"

Emily is Terry's baby. Sure, he brought us up like his own sons, but when Emily came along, the first girl in the family, it was the turning point for him. Rather than encouraging her to learn about the family business, he was determined to do everything in his power to keep her out of it. Like a parent warning their eldest child not to spoil the magic of Christmas for their younger siblings, he insisted that none of us ever divulged the true nature of our business to our baby sister.

So, Emily is still blissfully unaware that her mom, dad, and brothers are all part of one of the strongest mafia families in the city, even if we're not the most violent. She sailed through high school, got into Cornell, and is studying to be a vet. Sometimes, I envy her the normal path her life follows even if she does have the wealth behind her that most kids don't have.

But it means that she often views the world through rose-tinted glasses with no idea of the strings being pulled in the background to offer her this idyllic future.

Victoria is still watching me, waiting for me to respond to my sister's question, daring me to tell her the truth.

"Does this have anything to do with Mr. Dragonetti?" Emily asks. "He seems really nice. He came and said goodbye to me and Abigail before he left. Said that we'd be seeing a lot more of each other."

I could mention the shooting incident, but twenty-one years down the line, and Terry's warning is still imprinted on my brain with indelible ink. *Emily never finds out the truth. If I hear one of you told her, you'll have me to deal with*. I don't know what the don meant when he told Emily they'd see a lot more of each other, but my tongue remains firmly tied when it comes to telling her the truth.

"Okay," I relent. "You can come back to the apartment with me. But on one condition."

"I'm not getting Lauren to run errands for me." Victoria is still standing her ground, and I have the sudden urge to bend her over my knee, pull down her panties, and slap her ass. And yep, like fucking clockwork, my dick responds to the mental image.

"This is the twenty-first century." I force myself not to let my eyes travel any lower than her lips because if my gaze reaches her breasts I'll remember leaving my mark on them, and I might as well kiss goodbye to being the one in control. "We have internet."

"Speaking of." Emily swings Abigail up into her arms and

deposits her on the counter. "We've been looking at schools, haven't we, Abigail?"

Abigail nods seriously. "I want to go to Sudbury Valley."

Victoria moves closer, her hands instinctively fluttering towards the child to prevent her from toppling off the counter. "I don't know anything about Sudbury Valley, sweetie. I don't even know where it is."

"It's in Massachusetts," Emily chimes in. "My friend went there. It'll be perfect for Abigail because the children get to study whatever they want. They choose their own education. If Abigail wants to play with computers all day, that's what she does."

"What about the rest of her education?" Victoria's gaze flits between me and Emily. Curiosity has already gotten hold of her though. "What about reading and Math and history?"

"What about it?" Emily shrugs. "Have you ever used algebra since you left school? Why should every kid in the country be forced to take the same exams at the same time when they all have different abilities and different learning levels?"

"I can read," Abigail says.

Victoria wrinkles her nose. Pensive.

If I don't step in, she's going to drag me all the way to Massachusetts to look at a school where kids run amok. But then I remember that I don't know Brailand's whereabouts, and that I told Catherine Montgomery that we were not interested in sending Abigail to the Lutheran Prep Academy. Like her education is any concern of mine.

Massachusetts is what ... a three-hour drive from New York City? If they have boarding facilities, at least Abigail would be safe there with a bodyguard to keep an eye on her. Do people send their five-year-olds to boarding school? Would Victoria agree to it if she knew about Olivia?

"You want to go check out the school?" I ask Abigail.

"Can I?" She holds out her arms for me to get her down off the counter.

"I'm coming with you," Emily says.

Victoria isn't smug when we get back to the Wraith. She's withdrawn as if she has pulled her tough shell back around her shoulders and climbed inside, curled up on herself like a tiny snail wary of peering outside at the rest of the world.

She doesn't react when I leave her in the apartment and head down to the casino, and I realize that the silence is more disturbing than her yelling at me or demanding to come with me the way Olivia would. At least if she yelled at me, I would know what she was thinking. Now, I step out of the elevator wishing for the first time since the Wraith opened that I didn't have to show my face.

"Mr. Murray."

Denise Cartwright matches my stride as I march along the plush corridor that leads to the casino. The overhead lights are bright. The temperature is pleasantly warm, not so hot the visitors enter the casino with a sheen of sweat on their forehead, or so cold that their fingers are too cold to handle the chips. The artwork on the walls is subtle. We want visitors to focus on the entrance, we want them to be suitably wowed by the sheer scale of the floor when they step inside that they don't even remember how they got there.

"A position has come up in the restaurant. Someone walked out yesterday." Denise is breathless from trying to keep up with me. "How would you feel about me offering the role to Victoria?"

I sense her holding her breath. "That won't be necessary." I stop at the entrance, forcing her to stop with me. "Is there anything else?"

She shakes her head. "No."

I know it makes me sound like an asshole, but I can't risk anyone knowing about our arrangement. Denise might be easily replaceable, but playing God with people's lives for no reason isn't the way I roll. So, I walk into the casino, my straight spine informing her in no uncertain terms that the conversation is over.

The bartender has a drink waiting for me when I arrive at my usual spot at one end of the bar. Brandy on the rocks. It's a regular night at the casino. Busy. The low hum of voices providing the evening's soundtrack.

The tables are monitored. If a customer is on an outrageously high winning streak, an alert comes straight through to my phone complete with images of the table and the relevant figures. Tonight, the banker is winning. Which means that I'm winning, although even the brandy tastes sour after the last twenty-four hours.

There's something in the air though.

You don't sit in a casino night after night without learning how to read the atmosphere like a sailor tasting the weather. Leaving my drink on the counter, I wander around the floor, acknowledging the regulars with a nod and smiling politely at the women who catch my eye, slowly making my way to the exclusive room.

Ivan Petrov isn't hard to miss. The space around him is statically charged, his thick black hair standing on end as if he has rubbed it with a balloon. Aside from the almost audible crackle, his voice reaches me before the door has swung closed behind me.

As if sensing my presence, he turns away from the table, leaning to the left to peer beyond me as if he expected me to bring back-up.

My hackles are instantly raised.

"Ivan."

I force a warm smile and shake his hand which he reciprocates by grabbing my arm and holding on several beats too long. He smells of liquor. But this isn't what has me on red alert. A drunk I can handle with my eyes shut and both hands tied behind my back; a drunk with a proposition is an altogether different matter.

I take small comfort from the fact that Olivia Dragonetti isn't with him, but if Terry's informants were correct, Ivan Petrov knows exactly what went down last night, and who was responsible.

"Where's your wife?"

He rolls out his bottom lip in a petulant gesture worthy of a spoiled child. Ivan has a chiseled jawline and cheekbones, and dark eyes that shine like wet pebbles, runway looks, but they hide a vicious temper, and a lack of remorse generally associated with serial killers.

"I wanted to meet her for myself, dispel the myths that she bewitched you with some kind of evil potion and has taken to parading you around the Wraith with a collar and chain." He laughs, a sound without mirth, tips back his head, and drains his glass.

"We're having a new collar made." I smile. "If you're looking for a new fetish, I wholeheartedly recommend trying it."

He sniffs loudly, twisting his nostrils exaggeratedly.

"What can I get you?" The sooner we get this conversation out of the way, the sooner I can move Ivan on and get back to my wife. The casino has lost its appeal for me tonight.

Ivan checks out his empty glass. "Whisky. Neat."

I signal the bartender and lead Ivan to my private table in a booth at the far end of the room. The drinks appear on the table before our butts touch the seats.

"I don't know what went on between you and Olivia," Ivan begins, "but I half-expected to see images of your wife's corpse splashed across the tabloids this morning."

I don't react. I've seen too many mafia wives crushed by power struggles and revenge. It's the reason why I work seven days a week, three-hundred-and-sixty-five days a year, so that, when the time comes, I can step away from this life and keep the people I love safe. When a mafia boss falls in love, all bets are off.

"Something must've gotten lost in translation." I play dumb. "I heard there were bigger fish to fry."

His mouth contorts into a sinister smile. "How are things at the Rinse these days? Seems Ms. Dragonetti has set her sights on bagging herself a well-established casino resort if the rumors are to be believed."

I sip my drink. "I prefer to trade in facts not rumors."

"Now you're talking." He leans back in his seat, downs his drink in one. His eyes dart around the room, missing nothing. "There's a little indictment sheet floating around the commissioner's office with Cassius's name on it. I'll give you that one for free."

"It won't be the first time, and it probably won't be the last."

He sits forward, his boozy breath mingling with mine. "I wouldn't be so sure of that. You throw enough shit, some of it is bound to stick eventually."

I signal the waiter for another drink for my guest. He might not get what he's hoping for from this conversation, but I'll make damned fucking sure that he remembers my hospitality.

"I appreciate the heads-up," I say once the server walks away.

"My family can make it go away." He swallows half his drink and releases a sigh.

"That won't be necessary."

He leans across the table and slides my drink towards me. "You misunderstand me. We're not in the habit of greasing the commissioner's palms out of the goodness of our hearts. An alliance between the Petrovs and the Murrays will chase the Dragonettis out of the city with their tails on fire."

Don Dragonetti is one of the original linchpins of organized crime in New York City. Taking him down would be like dismantling the Empire State Building and starting over with the wrong color bricks, and much as I want to take Olivia out of the equation, the intention doesn't stretch as far as her father. I respect the don. This isn't how it is supposed to end for him.

"I know what you're thinking." Ivan empties his glass, swilling the liquid around his mouth before swallowing. "But this is the twenty-first century. Time to move on and reach new heights, my friend."

I down my drink in one and stand, offering the other man my hand. "I hear you, but the Murrays are not in the market for an alliance."

He hesitates. This handshake isn't quite as warm or as friendly as the first. "In that case, I thank you for your time." He goes to walk away but stops and turns back to face me. When he speaks, his voice is low. This is for my ears only. "Don't let this be your first mistake. No one is invincible."

My conversation with Ivan Petrov is still replaying inside my head when I return to my apartment. It wasn't even a veiled threat. Olivia told him about our potential alliance with the Dragonettis, so if it goes ahead now that I've rejected his offer, there will be repercussions.

The kind of repercussions we've been careful to avoid. Until now.

I step out of the elevator and spot a soft toy on the steps leading down to the living room. What the fuck. It's a couple of beats before I remember that Victoria and Abigail are staying here, which makes the earlier threat even more unsettling. Until the situation with Olivia is resolved, it isn't only about me.

For the first time, I can relate to how Terry felt when Emily was born, and he finally handed over the business. He would do whatever it takes to protect his family—still does—but it's the word 'family' that's suddenly taking on new meaning for me.

"Caleb?"

The voice jolts me back to reality. Victoria is curled up on a sofa in the living room, an open book on her lap. Her hair cascades over her shoulders when she folds the book, places it on the coffee table, next to an empty coffee cup, and stands. She's wearing faded jeans and a green-checked flannel shirt, open at the neck, and I've never wanted to fuck her more.

"Is everything okay?" Her gaze drops to the soft toy in my hand, and she chews her bottom lip as if worried that she might be the cause of my problems. If she only fucking knew.

"Long night."

I head straight to the brandy decanter on the drinks cabinet and half-fill a crystal tumbler. It burns as it goes down but does nothing to erase the Petrov family offer from my mind.

Victoria watches me without moving.

The brandy softens my mood a little and replaces one problem with another. Should I tell her how badly I want to fuck her, or should I keep her at arm's length, keep this arrangement on a business level as originally planned?

My cock already seems to have other ideas.

"Caleb..." She takes a deep breath, her breasts swelling beneath the shirt, and my pulse starts racing. "I need to tell you something."

Fuck. I swallow the rest of my drink and refill my glass. "Go on."

"Earlier, at your mom's house." She pauses. "I was talking to Emily on the decking about ... our arrangement." I don't speak. I've never heard the silence in this apartment before now. "I didn't realize that Mr. Dragonetti was standing inside the kitchen watching us."

Fuck!

Deep breath. Count to three.

On two, I ask, "Did he hear?"

"I-I don't know." She casts her eyes down to the floor.

"How can you not know? You spoke to him. What did he say?"

"He didn't say anything." She pauses. "He said he can understand why you married me."

He heard. It's only a matter of time before he does something with the information. His comment to Emily, that they'll be seeing a lot more of each other, suddenly takes on a whole new meaning.

I slide my phone out of my pants pocket. I need to warn Kyle and Terry. Especially Kyle since our meeting this morning. If Olivia knows, then that loose cannon will be firing in all directions before we can reverse the damage.

"Caleb, I'm sorry."

I hear her voice catch, but I'm too busy letting my family know that shit's about to go down thanks to her carelessness. It's my fault. I should've warned her what she was getting into, but I thought her innocence would serve her better than a summary of mafia life. Maybe I should've just married Olivia and sucked up the consequences.

"Maybe he won't tell Olivia." Her voice has shrunk, which only irritates me more.

"Maybe we'll all be living on the fucking moon this time next year." I can be an asshole when I want to be, but right now, I'm not about to put her feelings first.

So, I don't even hear her move until she thumps the elevator button to close the doors.

"Victoria?"

I cross the room and mount the three steps up to the elevator in one fluid movement, thrusting my arm between the doors just as they're about to close. I don't even think about it. I step inside the elevator, press her up against the back wall, and kiss her.

17

VICTORIA

When his lips meet mine, and I feel his tongue filling my mouth, I lose the ability to think. Any anger I felt towards him is instantaneously converted into lust, and I find myself reaching for his shirt buttons, fumbling to unfasten them so that I can run my hands across his inked chest.

He grips my wrists in his fists, raises my arms above my head, and holds them tightly with one hand, his other hand ripping open my shirt.

I gasp, but the sound is swallowed by his mouth.

Somehow, my bra follows my shirt onto the elevator floor, and he pinches my nipple until I cry out. His eyes meet mine. A silent warning not to stop him. His hand slides down to the waistband of my jeans. I feel his knuckles digging into the soft flesh of my abdomen as he unfastens the button and pulls down the zipper, and my pussy starts throbbing.

I want him so badly it's like an ache inside that only he can soothe.

His mouth pulls away, and I find myself reaching for him, my swollen lips lost without him. "Don't move." Caleb waits for me to nod that I understand.

Then he drops to his knees in front of me. He drags my jeans and panties down over my hips, exposing my sex to the open elevator doors and the apartment beyond, and I feel the dampness between my legs. I could lower my arms. I could cover my nakedness, entwine my fingers through his hair, turn around and bend over so that he can fuck me from behind. But I don't. I keep my arms raised above my head just like he told me to.

He spreads my thighs, and I open my legs wider, needing to feel his tongue inside me. He's rough, dragging his tongue across my clit until it's engorged and then sucking on it, until I'm bent double over him.

He sits back, hands still holding my sex apart. "I told you not to move, Victoria."

"Sorry." I'm panting, breathless, my orgasm so close, I could make myself come just thinking about his tongue.

"What do you want me to do?"

"Lick me." It's barely more than a whisper; the words are so unnatural to me.

"Give me one good reason why I should lick you." His eyes never waver from mine.

"Because… Because I want to come."

"Maybe I don't want you to come yet." He stands, leans over me, both hands against the wall on either side of my head so that I can't move.

"Please, Caleb." I'm throbbing so hard I'm going to explode with or without him.

"You'll wait if I tell you to, won't you?" A groan escapes my lips, and Caleb flicks my nipple. "That just cost you a couple of minutes."

I swallow. "I'm so close, Caleb. Please…"

He cups my pussy with one hand. "You're throbbing, Victoria."

He smothers my mouth with his, but keeps his eyes on me, gauging my reaction, inserting a finger into my sex at the same time. He leaves it there, sitting inside me, not moving but feeling what I'm feeling.

"How badly do you want it?" His breath mingles with mine.

I don't know how to answer this, so instead, I lean into him, stick my tongue in his mouth, and kiss him.

Caleb pulls away. "Answer the question. How badly do you want it?"

"Badly," I whisper.

He smiles. "Badly enough to wait for it?"

"Yes." Even though I don't know how much longer I can wait without finishing myself off.

"Badly enough to come when I tell you to."

"Yes." Louder now. More demanding.

He slides his finger out of me and places it between our mouths, watching me lick my taste from him, amusement glinting in his eyes.

"Good girl." He pulls away from me, turns around, and hits the down button on the elevator panel. The doors shush together, and my stomach twists when we start moving.

"Caleb." My eyes widen. "What are you doing?"

He smiles. "I'm waiting for you to come."

I stare at the panel, the levels counting down slowly. I know that the elevator opens directly onto Caleb's private parking bay, but I don't know if his driver will be there waiting in the car. Or his brother maybe.

"But what if someone sees us?" I sound desperate even to my own ears.

"Then they'll know how badly you wanted it too."

"But—"

He presses his finger to my lips. "*Now*, Victoria. I'm going down, and I want you to come before we reach the parking lot."

My mouth is dry. My heart is racing so frantically it's making me feel nauseous. But my traitorous pussy gives me away by clenching around Caleb's tongue.

I spread my legs as wide as they can go, groaning in response to his tongue filling me up. I spread my arms above my head too as if I've been shackled to the elevator walls and give in to the orgasm that is threatening to explode all over Caleb's tongue.

"Oh. My. God." I hear myself say in a husky voice that doesn't even sound like me.

My orgasm just keeps coming and coming. My entire body convulses against the elevator wall, and when the doors open at basement level, I'm still spreadeagled against the far wall, Caleb's head between my legs.

There's a rush of cold air from the parking lot.

"Don't look." Caleb stops licking briefly. Then his fingers are inside me, and he's fucking me with them while filling my mouth with his tongue and breathing into my mouth, "Mianach, Victoria. *Gach mianach.*"

And I do as I'm told. I keep my eyes closed as we ride the elevator back up to the apartment, and practically fall through the doors, my legs wrapped around Caleb's waist, his cock inside me.

Caleb is gone when I wake up in his bed the following morning.

Every part of me aches. I roll onto my back, and my swollen sex flinches at the feel of the sheet brushing against it. My nipples are sore. My lips are puffy, and my eyes feel gritty with lack of sleep. But I can't help smiling to myself when I try to recall how many orgasms I had.

I remember the elevator, and my eyes fly open.

Fuck!

Did anyone see us? How will I be able to look the driver in the eye?

Then I hear Abigail padding about in her room and my chest floods with guilt that she might've woken up and seen us having sex on every available surface in the living room. Worse than that, I didn't even think about how she would feel if Caleb had let me go, and she'd woken up without me here.

How could I have been so hot-tempered and selfish?

I don't even have to think about the answer. I'm sore. I can't even think about pulling on a pair of jeans this morning, but I want to do it all over again tonight. I want Caleb to fuck me every night for the rest of my life.

But the problem is, I still don't know what he wants. All those sexy Gaelic words that he whispers to me in the heat of the moment mean nothing to me.

It appears that we are drawn to talking to each other through our bodies, and as enlightening as Caleb's body has been, I don't know how long I can keep up the pretense of our arrangement without knowing what this is between us. I need to stop bottling it up and choose the right time to ask him how he feels. Which isn't easy when he's either working or bending me over and screwing me from behind.

My cheeks flush at the memory of Caleb fucking me from behind in front of the apartment's floor-to-ceiling windows the night before. Sure, we're fifty stories up, and the walls are black mirrors, but there's a small possibility that someone might have seen us. Someone with binoculars perhaps. A voyeur with a fetish for peering through other people's penthouse apartment windows.

I swing my legs over the side of the bed and wince at the soreness between my legs. My mind is already figuring out how to make it better by tonight.

Sienna will know. A tiny jolt of uneasiness stabs my chest. She didn't return my calls or text me to let me know that she was busy. We rarely spend a day without speaking, so my uneasiness is justified. She doesn't even know about the shooting incident at Cesar two nights ago.

I try calling her again, and her phone is dead. I get the standard message: *The number you are calling is currently unavailable. Please try again later.*

What's the point? I already know that later will provide the same results.

So, I'm going to do this the old-fashioned way. I'm going to go find her myself.

I shower quickly, get Abigail washed and dressed, and try to ignore the tingling between my legs. There's a time and a place to think about Caleb's naked body pressed up against mine, and this isn't it.

"Where are we going?" Abigail watches me closely like she can see right through me. Which would be pretty catastrophic if she could view the images of the night before currently playing out inside my head like a movie preview.

"We're going to find Auntie Sienna."

"Is she lost?"

Her eyes are so wide and innocent that I sometimes think I hate this world she's growing up in. If only adults could view each other with this same purity of heart the world would be so different.

"She isn't answering her phone." I can't lie to her, but I need to protect her from the truth.

"Is it broken?"

"Maybe." I smile. I wish I could believe that. "So, we'll go to her apartment."

"Is Caleb coming?"

I'm astonished at the ease with which Abigail has accepted Caleb into her life. There has never been a string of partners walking in and out of our existence—I never date, and Mason... Well, who knows what Mason does most of the time. So, I always thought that introducing her to a man I had serious feelings for would be hard for her to adjust to. Seems I was wrong.

I'm not sure how this makes me feel. I mean, has she been missing out on having a decent male role model in her life? It sucks when I think how hard I've tried to be both parents to her while Mason has been racking up a string of debts in casinos.

"No, sweetie, Caleb is working."

"What does he do?"

I perch on the edge of her bed while I braid her hair. "He runs the hotel."

She's quiet for several moments. Then: "He has other people to do that for him."

I can't help smiling at how smart Abigail is. "But Caleb tells the other people what to do." My cheeks flood with heat when I think of the elevator carrying us down to the basement with Caleb's face buried between my legs.

Including me.

A guy I don't recognize wearing a black suit and black roll-neck sweater is waiting in the elevator when the doors open.

Surprise must register on my face because he smiles at me and

Abigail and says, "Mr. Murray asked me to escort you wherever you want to go."

I'm not a prisoner, but I'm not allowed to go anywhere without Caleb knowing about it. Part of me feels safe within this cocoon Caleb has woven around us, but the other part of me, the independent part just wants to feel normal again.

I step into the elevator and face the doors as they slide shut, fighting the urge to ask the guy if he was on duty yesterday evening. Caleb was right: it's easier to keep my eyes shut and remain blissfully ignorant.

They must have a secret way of communicating because the driver is waiting next to Caleb's car, the rear passenger door already open, and the engine running. Either that or Caleb has invisible cameras inside the elevator.

Oh God. If that's true, then someone, somewhere, could be watching back the footage right now.

The driver keeps his eyes discreetly on Abigail, and I tell myself to stop overthinking it. It's done now. Too late to go back and change it, and even if I had the chance, would I do things differently? Probably not.

Abigail stares out of the passenger window, seeing the city through the fresh eyes of a child. One day, she'll see things differently. I only hope I can prolong that moment for as long as possible.

There's no answer when I ring the outside buzzer to Sienna's apartment. I peer up at the second-story windows; maybe it's my imagination, but it feels as though the apartment is empty. Abandoned. I think I'm letting everything get to me.

I step away from the door, still studying the windows. It's a gray morning, the heavy sky threatening the kind of drizzly rain that saturates you without you even realizing, but there are no lights on inside. It's Saturday. Sienna won't be working, which means that maybe she was out last night and ended up back at someone else's apartment for an after-party. Or maybe she hooked up with a guy.

But this doesn't feel right either. After the accident, Sienna changed. The flamboyant party animal was replaced by someone who was embarrassed to take her clothes off even in front of her best friend. She brushes it aside when I try speaking about it. Wears clothes that cover up the scars, but I think it was more than just the skin grafts that damaged her confidence. I think the guy who left her for dead obliterated her trust in men.

Besides, if she'd met someone she liked enough to hook up with, I'd be the first person she would tell.

I hold Abigail's hand. "Come on."

We walk back to the sidewalk, climb into the passenger seat of Caleb's car, and I give the driver the address of the art gallery that accepted Sienna's piece.

It's a small building, approached via an alleyway between buildings, making it invisible from the busy tourist-filled streets. The bodyguard, whose name is Martin, walks with us to the entrance and waits outside. The door is painted a smart navy-blue, which does nothing to prepare me for the way the interior opens up into a spacious modern room, the walls of the foyer covered with bold statement pieces. Sienna's artwork will fit right in here; no wonder they snapped up her piece.

A petite woman with black hair tied back into a severe ponytail comes out to greet us. Her smile remains firmly fixed in place even when her gaze settles on Abigail, and she decides that we're not looking to buy.

"Hello, I'm so sorry to trouble you," I begin. "I'm looking for Sienna Walker and wondered if she might be here."

The woman's expression remains perfectly bland. "She isn't, I'm afraid. I've been trying to get hold of her myself."

My stomach lurches, and I instinctively squeeze Abigail's hand tighter. This opportunity is so important to Sienna, there's no way she wouldn't be returning the gallery's calls. "When was the last time you spoke to her?"

The woman's eyes flicker briefly. "When she came here to discuss including her piece in our exhibition."

Days ago. I met Sienna for coffee after the meeting and haven't spoken to her since. Did someone see us together? Is she in danger because of me? Right on cue, the graze on my upper arm starts stinging, reminding me of what happened outside the restaurant.

Moving on autopilot, I thank the gallery owner and head back outside, my thoughts spinning. Where is she? I wish I could piece together her movements before we met for coffee, but I've been so wrapped up in Caleb and this new, surreal existence I'm living in that I've hardly thought about anything else.

"Everything okay?" Martin asks, escorting us back to the car.

I nod even though everything is a million miles from okay. Sienna wouldn't simply take off without telling me. Especially now when things are finally slotting into place for her. I don't know where else to look. Her other part-time jobs are in schools which will be closed for the weekend, and I can't wait until Monday, not knowing where she is.

"I want to walk," I say to Martin.

I need air and space to breathe, to reassemble my thoughts. Because with every passing moment I'm more certain that Sienna is in some kind of trouble.

Martin signals to the driver and falls into step behind me and Abigail. I try to zone him out of my mind. I pretend that he's just some guy out shopping for a gift for his wife, which is more difficult than I thought it would be when the driver appears from nowhere.

Great. So now we have two shadows.

How does Caleb even think when he never gets a moment alone?

I wander the streets, matching the city pace of the other pedestrians, gripping Abigail's hand so tightly, she squirms in my grip. "Where are we going now?" she asks.

"We're still looking for Auntie Sienna." I glimpse Martin and the driver, a few paces behind us, out of the corner of my eye. This would be easier without them tailing us like private investigators.

My heart is racing, and my mouth is dry. This is like looking for a speck of glitter on a thick-pile rug. There are millions of people in this city, and they all seem to have spewed out of the buildings and onto the streets at once.

Without thinking, I dip inside Macy's department store. The heady aroma of perfume, rather than making my head spin like cotton candy, almost feels welcoming. I worked here for six months when Abigail was a baby, so my brain instinctively associates the smells, and the buzz of sales taking place over counters laden with glamorous bottles, with safety.

I scan the aisles, but there are too many people moving in both directions for me to pick out individual faces.

Then, I catch a glimpse of a black leather jacket, collar bunched awkwardly around the back of the wearer's neck, hair the same color as mine and Abigail's.

"Mason?" I pick up speed, dragging Abigail along with me.

"Daddy?" She runs to keep up with me. "Where is he?"

"Mason!" Louder this time. But he doesn't hear me because he keeps moving, doesn't even glance over his shoulder.

A group of Asian women—tourists maybe—loaded up with shopping bags, blocks our path, and I quickly dart between perfume counters and out the other side, craning my neck to view the next aisle for a glimpse of a beaten-up leather jacket.

I can't see him now. Where did he go?

Sienna is forgotten momentarily. If I can find Mason, it will be one less person to worry about, and maybe then, I'll stop adding up the coincidences and start looking at Sienna's whereabouts logically.

We dart between counters, dodging shoppers and sales assistants. I remember the layout of the store, and when I reach the escalator, I drag Abigail onto it, brushing past people checking their cell phones and the contents of their shopping bags, and don't turn around until we're halfway, so that I scan the lower level before we reach the top.

Maybe I was so desperate to find him that I imagined Mason. There's no sign of a leather jacket anywhere now. My eyes dart to the exits, praying that, if he's here, I'll catch him before he leaves. But no one even remotely resembles my brother.

It isn't until I reach the cosmetics department on the third floor that I realize we're no longer being followed. I stop and scan the men's Levi section and the windows of Starbucks.

"Where's Daddy?" Abigail asks.

My shoulders slump. I raised her hopes for nothing, and now I have to let her down all over again.

Crouching in front of her, I keep my voice lighthearted. "I don't think it was him, sweetie. I'm sorry." I smile. "Did you see where Martin went?"

She shakes her head. "I heard them calling us."

"You did?" I must've been so focused on finding Mason that I didn't even hear them.

I stand up, peering around the store at the busy counters, the men rifling through racks of denim, the women getting their complimentary makeup done, reclining on comfy seats, eyes closed. There are people feeding stringy pizza wedges into their mouths at the pizza bar. Friends sharing caramel lattes inside Starbucks. Sales assistants eyeing up their next sale.

I feel like I can breathe again without our shadows. Like I'm just Victoria Callahan out running errands with her niece, and not someone who associates with billionaire bachelors like Caleb Murray.

"Well," I say to Abigail, "now we can look for Auntie Sienna without worrying about them following us."

"There they are." Abigail points in the direction of the escalators at the two men in black suits.

Without thinking, I dart into the stairwell, tugging Abigail along behind me. "Do you want frozen yogurt?" I don't even wait for her to answer. I know that she loves frozen yogurt.

We're both breathing heavily by the time we reach the seventh floor. I quickly buy a tub of yogurt for Abigail and then head to the elevators. I'm taking a chance that the men will stick to the escalators; it would be impossible for two men to cover all levels and all methods of moving around the store. But I also realize that they'll probably call for backup when they can't find us.

"Come on." I stare at the panel inside the elevator, willing it to go faster, and praying that the doors won't open to reveal one of the men waiting for us. Because now that we've evaded them, I just want to be left alone to find my friend.

We make it outside to W 34th Street, and I glance around the sidewalk, making sure they're not waiting for us.

They're not. I don't know how we managed it, but I get a small thrill of pleasure at the thought of losing Caleb's bodyguard in Macy's department store.

Walking quickly, we head towards Madison Square Garden. The streets are busy. Tourists stand outside the building taking selfies. Businessmen in smart suits walk briskly with their cell phones held in front of their faces. Yellow cabs beep their horns at the slow-moving traffic. There are sirens in the distance, the emergency services battling the Saturday morning chaos to attend whatever incident they've been called to.

I don't know where I'm going. But I do know that I can't sit around waiting for Sienna to call me back and let me know that she's okay.

I stop to get my bearings and catch the eye of a young man clad head-to-toe in black. He half-turns away and peers into a store window. I don't know why, but I wait for him to look around and meet my eye again, which he does.

My knees tremble. Is he following us? He can't be one of Caleb's men because he would come over and make himself known. Perhaps this is simply my overactive imagination making something out of nothing.

I keep walking, chatting to Abigail about what we should do for the rest of the day, and stop again. Spinning around abruptly, I notice the man in black peering into another store window, the distance between us having closed a little.

I crouch in front of Abigail again. "Sweetie don't look around, but the station is behind us. We're going to go inside and find somewhere quiet to sit down for a while."

"Why?" Abigail blinks her wide eyes at me but doesn't look around.

"Because I'm tired. Aren't you?"

She wrinkles her nose. "I guess."

I glance over her shoulder; the guy is still watching us, hands in his pockets, trying to look nonchalant while tourists and pedestrians mill around him. "Then we can think about where Auntie Sienna might be."

"Okay."

"Good girl." I straighten. Now is not the time to think about Caleb praising me for being a good girl too.

We walk as fast as we can without drawing attention to ourselves. Inside the station, lots of people are wandering around or sitting on benches waiting for friends or family to arrive. But the space is so huge that the guy will spot us the instant he walks in.

I realize that time is limited. If he is following us as I suspect, he will have reacted the instant he saw us dart inside the station. My heart is thumping, but my brain is thinking logically. I try to get inside his head. Where would he instinctively look for us? The restrooms are the first place that spring to mind.

Shrugging out of my coat, I drape it over a carryon while the owner is looking the other way and tell Abigail to take off her coat. Fastening her coat around my waist by the sleeves, I cut through the middle of a ticket booth line and make Abigail wait for me behind a giant stone planter. He will be looking for a woman and a child. I pray that he won't pay too much attention as I turn around and make conversation with the blonde woman waiting in line behind me.

I spot him standing just inside the entrance and force a wide smile, tugging my hair forward to half-cover my face. He turns three-sixty, eyes narrowed, scanning the vast atrium. His gaze skims past the line as he starts heading towards the food court.

"Hey, the line is moving," the blonde woman says.

"What?" My eyes dart back to the gap in front of me, and I instinctively move forward. But when I turn back, the guy in black is gone.

"What the hell..."

I step out of line. Where did he go? Abigail is still hiding behind the planter, but I can't risk him finding her. I realize with a jolt that this would never have happened if I hadn't lost Martin and the driver. I reach for my phone to call Caleb, but I left it in my coat pocket, and my coat is nowhere to be seen.

I grab Abigail and start running.

18

CALEB

Victoria almost collides head-first with me as I enter Penn Station.

"Whoa!" I don't think she even realizes that it's me until I pick Abigail up and reach for Victoria's hand. "What's wrong?" My gaze instinctively slides towards the busy station entrance like it might be on fire. "What's happened?"

"Caleb?" She pulls away from me, her eyes darting back and forth between me and the building. "What are you... How did you find us?"

"It doesn't matter. Stop. Take a deep breath. And tell me what's going on."

When Martin alerted me to their disappearance in Macy's, I hoped it was simply Victoria making a stand against me offering her and Abigail protection. I blamed myself. Even after the shooting incident, I refused to cloud her image of my dazzling world of casinos, designer outfits, and friends in high places because... Well, because her innocence is all part of this inexplicably overwhelming attraction I feel towards her.

I see now that it's too late. Victoria's life will never go back to the way it was before. Not that it was an enviable position to be in. But she's a part of this world now whether she likes it or not.

"A man was following us." Victoria's breathing is shallow, sweat beading on her forehead.

I set Abigail down between me and Martin who comes running up behind us. I focus on Victoria. "Listen to me. I need you to concentrate and copy me. Breathe in." I suck in a deep breath through my nose and hold it along with her gaze. On the count of five, I breathe out through my mouth.

Victoria mimics me, her breathing slowly regulating as tears collect on her eyelashes.

"Now tell me slowly what happened." I don't release her. I'm still worried that she'll bolt if I let her go.

"There was a man ... dressed in black. I spotted him over there." She raises a trembling hand and points towards Madison Square Garden. "He was following us. I ran into the station and tried to hide. But then he came in, and I needed to get Abigail out of there. I couldn't let him take her..." She's sobbing now, and I pull her against my chest and hold her close.

Her heart thuds against my ribcage, out of sync with my own heartbeat, which has slowed to a steady da-dum, da-dum, while I manifest a violent ending for the guy who did this to her. Above her head I gesture for Martin to send a couple of men inside the station.

I don't know how she did it, but I'm going to quadruple the protection around her and Abigail. She won't be able to make a slice of toast without me knowing whether she likes it just with butter or with strawberry jelly too.

When she is calmer, I hold her at arm's length. "Can you describe him to me?"

"Dark hair. Olive skin. He wore black clothes. I don't know…" She shakes her head as Martin's men come back empty handed. "Maybe I overreacted," she adds in a small voice. "Maybe he was just catching a train."

"Victoria, I want you to listen to me. If you thought that you were being followed, then I trust your instincts."

"You do?" She peers at me from beneath those goddamned thick lashes, and I have to stop myself from marching inside the station myself and ripping the place apart.

"Why didn't you call me?" I want to ask her why she gave Martin the slip, but it can wait for later.

"I ditched my coat. My phone was in my coat pocket." She covers her face with both hands. "Sienna won't be able to get hold of me now. I don't know where she is. I was looking for her…"

Something cold and slimy settles in my stomach. Mason Callahan, Brailand Voth, and now Sienna. "We'll find Sienna."

She lowers her hands and glares at me. "Have you found Mason?"

I flinch. "No."

"How did you know where to find me, Caleb?"

"I gave Abigail a phone, so that I could track her."

She squeezes her eyes shut briefly; when she opens them again, her eyes are filled with accusations. "You were tracking Abigail?"

"It's for her own protection. If you'd stayed with Martin and Kev, I wouldn't have needed to track her." I feel my own voice rising a notch but I'm powerless to tone it down. The thought of losing Victoria to someone who has a beef with the Murrays sets my thoughts on fire.

"I got a picture of the man." Abigail's voice jolts me back to reality.

"Abigail?" Victoria furrows her brow. "What are you talking about? Which man?"

"The man who was following us." She slides a slim phone from the pocket of her overalls and offers it to me rather than Victoria.

"How did you know the man was following us?" Victoria asks while I unlock the phone and find the image.

I zoom in. It's grainy, but it's better than nothing. I send the image to Terry, and hand the phone back to Abigail. "Good job." I high-five her, and she knows exactly what to do.

"You kept looking at him," Abigail says in response to Victoria's question. "Then you told me to hide. I waited for him to come through the doors and then I took a picture."

"Caleb, what is going on?" Victoria drags her eyes away from her niece. "Do you know who that man is?"

"No." It isn't a complete untruth.

I'm hoping Terry will come back with a name, but even with a hazy photograph snapped by a five-year-old, I can hazard a good guess at what is going on here. I think the guy works for the Petrovs. Ivan's unscheduled visit the evening before hot on the heels of the shooting incident is more than just a coincidence. I think that he and Olivia are in this together, and whatever game they're playing, the only outcome they're looking for is one that will benefit the two of them and no one else.

I need to warn Kyle. I was already uncomfortable with him volunteering to take Olivia on, but now it can't go ahead. I'm almost certain that Don Dragonetti has no idea what his daughter is up to; if he did, he'd have shut it down before it even crossed the starting line. I'm equally certain that Olivia has convinced herself she doesn't need her father's protection. Perhaps she is replacing Daddy with Ivan Petrov.

An image of the two of them together, racing around the city in Olivia's Lamborghini and blowing up the other mafia families fills me with a sickly sense of dread. They're both volatile. Their behavior is erratic at best. They probably imagine themselves as a modern Bonnie and Clyde, armed and dangerous, and laughing at the other families as they ride off into the sunset.

"Caleb?" I've known Victoria for less than a week, but it already feels like she can see right through me. "Who is he? Do you think he might know where Mason is?" She catches on quickly.

"I think we should get back to the Wraith." It's a cop-out, and she knows it, but she doesn't argue.

"No." Kyle shakes his head. "I bumped into Olivia in her favorite nightclub yesterday evening, and we hit it off straight away." He helps himself to a glass of iced water and sits on one of the sofas in my office.

I've already instructed Lauren to hold my telephone calls for the rest of the day, and to let the rest of the family in as soon as they arrive.

"It's too dangerous." My brandy goes down without the burn. Typical. "We'll find another way."

"I thought you already did that and look where that's got us." Kyle doesn't use sarcasm; he's merely telling it like it is. And it hurts.

I can't deny that events have escalated since I introduced Victoria to Don Dragonetti and his daughter, but this is no reflection on Victoria. It's all down to the loose cannon named Olivia Dragonetti. She's the loaded gun, and now Ivan Petrov is waiting to pull the trigger.

"Ivan Petrov was in the Wraith last night." I say, and Kyle sits forward, elbows resting on his knees. "He offered me a deal to throw in with his family."

"Go on."

"I told him the Murrays were not on the market."

"Which he obviously doesn't believe."

I refill my glass; I sip this one slowly. After recent events, it will hit me later, and I want to be sober when I face Victoria. "Olivia might be crazy, but she isn't gullible. She'll know you're not interested in her."

"So, I have to make it believable."

The door opens then, and Terry walks in with Mom. I fix them both a drink, Terry's on the rocks, Mom's neat. Cash gets his ability to drink his friends under the table from our mother.

"Guy's name is Riki Kuznetsov." Terry tosses a printed sheet of paper onto the coffee table. "Ivan brought him back from his sabbatical in Europe. From what I hear, we got lucky today. This guy will fire a bullet if you mispronounce his name."

I enlighten them about Ivan Petrov's offer. "We can't proceed with the Dragonetti alliance without squaring things with the Petrovs first, and it still all revolves around Olivia. Whatever she promised Ivan, he's bought into it."

"Only because there's nothing better on the table." Terry swallows a mouthful of brandy and crunches an ice cube with his back teeth.

"Terry's right," Mom says. "We didn't get lucky. What happened today, and outside Cesar was exactly what was supposed to happen. A warning. Ivan is hedging his bets. Going along with Olivia because keeping her happy is his safest option until he figures out his next move."

"I'm not cutting a deal with the Petrovs." I address Terry. If he suggests that I reconsider, then I'll listen, but I already know his feelings on the matter.

Terry shakes his head. "We don't have to."

"We proceed as planned," Mom joins in. "Olivia Dragonetti won't be able to stop herself. The instant she reveals her true intentions regarding cutting you out completely unless you marry her, Ivan will back off. He'll have no choice. He'll do it to save face."

"Or risk being banished again," Terry adds.

"Kill two birds with one stone." Mom drains her drink and slides her glass my way for a refill. "The Petrovs stand down, leaving the way clear for Don Dragonetti to step in. Win-win."

When the door opens a second time, it catches us all by surprise. Victoria is standing there, a red-faced Lauren trying to skirt around her and speak first. "I'm sorry, Mr. Murray. I tried to stop her, but she—"

"It's okay, Lauren." I avoid Kyle's eye. He has always claimed that he would rather face a scathing lawsuit than the wrath of Miss Ingram, and it shows in the way he visibly shrinks in his seat.

The older woman reverses out of the room, closing the door behind her, but not without glaring at Victoria's back.

"Is this about what happened today?" Victoria's gaze flits around the room and finally settles on me. It must've taken a lot for her to come down here and gatecrash a family meeting, and she already looks as if she has lost her momentum.

I stand and gesture to the seat next to me where we sat only days ago with Abigail between us. "Come and sit down." So much has altered since then that it feels as if it was a lifetime ago, a memory of a meeting that happened to two very different people.

Victoria sits between me and Mom. "If Abigail is in danger, then I have a right to know. Until Mason comes home…"

"She's under my protection."

I half-fill a glass with water and hand it to her, but she shakes her head. I add a splash of brandy, and she glugs the first mouthful, wincing as it goes down.

"Abigail is safe here." Mom's voice is steady. It's impossible not to believe my mom, she always speaks with such utter conviction and loyalty, that no one dares question her. "Today's unfortunate situation should never have happened but—" she takes Victoria's hand and rubs it as though trying to coax her to dive into the deep end of the pool on her first swimming lesson "—we'll all learn from it."

Victoria swallows. The inference that she should have stuck close to her bodyguards isn't lost on her. "I-I thought I saw Mason. I was trying to catch up with him before he left Macy's, but I lost him and then..." Her voice trails off. "Then he was gone."

Mom smiles and releases Victoria's hand. "No harm done. You're both safe and well."

"I've increased security at the Wraith," I confirm.

Victoria seems to slump against me, the fight draining from her as she realizes that this is out of her control. Just like when I fucked her in the elevator.

"Does this mean that I'm stuck in your apartment?" She sucks on her bottom lip, and I can't help wishing that I was the one doing the sucking.

"On the contrary," Mom says before I can respond. "We want you to continue as if nothing has happened."

"Mom." The warning note in my voice is totally missed by my mom but not by Terry and Kyle who both hide behind their drinks. "I'm not risking Victoria—"

"No one is risking anything." Mom talks over me. "Your wife is going to plan her wedding reception, buy an outfit worthy of the cover of *Vogue* magazine, get her hair done, visit her new family, and act like the happy new bride everyone expects her to be."

"But I—" Victoria begins.

"One thing you must learn about our family," Mom continues

regardless, "is that we provide the tabloids with a united front. No matter what happens."

Her gaze slides my way and back again, a warning not to undermine her even when the discussion relates to my wife.

"We will all be beside you every step of the way. No one will get to you unless they get through us first."

Victoria smiles tentatively. "What about Abigail?"

"Goes without saying." I reach for Victoria's hand and entwine her fingers with mine, a gesture that isn't missed by my mom. "But you must let the bodyguards do their job."

Victoria lets out a sound halfway between a chuckle and a sob. "Will there..."

She blinks back tears, and I'm reminded how overwhelming this whole situation must be for her. She's sitting in a room with one of the wealthiest and most prominent families in New York City having been shot outside a restaurant and followed by a mafia mobster while we all discuss keeping her and her niece alive. She probably regrets the day she accepted the job as temporary concierge at the Wraith, and who could blame her?

"Will there be trouble at the wedding reception?" she asks in a small voice as though scared to voice her concerns out loud.

"Not on my watch." Terry drains his drink, and peers into his empty glass.

"You have nothing to worry about," Mom says. "You have the word of every single one of us in this room."

Kyle clears his throat. "I don't think we can guarantee there'll be no trouble at the wedding reception."

"I've told him to abandon the plan we agreed on yesterday." I refill my glass, and tip Victoria's towards her lips.

Despite the gravity of the conversation, my mind is already drifting towards fucking a tipsy Victoria later when I have her all to myself. Sober, she offers me her body with complete and utter abandon; I can't wait to see what happens when she's softened by booze.

"What plan?" Victoria asks.

Kyle answers. "It's fair to say that my brother's fake marriage, rather than prompting her to back off, has ignited a fuse beneath our friend Olivia Dragonetti. So, we decided to provide her with a distraction. Aka me."

"No." Victoria shakes her head, and Mom flashes me a warning glance. *Control your wife; she isn't part of this family.* "Why would you do that? What about Suki?"

Kyle smiles. "Suki was just a date. She was happy to be seen out with me because it keeps her social media profile current."

"But Olivia Dragonetti..." Victoria swallows the remainder of her drink in one mouthful as if requiring fortification. "She told me that Caleb's car was waiting for her outside the restaurant the other night."

"Precisely my point." Kyle spreads his hands wide like he's addressing members of the jury rather than his family. "I realize that she'll use me to get to Caleb, so I intend to drip feed her tiny crumbs of information about my brother's rocky relationship with his bride of a few weeks."

My fists clench, and I set my glass down on the table before I crush it. "No. I'm not faking a rocky marriage with Victoria." I realize the irony a beat too late when Kyle shakes his head.

"Caleb, hear him out." Victoria sits forward so that she doesn't miss anything. "You want her to believe that she's in with a chance."

I can't believe what I'm hearing. "She has never been in with a chance. If she doesn't get it after ten years—"

"But don't you see?" There's excitement in Victoria's voice now. "Her brain obviously isn't wired the same way as other people's."

"The closer it gets to the wedding reception," Kyle joins in, "the more desperate she'll become."

"Which will spark Ivan Petrov's fury at being used." Even Mom is on board with this now. "She'll be on her own when she realizes that Caleb and Victoria are happy, and that's when she'll get careless."

"Abigail will be at the wedding reception." I already know that my input is washing over their heads.

"We'll be waiting for her," Terry says. "It's the only way to make sure her father understands what a monster he has raised, and it will offer us a way out from the Petrovs when they have to confess to Ivan helping her."

"I don't like it. Too much can go wrong."

"Oh, Caleb." Mom smiles. "Too many things can go wrong every minute of every day. It's the world we live in. It never stopped you before." She gives Victoria a sideways glance. "Wouldn't you agree, Victoria?"

"I know Olivia is..."

"Crazy?" I suggest. "A nutjob with psychopathic tendencies?"

Instead of being deterred, Victoria smiles. "But maybe this is the only way to get her out of your life for good. And you have your family on your side."

Her tone is gentle, but I sense the wistfulness behind the comment. I don't know her history, but it's obvious that Victoria has been the one holding her family together. Perhaps she is more like my mom than anyone realizes.

A sudden image materializes inside my head: Victoria, twenty years from now, sitting around a table with our sons, reminding them that family is everything, and that together, they can rule the world. I don't know where it came from, but it's so vivid, my breath hitches in my throat, and I find myself nodding in agreement.

"Good." Mom and Victoria exchange glances, and I don't know how the meeting slipped into their hands so easily, but I feel as if they ganged up on me. And won. "I think this calls for a toast." Mom clinks her empty glass against mine.

I top up our drinks—including Kyle's—and we toast our futures.

Victoria's bottom lip disappears behind her top teeth, and I make a mental note to tell her not to do that in public unless she wants to risk me ripping her clothes off and fucking her with an audience.

"What about Sienna and Mason?" she asks. "Do you think Olivia has something to do with their disappearance?"

"I'm already on it." Terry sets his glass down on the table; he has barely touched his drink. "The Petrovs have been keeping a low profile while Ivan was off the scene. Expanding their business into computer equipment."

Computer equipment?

My face must reflect my bewilderment because Terry grins. "My sentiments exactly. It's a front for something else—my guess is weapons or drugs."

"Or both," Kyle suggests.

"Or both." Terry inclines his head. "Either way, storage capacity within the city is at a minimum. I've put out feelers to locate their warehouses. With Ivan involved, it's as good a place as any to start looking."

19

VICTORIA

WAREHOUSES FILLED WITH DRUGS AND WEAPONS. IT'S like something out of a movie, but Caleb and his family don't even flinch when they speak these words out loud. My heart aches to think that Sienna and Mason are mixed up in this because of me.

I was angry with my brother when he didn't come home after the fight with Killian. I blamed myself for always being around to pick up the pieces so that he never bothered to learn from his mistakes. But now, I realize that he is missing because of my involvement with Caleb. Because of me, Abigail doesn't have her father around.

What if... I can hardly bear to think about the worst-case scenario, but what if he never comes back? How will I live with myself?

"Why are you sad?" Abigail's voice penetrates my morbid thoughts.

We're on the rooftop decking of Caleb's penthouse apartment. After the meeting, Caleb stayed with Kyle in his office, and I didn't question it. Instead, I spent the rest of the day with Abigail, playing video games on the tablet Caleb gave her, and getting beaten by a five-year-old every time.

We ordered pizza for dinner from the restaurant downstairs which was delivered to the penthouse and received by Martin at the elevator—seems I'm not allowed to speak to the servers either now— in case Olivia has somehow gotten to them first. For dessert, I requested ice cream to be brought up along with a couple of sodas, and Abigail and I made our favorite: ice cream sodas. We mixed the bubbly liquid and a couple of scoops of ice cream in tall sundae dishes and scooped it out with long-handled spoons on the decking with the stars twinkling overhead.

It's magical up here. The entire rooftop is strung with fairy lights, the pool alive and shimmering with golden ripples. Caleb must've designed the space with relaxation in mind, but I wonder how often he uses it. I get the feeling he has gotten himself into a rut of working all day, and staying in the casino all night, and has forgotten how to switch off.

Now, I peer down at Abigail, the glow of the fairy lights casting a gentle sheen across her cheeks. If this feels magical to me, I can't even begin to imagine how special it must feel to her. She will never ever forget this period in her life when she was thrown into a world that exists only in movies and fairy tales, and I wish that I could tell her that this is real.

"I'm sad because Daddy and Sienna are not here." There's no point lying to her, she can see right through me. "When will they be back?"

"Soon." I hope. "Caleb is trying his best to find them."

Abigail nods and rests her head on my shoulder. I stroke her hair. The weight of her small body against me is the most special feeling in the world. A reminder of how precious life is.

"Will I have to go home with Daddy when he comes back?"

It's like a stab straight through my heart. Our future isn't here. Our future isn't with Caleb Murray, living in the penthouse apartment of the Wraith and spending cool spring evenings on the rooftop under fluffy blankets with the lights sparkling all around us.

"We both will, sweetie."

"Why can't we stay here with Caleb?"

I squeeze my eyes shut and feel the tears collecting in the corners. "Because Caleb has been very kind allowing us to stay, but ... well ... think of this as a vacation."

It seems to satisfy her because she doesn't ask any more questions, and within minutes, her breathing slows, and her limbs grow limp.

And I'm left alone with my thoughts.

I meant what I said to Abigail—we'll both go back to our previous life eventually, only I can't imagine being anywhere else without Caleb, and he belongs here. Without us.

I tuck the blanket around Abigail and lean my head back against the outdoor sofa. The sky is velvet-black, the stars merging into a mysterious silver glow when I allow my eyelids to droop. The vastness of space is overwhelming. I'm just a tiny speck on a rooftop in a universe that is too huge to even comprehend, and it makes all our lives seem so inconsequential.

Olivia Dragonetti might be dangerous, but even she is only a speck in the universe. She isn't all-powerful. She isn't an omnipresence, a mystical being with powers beyond comprehension. She isn't immortal as she seems to believe she is with the power to mess with other people's lives. She's just a spoiled princess with mafia roots.

And I'm fucked if I'm going to sit back and let her hurt my brother and Sienna.

I must doze because I'm woken by the warmth of Caleb's fingers on my cheek. Startled, I open my eyes and blink away the remnants of sleep, to find his face so close to mine I can feel his breath on my lips.

"Sorry. I didn't want to wake you. You looked so peaceful."

I smile sleepily. My left arm has gone numb with Abigail's weight on me, and I wince as I try to flex my rubbery fingers.

"Here, let me." Caleb doesn't wait around for my permission. He slides one arm underneath Abigail's legs, his other arm wrapping around her and stroking my breast beneath the blanket at the same time.

My skin tingles with his touch, my nipples instantly erect. If he notices, he doesn't say anything.

I go to stand up, but he tells me to stay where I am. "I can put her in her bed. I'm not completely useless, you know."

I smile at his receding back, the scent of vanilla lingering in his wake. He carries Abigail as if she were no heavier than a sack of feathers, his back muscles rippling beneath his shirt. My pussy responds of its own free will, tightening and tingling, and I reflexively chew my bottom lip. I don't know how many times I can do this when I still don't know what 'this' even is, but I also know that if he comes back to the rooftop and orders me to lie down and open my legs, that's exactly what I'll do.

I can't help smiling when Caleb returns a short while later having swapped his shirt and suit pants for jeans and a jersey sweater that defines every muscle of his upper body. He's holding a bottle of champagne and two crystal flutes.

"What are we celebrating?"

"Do we need a reason to drink champagne?" He sets the glasses down on the table and pops the cork, the bubbles froth over his wrist before they settle. He fills a glass and hands it to me.

I've only tried champagne a handful of times, and it always goes straight to my head, so I sip it slowly, the liquid fizzing behind my top teeth.

Caleb fills his own glass and sits beside me, his thigh pressed up against mine, his warmth transferring to me through our clothes. Whenever I'm in the apartment, I change into my own clothes—I don't want to get comfortable wearing the outfits Caleb bought for me or it will be even harder to hand them back when it's time for me to leave.

My heart is thumping. I wonder if it would always be this way if we were to stay together or if this physical attraction would become muted over time. Would his presence eventually produce a warm glow inside me instead of this red-hot passion? Would I be disappointed when this happened, or would it be such a gradual thing that neither of us would even notice?

Tears well in my eyes.

"Hey." Caleb catches a teardrop on his fingertip. Holding it up to the glow of the fairy lights, he studies it closely and then places it on his tongue. "We'll find Mason and Sienna."

I swallow another small sip of champagne. Does he really think the tears are for my brother and my friend? Or is this his way of avoiding a conversation about us?

"Caleb..."

"Shh." He puts his glass down and leans closer, smoothing my hair away from my face. "You know how gorgeous you are, right?" He cups my face with both hands and kisses my eyelids, the tip of my nose, my earlobes.

"No, I—"

He kisses my lips. I want to tell him that I've never felt as beautiful, as special, as desirable as he makes me feel, and I doubt that I will ever feel this way again. I want to tell him that, for me at least, this is way more than a marriage contract. That I never intended to develop feelings for him, but now that I have, he has grown roots inside my heart that I will never be able to cut down.

I want to ask him if he feels the same way.

But my body is talking its own language, and I also know that I'm powerless to stop responding to his touch. So, when he slides my hips towards him and leans over me, I comb my fingers through his hair and kiss him like this is the last time we will ever get to do this.

Caleb unbuttons my shirt without popping the buttons. He unfastens my jeans and slides his hand inside my panties, his cold fingers slipping easily inside my sex. I gasp against his lips.

"You're so wet." His breath mingles with mine when he

speaks, and I smile. "You're dripping like a fucking waterfall. Is this just for me?"

I don't answer. I pull him towards me and kiss him, feeling my pussy clench around his finger.

"Say it. Say it's just for me."

"It's just for you," I breathe against his lips.

"Tell me you're mine, Victoria." His voice is husky. I can't read the gleam in his eyes, but it's enough for me to know that it's all for me.

"I'm yours, Caleb."

He kisses me deeply, his tongue filling my mouth, his free hand stroking my neck.

Then he pulls away and stands abruptly, leaving my lips still parted, my tongue still searching for his. He offers me his hand and pulls me onto my feet.

"Take off your clothes m'áilleacht."

"But..." I peer around the rooftop.

We're alone up here. Abigail is sound asleep in her bed downstairs, and the only way anyone can reach us is by going through Martin and his men guarding the penthouse elevator. But it isn't the fear of getting caught that's stopping me. I've never undressed in front of a man before, and I don't know how to make it look sexy.

"Take off your clothes, Victoria." His voice is firm; it's an order.

I shrug my shirt over my shoulders and drop it onto the floor. My jeans are already undone, so I slide them over my hips and step out of them, kicking them aside too.

"Continue."

I reach behind me and unhook my bra, letting it fall from my breasts and land on the floor at my feet. The cool night breeze and Caleb's gaze on my breasts makes my nipples stand erect. Watching him closely, I slide my panties over my hips and nudge them aside with my bare feet.

I thought I would feel self-conscious standing naked in front of him, but I can tell by his appreciative gaze that he likes what he sees.

"You're so fucking beautiful."

And in the moment, I believe him.

Caleb tugs his sweater over his head and tosses it on top of my discarded clothes. Then he removes his jeans. He's commando underneath, and his cock springs free, standing thick and proud.

He walks toward me and caresses my breasts with his fingertips, lingering on the marks he gave me, while he kisses me on the lips. It's a tender kiss, quite unlike any we have shared before, and a shiver runs down my spine.

"Get in the pool."

My gaze drifts towards the water that's still shimmering golden with the twinkling fairy lights. "The pool?"

"I'll count to three, and if you're not in the pool, I'll throw you in." He says this with a wicked smile.

I do as I'm told. I've always thought of myself as an independent woman, but there's a huge part of me that wants to be dominated. It's like this is the one area of my life that I can relinquish control to, and I know that I will do whatever

Caleb tells me to do. And I will enjoy it more than I have ever enjoyed anything else.

The water is heated, but still, goosebumps pop on my flesh as I walk into the water. Caleb follows me. He stands in front of me, the water up to my waist, and kisses me before trailing his tongue down to my nipple. He sucks hard with one arm around my back, holding me tightly so that I can't move.

His other hand finds my sex under the water. He inserts a finger, and I instinctively spread my legs. Two fingers. Three. I don't know where the water ends and my wetness begins, but I want him to fill me up, so I raise my feet from the bottom of the pool and float towards him, his fingers supporting me in the water.

Caleb submerges my upper body; his mouth still finds my nipple under the water's surface. I reach for his cock, wrapping my fist around his girth. He rams his fingers inside me, the water lapping the sides of the pool with our movements.

Without warning, Caleb removes his fingers, carries me to the side, and sits me on the edge. He spreads my legs wide, gripping my thighs to keep them open. Then he pushes his tongue inside me.

I lean backwards, rest my head on the tiled floor, and arch my spine, forcing myself onto him. I stare at the stars. All I can think about is the feel of Caleb's tongue inside me, rasping back and forth across my clit. The tingling, and the throbbing. I want it to last all night, but I'm powerless to stop my orgasm from bursting out of me.

Panting, I barely feel Caleb pushing my thighs backwards, raising my ass off the side of the pool. His tongue travels between my sex and my butt, while his fingers play with my orgasm. They keep it coming and coming. I think he says,

"Good girl," but colors explode behind my eyelids, and the stars, when I open my eyes, are twinkling just for me and Caleb.

I lie there, limp and spent until he picks me up and slides me onto his cock. I wrap my legs around him, and he walks back towards the middle of the pool, our bodies submerged up to our chests. Arms around his neck, Caleb's hands still gripping my thighs, I ride him under the water until he comes inside me, his warm cum mingling with the pool water trapped inside me.

After, we lie on the decking side by side, our skin tingling as it dries, and sip champagne. Caleb leans over me and dribbles champagne from his mouth to mine, his fingers making a trail around my breasts.

He doesn't speak, but everything about tonight is so tender, so perfect, that I feel the glimmer of hope that this is way more than either of us expected it to be, sparking inside me.

Breakfast is waiting for me the following morning when I wake up in Caleb's bed: poached eggs and oak-smoked salmon, a rack of brown toast, jelly and marmalade and neat curls of butter, steaming coffee and cream, and a selection of pastries for me to share with Abigail. A note is tucked inside a pristine white napkin with the Wraith emblem in one corner.

The car is waiting to take you to the Titan.

I swallow hard. A moment ago, I wanted to devour everything on this tray, but now the smell of the smoked salmon is making me feel nauseous.

I push it away, shower quickly, and carry the tray through to the kitchen to eat with Abigail. Still, I only manage to nibble a slice of toast while my eyes devour the food.

Moira and Emily are waiting for us when we arrive. Emily takes Abigail to the playroom used by some of the employee's children, while Moira and I check out the ballroom.

The Titan doesn't have the sleek, dark splendor of the Wraith, but it does reflect the golden era of Hollywood. The pale gold walls shimmer with the glow of tasseled wall lamps. The overhead chandeliers appear to sprinkle golden raindrops on our heads. The floor is so highly polished that it looks wet, and there are framed black and white photos of celebrities hanging on the walls.

I stand in the middle of the ballroom and turn three-sixty. I'm gaping but I don't even care. The ceiling is ultra-high, and when I let out a giggle, it echoes off the walls. I didn't expect to be this wowed by it, given the situation with Olivia, but it's perfect for a wedding reception.

When I turn around to face Moira, her face is beaming. "You love it, I can tell."

"I do." I hesitate.

"But?"

"But... Moira, I don't..." Jeez, I can be such a wimp when it comes to saying how I feel about stuff. "I feel bad knowing that this is all ... for show." It sounds way worse when I say it out loud than it did in my head.

Moira's expression relaxes into a smile. "Why don't you let me worry about that, huh?" Her perfectly shaped eyebrows slant upwards. "One thing you should know about this family: we don't do things by halves. We could make this a small intimate affair. Or we could forget all about it, carry on as if my new daughter-in-law doesn't care about being introduced to our friends and family."

Her tone is pleasant, but I understand what she's saying. We have no choice. Caleb Murray would throw an extravagant party, he would invite everyone he knows to meet his bride, and he would take immense pleasure from showing her off.

If only this were real.

It's now down to me and Caleb to make everyone believe that this is real, and with memories of last night lingering in my mind, it shouldn't be too difficult.

"Good." Moira nods once. "Come, I'll introduce you to Bastien."

Bastien, or Bash as he's affectionately known to his family and friends, is waiting for us at a corner table in the Titan's restaurant. He stands when we enter and kisses Moira on both cheeks before taking my hand and greeting me the same way.

The glitz and glamor are evident in the restaurant too, and I wonder if the décor in each building reflects the brothers' personalities. The sleek black charm of the Wraith and the extravagant glam sparkle of the Titan.

"So, how is married life with my brother treating you?" A half-smile plays on Bash's lips.

Color immediately rises from my neck to my cheeks, and I wish that I could control it. "It's ... different."

Bash laughs; it's an easy infectious sound. "I see Caleb has made an impression on you."

Fuck! Is it that obvious? I lower my eyes and pray that Moira doesn't notice or ask him what he means.

She doesn't. "Ignore my son, Victoria."

She helps herself to brandy from a decanter on the table and offers to fill my glass. I decline and sip my iced water instead. I don't know how they all drink so much liquor and still function like normal human beings.

"Victoria has her own ideas about the ballroom for the wedding reception," she continues. "Whatever she wants..." She leaves the sentence hanging.

"Sure thing. You're family now." He winks at Moira who raises her glass to an invisible toast.

I wish I could read their expressions or their body language, but these people might as well be aliens from another planet, and I feel so out of my depth that I sip my water waiting for a suitable response to spring to mind.

I almost choke on the liquid when a woman approaches the table and says my name. Heart racing, I peer around to find Denise watching me as if she had just seen a ghost.

"Denise." I hear the tremor in my own voice. I realize how it must look and feel guilty for not telling Denise what happened after Caleb fired me from the concierge position.

"You two know each other?" Bash asks.

"Yes... I... That is, Denise knows my mom."

I stand and excuse myself from the table so that I can speak to Denise out of earshot. When we are alone in the corridor outside the restaurant, I suck in a deep breath, psyching myself up to explain what's going on.

"Denise, I'm sorry I didn't tell you sooner but... It all happened so quickly, and when I tried to find you, you were not at the Wraith, and then it all kind of spiraled out of control, and..."

It's such a crazy, unbelievable situation that I don't know how she will react to the news that I'm married to her boss, and I realize that I still desperately want her to be on my side.

"And...?" Her voice is cold, and my stomach is lurching.

Deep breath. Here goes. "After Caleb Murray fired me, he came to me with a proposition. He asked me to marry him. On paper. We're not really married, at least, there hasn't been a wedding." The words are tumbling out, and I glance around to make sure that no one can hear us. "It's a long story."

"Wow." Denise blinks at me. "So, you're here because..."

"Because we're going to hold our wedding reception at the Titan. Our *fake* wedding reception."

Denise shakes her head, trying to process the news. "You and Caleb Murray."

I wince. "I know how crazy it sounds. I just happened to be in the wrong place at the wrong time."

She narrows her eyes. "Or right place, right time, depending on how you look at it."

"I've never met anyone like Caleb Murray before." I blurt it out before I can stop myself. "He's going to help us, Denise. He's going to give me enough money to clear Mason's debts." It occurs to me then that she doesn't know about Mason, but I don't want to overload her with information.

Finally, after what feels like an age, Denise shrugs. "Will I get an invitation?"

I smile. "Of course." Pause. "But, Denise, please don't tell Mom."

She regards me coolly. "If that's what you want. I guess it's better coming from you, anyway."

"Thank you." I hug her tightly.

She pulls away and teases a lock of my hair over my shoulder. "Just be careful, Victoria. I don't want to see you get hurt."

Too late for that, I think as I head back inside the restaurant.

After the Titan, Moira takes me shopping on Fifth Avenue, ignoring my protests that there are enough outfits in my dressing room in Caleb's apartment to clothe me for an entire year.

"This is your wedding reception, Victoria." We're passing the Prada store as she says this. "You deserve to wear something special."

I've never shopped on Fifth Avenue before. Sure, I've walked along here plenty of times, I've even window shopped, staring open-mouthed at ball gowns that cost more than I earn in a year, and diamond rings that would feed an entire country for a month. But I've never been here knowing that I could buy whatever I want.

It's a giddy feeling. It's like having an out-of-body experience and watching myself from above. Moira peers in windows, oblivious to the bodyguards trailing us at a discreet distance, then comes to an abrupt halt outside Vivaldi.

"What color are you thinking?"

"I-I haven't thought about it."

I follow her inside and wait while she speaks to the store assistant. It's like a scene from *Pretty Woman*—my favorite scene—where Julia Roberts sits down, and the assistant brings her gown after gown to get her approval.

It feels surreal trying on outfits that feel expensive even without looking at the price tag. Maybe it's my imagination, but the fabric is heavier, it lays differently against my skin, and when I peer at my reflection in the mirror, I barely recognize myself. I look like the kind of woman I would expect to see on Caleb Murray's arm in a glossy magazine.

Moira studies each gown with a critical eye. When she eventually raises her eyes and smiles, I know we've found the right dress. It's floor length, fitted, in soft wine-red fabric, with a plunging neckline offset by bold ombre petals on either side of my exposed flesh.

"This is the one." Moira stands and circles me, examining the dress from every angle." You look beautiful, Victoria."

I undress in a daze and accept the bag containing my dress from the assistant with a polite thank you. After everything else that has happened, this is the most surreal, shopping on Fifth Avenue with my fake mother-in-law for an outfit to wear to my fake wedding reception.

"I need a coffee," I mutter to myself when we're standing outside the store.

"Oh, I think we can do better than that." Moira covers my hand with hers. "I know you probably dreamed of shopping for a white wedding gown with your mom, Victoria, but I just want to say thank you for letting me be a part of your experience."

VIVY SKYS

There are tears in her eyes, and for one wild crazy moment, I allow myself to believe that this is really happening.

20

CALEB

Lauren hands over two tickets to see *Wicked* at the Gershwin Theater on Broadway.

"Will she enjoy this show?"

Lauren's eyes flit between me and the tickets in my hand, and her customary pursed lips soften into a smile. "She'll love it. I've seen it five times."

"You have?" I've never thought of Lauren's life outside the Wraith, never even considered that she might be married or have a partner, kids even. How does she find the time?

"Mr. Murray." After all these years, we're still on formal terms. "I apologize for yesterday, for letting your ... well, for allowing Mrs. Murray to interrupt the family meeting. It's just that you said to bring family straight through and I didn't... That is to say, I didn't know if I should..."

"It's fine, Lauren. Victoria is family now."

Lauren closes the door to my office on her way out, and I stare at the tickets. If I'm being honest with myself, Victoria is more than family. She's everything that I ever imagined I wanted in a wife. Beautiful. Sexy. Affectionate. Feisty. I can't help smiling when I think of her with Abigail. She's everything that I would want the mother of my kids to be too.

Perhaps there's a reason why she stumbled into the Wraith when she did. I don't pay much attention to motivational quotes and all that 'Trust the universe' shit, but there has to be a reason why she was there when I needed her. I can't even imagine asking anyone else to pretend to be my wife, and yet she has settled into the role as if it was always destined to be hers one way or another.

I hide the tickets inside the desk drawer and stare at a spreadsheet on my screen. The figures merge into one fuzzy gray mass in the background when I think about Victoria lying on the edge of the rooftop pool with her legs open. My cock grows inside my pants. I could ride the elevator up to the rooftop now and fuck her until she begs me to stop, and it still wouldn't be enough.

I'm insatiable for her. Like a drug, the more I have of her, the more I want, and I don't know what's going to happen when this is all over.

I open the drawer again and check the start time for the show. 7 p.m. We've got a couple of hours to kill, and I'll achieve nothing while my brain is occupied with the soft groans of Victoria reaching an orgasm on my tongue.

I stand, adjust my cock inside my pants, and tell Lauren to finish early for the day as I pass her desk on my way to the elevator.

"Early? But, Mr. Murray, what about—"

I don't wait around for her to finish.

Victoria is on her hands and knees in the bathroom, cleaning the bottom of the shower when I walk in. Her ass in the air is enough to make my cock bounce. It's tempting—*so fucking tempting*—but I want tonight to be different. I want it to be special. I want to prove to her that I'm not a sex-crazed mafia king who thinks with his hand in his wallet or on his dick.

"What are you doing?"

Victoria visibly jumps, banging her elbow on the shower door. "Caleb." She sits on her haunches and faces me while she rubs her elbow. "Why are you here?"

"I live here, remember?"

She wrinkles her nose. "I mean, why are you back so early?"

"We're going out."

"Out? Where?" Her eyes narrow like she doesn't believe me.

"To the theater."

The tickets are burning a hole in my pocket, but I don't want to show them to her yet. I don't know much about my wife, but I get the sense that she enjoys surprises, and I want to see her face when we're standing outside the theater.

She stands slowly and tugs the latex gloves off her hands. She half-smiles with a sideways glance. "Is this like a date?"

I shrug, trying to keep the smile off my own face. "Maybe."

Victoria crosses the bathroom, stands on tiptoes and kisses my cheek. "Why, Caleb Murray, you never cease to surprise me."

I can't resist. Pushing her up against the wall, I pin her down with my body and force my tongue between her lips. She reciprocates the kiss, as I knew she would, and I pull away before I go too far and take her on a date to my bedroom instead.

"Should I change?" she asks.

My breath catches in my throat as my fingers drift down and sneak underneath her sweater. "No. You're perfect as you are."

Her expression is unfathomable, but it soon rearranges into her familiar smile as she brushes past me on her way to her room. I follow her with my eyes. What the fuck is happening to me? She's wearing faded jeans and a plain pink sweater, but the promise of what lies underneath her clothes is almost too much for me to bear in such close proximity.

Five minutes later, we're in the car and heading for Times Square. Victoria's hand is on the seat between us, and I cover it with my hand, raising a smile from her that warms me inside. If anyone ever touches her, I'll happily spend the rest of my days behind bars.

We join the throng of tourists in Times Square, following them hand in hand, Martin trailing a few discrete steps behind us. The sky is a moody shade of purple-gray, but this is already overshadowed by neon lights and flashing virtual signs. Victoria squeals as a woman appears to fly out of a gigantic 3D billboard above our heads. Like a child, she wanders around with her head tilted back towards the sky so that she doesn't miss anything.

"You've never been to Times Square before, huh?"

She laughs. "Plenty of times, but never as a tourist."

It strikes a chord within me. I've never done the whole touristy thing around my home city either, and it's refreshing to view the sights and sounds through her eyes.

We stop at the Royal Grill cart and buy lamb over rice for Victoria and Philly steak over rice for me, eating as we walk, the flavors exploding on our tongues.

"Oh my God this is amazing." Victoria licks sauce from her fingers, grinning like the cat that caught the fattest mouse.

"Better than the Wraith?"

Her smile fades and she scrunches up her nose in a gesture that makes me want to drag her down an alleyway and fuck her up against the wall. "Sorry. I didn't mean—"

I laugh out loud. "It's the best Philly steak I've had in years."

"You're just saying that now to make me feel better." She nudges my arm with her elbow, and I nudge her back.

When we eventually stop outside the Gershwin Theater, and she sees the *Wicked* sign, she squeals again, eyes wide and glittering with tears. Then she throws her arms around my neck and kisses me on the lips. No tongues. Just a happy kiss, and I hold her hand as we enter the muted sounds of the theater foyer.

I barely recall much of the show. I'm too busy watching Victoria who rests her arms on the ledge of the box, her chin on her arms, mesmerized by the stage, the costumes, the songs.

Outside, she walks in a daze, her mind still back inside the theater, the songs replaying inside her head. Each time she looks at me, she recalls another moment from the show that stole her imagination.

"What would you like to do now?" I ask when we're back in the car.

"We should go pick up Abigail from your mom's house. It isn't fair on Emily."

"Victoria." I hold her gaze and force her to listen. "Stop worrying about Abigail for once. I asked Mom to keep Abigail at her place overnight. Tonight is yours."

Her eyes grow large with tears. "Anything?" she whispers.

"Anything."

She twists her mouth to one side. "You're going to laugh when I tell you what I want to do."

"You're not going to tell me that you want to go home and watch a movie."

She grins at me. "No. Better than that. I want you to take me out on your Harley."

At first, I think she must be joking, but then I realize that she's watching me closely, waiting for me to react. "You're serious?" She nods. "Have you ever been on a motorcycle?"

"Nope. Never."

"You know it's dangerous." She nods again. "You know how fast a Harley can go. Riding a bike isn't like sitting in the back of a fast car."

"I know." Her eyes are still wide, eager, hopeful.

"First time riding pillion can be scary." It sounds like I'm trying to talk her out of it, but I just need to be certain that she understands the risks.

"I'm not scared, Caleb. I trust you."

That does it for me. "I've got a helmet and leathers back at the Wraith that will fit you."

Her smile is wider than ever.

"Where do you want to go?"

"Surprise me."

We head out of town, pick up the Upper Delaware Scenic Byway, and drive until we find a spot by the river with spectacular views of the New York City skyline. With Victoria riding pillion, her arms wrapped around my waist, her thighs pressed against mine, my adrenaline rush is drastically altered.

Her presence fills my head. Her body consumes my every thought. Her trust in me is like every orgasm I've ever experienced bottled into an exotic cologne that I could make billions from.

I offer her my hand and help her to dismount the bike when we stop. She stands in front of me, her face pale in the moonlight, and doesn't move while I take off her helmet. She's trembling, I realize.

"Are you alright?" I lower my face so that our eyes are level.

Victoria's eyes are wide and dark. Her lips are so pale they blend in with her skin.

"Did I go too fast? Did something happen? Breathe…"

She shakes her head, and a wide smile sets her face aglow. "That was amazing." She laughs, a mixture of emotions, shock, exhilaration, pleasure, playing across her face. "Why did no one ever tell me it would feel this good?"

"Because you never met me till now."

I pull her into my arms, and we stand there by the side of the road enjoying the view of the city lights, her head resting against my chest.

I've explored the Byway before. I've pushed the Harley to its limits, the speed and the adrenaline rush erasing my thoughts and setting me free like a bird released from its cage if only for a few hours. But it has never felt like this before. I've never paused to breathe and feel and just be me.

I don't know if it's having Victoria in my arms, or the view, or simply a combination of an evening spent being someone other than Caleb Murray, but there's a sensation rushing through my veins and shouting in my ears that this is what I've been missing. It's the same feeling that prompted me to search for Sandy. A feeling so extraordinary that letting it go would be like telling my heart to stop pumping.

"Victoria, you don't have to go ahead with the wedding reception." The words appear from nowhere, but now that I've said them out loud, it's like slotting the final piece of a jigsaw puzzle into place.

After the party, once Victoria has been introduced to the rest of the world, we can think about cutting short the agreement. It's the tipping point, the peak of the mountain, passing the test you've been studying for your entire life and realizing that it's all downhill from here on. I'm not ready to let her go. I've barely even scratched the surface of Victoria Callahan, but if this is only the beginning, I'm not prepared to walk away without knowing more.

Plus, there's the niggling concern at the forefront of my mind called Olivia Dragonetti.

Victoria tilts her head back so that she can look me in the eye. "What's brought this on?"

"I... I know that you want to help. You didn't have to marry me, but you did. You accepted my fucked-up proposal and you've done nothing but keep your side of the deal from the moment you stepped into my office."

Her eyes are glittering with unshed tears, but she doesn't say anything.

"My family ... they can be persuasive when they want to be." She opens her mouth to speak, and I shake my head. I'm not finished. "They want the reception to go ahead because it works in our favor. It ties up loose ends. It may even, with a bit of luck, result in the alliance we've been trying to seal for years."

"It works in your favor too." It's barely more than a whisper.

"Depends which way you look at it." I smile. "Until now, I've used people to get what I want and never given them a second thought. It's what people like us do."

"People like us?"

"I'm not going to sugarcoat it. You've seen the way we live. The lifestyle, the trappings, the bodyguards. It all comes at a price, and I'm not prepared to barter with you and Abigail."

I feel her stiffen in my arms. Maybe I've said too much, but she needs to hear it like it is. She needs to know exactly what's in store for her if we don't walk away from each other as planned. As if the bullet wound and the stalker haven't made it blatantly obvious.

She shakes her head. "You're not bartering with me and Abigail. I came to you of my own free will. I'm a big girl now, Caleb. I make my own life choices, and I choose you. With or without the lifestyle and the trappings and the bodyguards." Her mouth twists into a lopsided smile. "Although I'll admit that the bodyguards are useful when you're being followed."

"So long as you don't lose them in Macy's."

"Yeah..." She winces. "Sorry about that." She looks like she has a whole bunch of stuff more to say that's eating away at her, and I wish she understood that she can talk to me. I want to listen.

"I need you to trust me, Victoria."

"I do." She leans back to get a better look at my expression. "What is it? What haven't you told me?"

"I'm calling off the reception."

"But—"

"I'm making an executive decision. It's what I do, if you hadn't already noticed." I'm making light of it, but I know I'm not fooling her. "We'll find another way to call Olivia's bluff. Fuck knows we have enough resources to throw at it."

"But what about your mom? Kyle?"

"I'll handle them. This isn't what's best for Kyle."

There's so much I want to tell her about Kyle. I want her to know that he isn't an asshole, that he would never leave a woman for dead to save himself, that he's not as strong as he looks. Baby steps. I haven't even told her how I feel about her yet because I'm still figuring it out for myself.

"You can stop Kyle, Caleb. He'll listen to you. They all listen to you." I sense a but coming. "But I think the wedding reception should go ahead as planned. You need this. Your family needs this. Maybe I..." For the first time since we stopped here on the Byway, she turns her face away and refuses to meet my gaze.

I take her chin between my thumb and forefinger and tilt it towards me. "Go on."

"Maybe I could talk to Olivia."

"No." I release her and step backwards, missing her presence in my arms instantaneously. "Don't even think about it. You don't know what she's capable of. You've not grown up in the same world as she has, so you wouldn't understand how little respect she has for anything or anyone."

"No, you're right." Her voice is brittle. "I don't belong in your world. Thank you for the reminder."

She goes to walk away, but I grab her arm and turn her back around to face me. "That isn't what I'm saying. I don't want you to belong in this world."

She glares at my fist wrapped around her arm until I let her go. "What do you want then, Caleb?"

Her chest is heaving with the effort of controlling her anger at me, and I hate myself for doing this to her. I asked her to trust me, and then I shoot her down the first time she asks me to trust her. It isn't one of my finest moments.

"I—"

My phone rings in my pocket. Terry's ringtone. He only ever calls me when it's an emergency; it's an unspoken rule that we keep communication to a minimum because you never know who's listening.

"I have to answer this." My cell phone is already in my hand, the screen unlocked.

Terry's voice buzzes in my ear. "Don Dragonetti has had a heart attack."

21

VICTORIA

The ride back to the Wraith is less exhilarating than the outward journey. I sense the tension through Caleb's leathers as I hold on to him from behind: the straight spine, the taut shoulders, the clenched muscles. He didn't confirm what Don Dragonetti's possible death would mean to him and his family, but I guess he didn't need to. Olivia is his only child. She would be the new head of the Dragonetti family, and it would not bode well for any of the mafia families in New York.

They might not have cemented an alliance yet, but I sense that Caleb has a lot of sentiment for Don Dragonetti. A lot of respect. His concern runs deeper than fear of Olivia holding the reins of the older man's empire. He might never admit it, but I think he cares about him.

We don't go to the hospital. The don is still alive, and it would be wrong to encroach on his family's precious moments with him. Instead, we return to the Wraith, and I go straight to his apartment while Caleb holds a meeting in his office.

The news has rubbed the shine from what had been one of the best nights of my life. Eating halal food in Times Square, the show, the motorcycle. Stopping on the roadside, just the two of us, no bodyguards, no family members, no reminders of real life.

Caleb was different somehow. Softer. Gentler. Unmasked. He was about to tell me what he wanted when he got the call about the don. He was so close... So close that my heart didn't know whether to slow down so that I didn't miss a word, or flutter around like an excited butterfly.

I change out of the leathers and into one of Caleb's shirts. Make coffee. Wander up to the rooftop decking and huddle under a blanket to watch the stars.

I think about Don Dragonetti in a hospital room somewhere surrounded by people who care about him. Is he sad that his entire legacy will be left to his uncontrollable daughter? Or is he so blinded by paternal love that he can't see the darkness ahead? I don't know the man well, but my heart aches for him.

The sky fades to gray and then lilac, the pink of dawn rising above the horizon, and still Caleb doesn't come back.

I head back inside, grateful that Abigail is safe with Moira and Terry, and lie down on Caleb's bed. When I wake up, the comforter has been pulled over me, but the apartment is empty. No note. No sign that Caleb was there at all.

The apartment seems even larger when I don't know where Caleb is. I switch on the sound system to drown out the silence, an old Fleetwood Mac album, the songs easy to listen to because everyone has grown up with them. I make more coffee and stand in front of the windows staring out at the city, but all I can think about is Don Dragonetti.

Caleb can't keep me here indefinitely without any news. Till now, Lauren might've been the only person who needed to know his movements, but I'm his wife. Okay, I'm only his wife on paper, but the nights we've spent together must count for something.

Caleb knows every inch of my body. He has tasted me inside and out. He was about to make this real last night on the Byway, I know he was, because two people don't share the kind of passion that sparks between us whenever we're together if they're just passing through. Do they?

Danny pops into my head, and for the first time in five years, I bat the images out of the ballpark. Danny isn't real, but Caleb is. This is more than just a one-night stand; this is what Danny and I might've had if only we'd found each other again, and the soreness in my breasts this morning only cements this. If this means what I think it could mean, then the universe is giving me a second chance. I just pray it isn't messing with me this time around.

I almost blurted it out to Caleb on the Byway, but I didn't want him to think that I was trying to trap him. I'm not Olivia Dragonetti. I'll fight fair and square for him, but I want him to want this as much as I do with or without whatever my body is trying to tell me.

I'm about to get dressed and go down to Caleb's office to find him when the elevator dings and the doors slide open.

"Caleb?" I run to the elevator, my pulse racing, and fail to hide my disappointment when Kyle steps out. "Oh, Kyle, what are you doing here?" My eyes instinctively drift back to the elevator, hoping that he isn't alone.

"Caleb asked me to come and check on you." He shakes his

head as if trying to erase the words and start again. "He doesn't want you to be lonely."

"Where is he?"

"He's with Terry and the twins. There's a lot to sort out." He shrugs, a smile that doesn't fully materialize half-forming on his lips. "Strange considering the business we're in, that a heart attack can throw the entire city into this kind of turmoil."

"It was unexpected." I peer down and realize that I'm still wearing Caleb's shirt and holding an empty coffee cup in my hand. "I'll go change and make coffee."

"I'm quite capable of operating a coffee machine." Kyle heads to the kitchen while I dash back into my room and tug on the jeans and sweater I wore last night for our date.

I can smell Caleb on my clothes. I want to feel close to him, to hold onto the memories of our first real date, to nurture the tiny nugget of hope that he was going to tell me how he feels about me. Kyle's arrival has driven home the stark reminder that this is Caleb's life, and that work will always take up much of his time.

Back in the kitchen, Kyle is filling two cups with steaming black coffee and buttering slices of toast. "See." He grins at me. "I'm the domesticated brother. You drew the short straw when you got Caleb."

He slides a plate of toast across the counter towards me, and I realize how hungry I am when I take the first bite. "Oh my God," I manage with my mouth full of buttery bread. "Is there anything better than toast when you're hungry?"

Kyle tilts his head to one side, pondering the question. "You know, I don't think there is."

We both laugh, and I climb onto one of the leather-cushioned chrome stools around the central island. Growing up, even when our mom was never really present, Mason and I spent most of our time in the kitchen. It was the hub of the family unit. It was small and cramped—a million miles away from Caleb's pristine kitchen—and there was rarely enough food to fill our tummies. But it was warm. It was where we both felt safe.

I hadn't thought about feeling warm and safe in Caleb's streamlined kitchen before, but with Kyle keeping the toast and coffee coming, I finally start to feel comfortable.

"We went out on Caleb's bike last night," I kickstart the conversation.

His eyebrows shoot upwards. "He let you on his bike?"

"Even said that I could keep the leathers and helmet." I lick butter from my fingers and help myself to another slice of toast.

"Wow, what have you done to my brother?" Pink spots appear on his cheeks, and I feel heat rising in my own face when I think of me and Caleb in the elevator.

Has he seen the video footage? Would Caleb show his brother? No. I immediately shake the thought from my brain; Caleb would never share me with anyone.

"Sorry," he says. "That was a stupid question."

A heavy silence settles on us. We both know that me being here is just an arrangement to serve a purpose, and that one day, I'll disappear from their lives as if I never existed. Unless Caleb tells them how he feels about me.

"Do you have a motorcycle too?"

It's a tough habit to break, this need to fill silences before they become awkward. It's like there's a time limit on them, fill them too soon, and you just sound needy, but leave it too long, and then anything you say sounds forced. Overthinking is another tough habit to crack.

"No." The toaster pops, and Kyle retrieves the hot slices. "I was involved in an accident five years ago. It kinda shook my confidence. I've never been back on a bike since." He pushes some more buttered toast my way.

I bite another mouthful of toast; I was hungrier than I realized because I skipped breakfast. I study him closely. No one could mistake the fact that he and Caleb are brothers, but there's something softer about Kyle, almost as if life has sanded down his edges to make them smoother, less abrasive. Or perhaps Caleb has simply developed a harder exterior. Comes with the territory.

Then I realize what he just said.

"Five years ago?" *Shit*. "What happened?"

"Long story." He swallows, his Adam's apple bobbing above his shirt collar as if he's munching on glass. "It was New Year's. Caleb and I had gone to a club. We got separated, and I met a girl."

Something cold and slimy slithers down my spine, and I suddenly feel nauseous.

"Something clicked between us." Kyle's eyes grow distant. "She was ... amazing. Wild. Full of life and energy and laughter. I'd honestly never met anyone like her before."

His gaze hops my way. Oblivious to the churning in my gut.

He's describing Sienna. She is all of those things, or at least she was before the accident destroyed her self-esteem.

"It was past midnight. I didn't want to let her go." His voice is barely audible above the thud-thud-thud of my heartbeat. "I don't know. I wasn't drunk, so it wasn't that; there was just something about her that I'd never found before. So, when she suggested that we drive out of the city and watch the sunrise, I said yes."

That's why they were on the highway. They were going to watch the sunrise together. Sienna never mentioned this before. She never spoke about the guy she was with like she wanted to erase it from her memory completely. I never pushed it because I knew how painful it was for her.

"What happened?" I whisper.

"It's all a bit fuzzy. There was a truck heading in the opposite direction. The cab was all lit up like a Christmas tree, and we laughed about it. I flashed the headlights. It was New Year. Everyone on the road was buzzing. Then a car came out of nowhere."

"A car?"

"Heading straight for us. On the wrong side of the road, like it was a game of chicken. It was level with the truck." His breathing is growing shallow, but I keep my eyes fixed firmly on the half-eaten slice of toast in front of me. "I hit the brakes, but I must've hit some black ice because the car swerved across the lanes." He pauses, wiping tears from his eyes with his thumbs.

I try to wash the toast down with a mouthful of coffee, but it's hard to swallow. Sienna must've been so frightened. They both must've been, but I'm struggling to muster any sympathy right now for the man who left my best friend to die in a car wreckage.

"Next thing I knew, Cash and Bash were there, and I was lying in the middle of the road." He puffs up his cheeks and releases a steady breath, remembering. "They said I called them. No one could get hold of Caleb."

No mention of the woman who was in the car with him.

My mouth is dry. My palms are sweaty, and the apartment suddenly feels claustrophobic even though there's only the two of us in a room that could easily accommodate an entire party.

I have to ask. "What happened to the woman?"

"She died."

She died? He wasn't with Sienna. This was a separate incident. Two wrecks on the same night, which I guess isn't so unbelievable especially on a night like New Year's.

My heart does a double take and starts racing to the tempo of utter relief. Kyle didn't leave Sienna for dead... Although this thought is accompanied by another icy shudder that travels the length of my spine.

"Did your brothers pull her out of the wreckage?"

He inhales deeply. "She was dead. There wasn't time. They called the emergency services and got me out of there. We couldn't afford to have the press get hold of the story."

"So, they left her there." My voice is cold.

I'm trying to picture the scene: Kyle lying in the middle of the road, perhaps fading in and out of consciousness; Cash and Bash feeling the passenger's pulse and trading her life for their brother; Caleb God only knows where. I shouldn't really blame Kyle, but there's something cold and heavy puddling in the pit of my stomach at the thought of this family protecting their own rather than saving the life of a young woman.

"I trawled the tabloids after." Kyle picks the loose skin around his thumbnail. I never noticed the pulpy flesh around his nails before. "I wanted to find out who she was, to pay my respects to her family, to tell them what happened. I hoped... I hoped that maybe we could all gain some closure from it."

"What was her name?" I grind out the words with clenched jaw.

"I..." Kyle shakes his head. "She told me her name was Ruby Tuesday, but she made it up. She was wearing a costume." He closes his eyes briefly. "She was Wilma from *The Flintstones.*"

Bile rises in my throat, and I cover my mouth, trying to swallow it. Kyle was trying to find closure for his survivor guilt, while Sienna would never have found him because his brothers covered up his part in the incident.

"She wasn't dead."

"Huh?" Kyle furrows his brow. His thumb is bleeding, and he covers it with his other hand as if he can make it go away. Just like his brothers did with the woman they left for dead in the car wreckage five years ago. "H-how do you know this?"

"Because the woman in the car was my best friend, Sienna." Tears spill from my eyes now, and I don't wipe them away. "She didn't die in the crash. After your brothers rescued you, the car caught fire. Sienna suffered burns on seventy-five percent of her body. She has been in and out of hospital ever since, having operations and skin grafts."

It sounds as if I'm reading from a script, but it's the only way I can recount Sienna's horrific story without breaking down.

"Sienna? Your friend, Sienna?" His voice has shrunk, and when I finally force myself to look at him, he seems smaller somehow too. "Is she... Did she ever..."

"If you mean did she ever talk about you, the answer is no. You left her to die in that wreckage." My voice rises a notch, but I don't even try to contain it.

"I didn't. I thought—"

"It doesn't matter what you thought." I cut him off. "Sienna knows that two people went into that car crash, and only one got left behind. That night changed her life, and not in a good way."

As the enormity of what I'm saying sinks in, Kyle's shoulders begin to shudder. "I'm sorry. I'm so very sorry. I never meant for any of this to happen." He hangs his head low, his chin almost touching the counter. "I need to speak to her."

"She's missing." Sienna was almost killed by a member of this family, and now she's missing because of them too. Or at least, because of my involvement with them. It amounts to the same thing. "She wouldn't want to speak to you even if she was here. Because of what happened that night, she has never dated anyone else since."

Kyle is on his feet in a heartbeat, his cheeks damp with tears. "I'll find her. I'll do whatever it takes, I'll scour the city, I'll scour the entire fucking United States of America to find her, I promise you. And when I do, I'll make everything right again."

"How?" I suddenly feel bone-weary, recent events pressing down on me and making my limbs heavy. "By offering her money? That's what the Murrays do, isn't it? You buy whatever you want, including people."

"No, not with money, that's not what I meant." He reaches for my hand across the counter, and I snatch it away. "You have to believe me, Victoria."

"Why should I believe you? Why should I listen to anything you have to say?"

I climb down from the stool. I have to get away from him, from the apartment, the bodyguard waiting in the elevator. I have to get away from all of them. Even Caleb.

Slowly, like the sun peeping out from behind the horizon, it dawns on me that I told Caleb about Sienna. I told him that the guy she was with left her in the wreckage, and I'm almost a hundred percent certain that I told him it happened at New Year's five years ago.

"He knew," I mutter under my breath.

"Huh?" Kyle furrows his brow. "Who knew?"

I start pacing back and forth, trying to get things straight inside my head. "I told Caleb about Sienna. I told him, and he never said that it was you."

I stop pacing and stare at Kyle. I hardly recognize him now as the suited lawyer who drew up the marriage contract that started all of this. All I can see now is the guy who ruined Sienna's life that night.

Kyle slumps forward over the counter and holds his head in both hands. When he peers up at me again, his eyes are pink and puffy. "He never told me either."

What other secrets is Caleb keeping from both of us? Why didn't he want either of us to know the truth? Was he worried that I would hate his brother and call off the fake marriage? And what about Kyle? If he knew that Kyle had tried to find Sienna, why didn't he tell him that she was still alive so that he could finally get the 'closure' he needed?

I grab my purse off the side and go to the elevator. I don't know where I'm going, but I do know that I can't stay here a moment longer.

"Victoria?" I hear the panic in Kyle's voice, but I don't turn around until I'm standing in the elevator. "Where are you going?"

"I don't know. Away from here." As the doors hiss shut, I add, "Tell Caleb not to try finding me."

"No, wait. Come back..." His words fade as the elevator starts descending to the basement.

In the car on the way to Staten Island, all I can think about is Kyle and Sienna in that car wreckage, and Caleb's silence when he discovered the truth. I know he must've had his reasons, but the fact is, all those reasons revolve around Caleb Murray. Everything that he does and says is with his own wellbeing and reputation in mind, and I hadn't realized until now just how self-absorbed he is.

How can I be with a man like that?

How can I be in love with a man who would cover up a serious accident to save the family name?

Hot tears sting my eyes. I am in love with Caleb Murray, but I don't even know who he is. Not anymore. Sure, the physical attraction is undeniably through the roof. It's explosive and sexy and passionate, and I'm wet just sitting in the back seat of the car thinking about it, but two people can't build a lifelong relationship on lust.

My tears turn to anger the closer to Staten Island I get. I introduced Abigail to this family. She's with Moira and Terry right now, and who knows what she might hear in a house where the guests are mafia mobsters and supermodels and police commissioners. The sooner I get her away from them the better.

I have no clear plan when the car pulls up outside Moira and Terry's mansion. I don't know where I'll go with Abigail—I haven't received any money from Caleb yet—but I do know that I'm not going through with the wedding reception. The thought of it makes my hands ball into fists. All that money and pretense and fake smiles.

I don't wait around for Martin to open the car door. I've unbuckled my seatbelt and am out of the car almost before it stops, approaching the front door with my heart still drumming a dull erratic beat.

The door opens, and Moira is there to greet me before I can ring the doorbell. Kyle must've called ahead. Of course he did. Family first.

"Victoria, come in." She holds the door wide. I don't know if she gestures behind my back to Martin to wait outside, but she closes the door and wanders to the kitchen, expecting me to follow.

"I've come for Abigail," I say while Moira fills two cups with coffee from the elaborate machine on the counter.

"Abigail is with Emily, she's fine." Moira smiles. "Let's talk first."

I sit down on a bar stool. This room is the kind of family hub most people could only dream of. It's bright and airy, the cabinets are glossy ivory, the appliances are coordinated, and everything about it yells home and comfort. The Murrays might put family first, but they're still the kind of people who would leave a young woman to die alone in a car wreckage.

"I want to cancel the wedding reception." I sip my coffee, but my whirring thoughts are still making me feel queasy.

Moira stands across the counter from me and cradles her cup in both hands. "Kyle told me about your friend, Sienna. I know what you're thinking. You think that my sons left a young woman to die to keep their names out of the tabloids."

It's exactly what I think, but I'm not going to agree with her. I feel like I'm betraying Sienna, but I want to hear Moira's version of events before I leave with Abigail.

"I've spoken to Bastien and Cassius. Cassius checked the young woman's pulse. When he couldn't find it, he called the emergency services. My husband Terry, believing that there had been a fatality, told him to get Kyle away from the scene." Moira places her cup on the counter and rests her chin on her steepled fingers. "I'm a mom, Victoria. I would do anything to protect my children. But I would never allow them to leave an innocent young woman to die. No matter the circumstances."

My tears start over again as the anger I'd cultivated on the car journey here evaporates.

"For all we knew the young woman, Sienna, was someone's daughter, sister, partner. Maybe even someone's mom. I couldn't even begin to imagine getting that terrible news from the NYPD. My sons believed that she was dead, and I know my sons well enough to believe that they're telling me the truth."

My sobs erupt then, and Moira pushes a silk-covered box of tissues my way. I bury my face in a wad of tissue paper, and cry. There are five years' worth of tears stored up inside me along with my own guilt at not being around when Sienna needed me most. Maybe my anger is directed at myself rather than the Murrays. I guess it would take a shrink and a whole lot of therapy to figure that out.

"I watched her change from a vibrant, fun-loving woman to someone who was afraid to get dressed up and party." I soak up my tears with a soggy tissue. "She thought he left her to die..."

"I know." Moira reaches for my hand, and I don't stop her. "And I bet you wanted to kill the bastard that did this to your friend."

I nod, and laugh, and cry all at the same time. Ugly messy tears. Maybe I needed this, and maybe it took an outsider, someone like Moira, to make it happen. "I told Caleb about Sienna. He promised to help her open an art gallery. But he didn't tell me about Kyle."

Moira pats my hand and sits back. "Kyle doesn't know this, but Caleb tried to find out who the young woman in the car was. He felt guilty for not being there when Kyle needed him. But he was looking for a death announcement. We didn't know her name. He called in some favors, got the names of every person that had passed through every morgue in the city. If we'd known she survived ... well ... it would've been quite a different story."

Caleb tried to find her.

On the way here, I'd made up my mind to get as far away as possible from Caleb once this was over. It made my heart ache, the thought of never seeing him again, of never tasting his kisses, or feeling him inside me, but I couldn't envisage a world with both him and Sienna in it, and I owe it to Sienna to put her first.

But now that I know the truth, that we were wrong about the guy she was with that night, that glimmer of hope has been rekindled. We can find Sienna, tell her what happened, give her the money to open her art gallery. Maybe she and Kyle might even fall in love someday.

Me and Caleb, Kyle and Sienna. It's the kind of story you read about in Romcoms, but it could happen. Couldn't it?

"My advice," Moira interrupts my rosy thoughts, "is to go ahead with the party. Wear the beautiful gown, Victoria, be Caleb's wife, and let us handle Olivia Dragonetti."

I suck in a deep breath. For a while there, I'd forgotten all about Dragon-face.

"I know you're in love with my son."

My breath seems to get stuck, and I blink slowly, thinking that I must've misheard.

"Anyone who can't see it must be either blind or extremely naïve." She pauses. "I know that he feels the same way about you too."

"Y-you do?"

She smiles, and for the first time, I think I'm seeing Moira the mom rather than Moira the mafia queen. "He might not know it yet, but he'll figure it out. You're good for him, Victoria. I can't remember the last time I saw him this happy, and that's really all I've ever wanted for my children, their happiness."

I don't know what to say. Is that what Caleb was going to tell me when I asked him what he wanted?

My phone vibrates, and my pulse races as I check the Caller ID hoping to see Caleb's name. Instead, it's a message from an unknown number. It says:

I know where Sienna is.

22

CALEB

"Why didn't you tell me about Sienna?" Kyle barges into the Rinse's boardroom and leans over the table, his chest heaving as he tries to fill his lungs, his face pink and blotchy.

"Kyle, breathe." I stand up, pushing my seat backwards, but he raises a hand, palm outwards, warning me not to come any closer. "Where's your inhaler?"

He fumbles inside his jacket pocket, and his hand comes back empty. His breaths are shallow, his chest caving as he tries to get enough oxygen to keep him upright.

I'm by his side before he can protest. I check his other pockets but draw a blank. It's been years since he has had a full-on asthma attack, so maybe he's given up carrying an inhaler around with him.

"Cash, pull some strings and get an inhaler here."

The twins both leave the room.

Terry helps me get Kyle onto one of the sofas, plumps up the cushions behind him to keep him upright, and loosens his tie while I fill a tumbler with iced water. I hold it to Kyle's face and tell him to breathe. I don't know why, but it used to help Kyle when he was younger, just breathing in the air surrounding a glass of water. Or maybe it was just an illusion, something that I convinced myself was a mystery cure when I was just a kid trying to keep him safe from our father.

"I'm fine." Kyle tries to stand up and then slumps back in the seat. "Don't fuss."

I sit down and nod at Terry to give us a few minutes alone.

I can hear Kyle's breath wheezing through his restricted airways, but at least he's calmer than when he first came in.

"I wanted to find Sienna before I said anything. I needed to be sure that it was the same person who was in the car with you that night. I didn't want to get your hopes up only to crush them again."

"You still … should've told me… I can help … you find her."

I breathe in through my nose, hold it, and breathe out through my mouth. Watching Kyle struggling to fill his lungs always has this effect on me, like my own lungs start shutting down in sympathy.

"I saw how you were after the accident. I tried to find her." He listens, his eyebrows lower making his eyes appear even more sunken with his labored breathing. "I didn't say anything, because I didn't want to admit that I'd failed. I failed you that night. I should've been there for you."

"This … doesn't change … anything. When was you … going … to tell me? After you let … Victoria go?"

I rub my hands across my stubble. It's been a long twenty-four hours. Victoria was asleep when I went back to the apartment to shower, and as tempting as it was, I didn't want to wake her. It isn't until Kyle talks about letting her go that I realize that I didn't get to finish what I was about to tell her on the Byway.

"Letting her go is no longer an option."

The corners of Kyle's mouth twitch into a smile. "I thought ... it would take you ... longer than this ... to realize."

"I'm learning." I sit forward, resting my elbows on my thighs. "Now do you understand why I was against you and Olivia?"

"Because of ... Sienna?"

"Kyle, there must've been something in the air that night five years ago because you fell for Sienna almost as hard and as fast as I fell for Sandy."

"And now...?"

"And now there's Victoria. She reminds me so much of Sandy it's uncanny."

"You should try ... keeping it in your pants."

I smile. At least we're good again. "It's more than that. She's ... I don't know." I'm not used to expressing my emotions, so I'm struggling to find the right words. "She's everything I ever imagined my future wife to be, I guess."

Kyle nods. "You look good ... together. I've never seen ... a woman ... eat so much toast before."

I can't help laughing. "You had breakfast with my wife?"

"Someone had to ... keep her company."

"How do you feel about Sienna now? I mean now that you know she survived the wreck?" I watch him closely. Even now, it's still my job to look out for him. Perhaps it always will be.

"Honestly, I don't know. Maybe you're right … maybe there was something … in the air that night … because I could hardly … take my eyes off her. But now…" He coughs into his hands, his eyes filling up. "Have my memories … made her into something special … because of what happened?" He shakes his head. "What if… What if she doesn't … live up to the images in my head?"

"Then it'll be time to let it go. Just think yourself lucky that you get a second chance."

"We have to find her first."

The door opens again, and Cash and Bash come in, closely followed by Terry and our mom. She comes straight in, sits beside Kyle, and hands him an inhaler. His breathing eases a little almost immediately.

"Thanks, Mom." Kyle looks sheepish, like a little kid again, and my chest swells with love for him.

"I'm not going to remind you to carry an inhaler around with you." Mom sits demurely beside him, legs crossed at the ankles. "You're old enough to make your own mistakes."

"It hasn't happened in a while." It isn't an excuse; Kyle is just stating a fact.

Mom inclines her head. "Now, about Sienna…"

Kyle snaps his head towards her; she has his full attention now that his lungs have some respite. "What about her? What have you heard?" His eyes hop between Mom and Terry, his breathing growing shallow again.

I place a hand on his arm. "Relax. Breathe. We're still looking for her. Right?" I address Terry.

"Let your mom speak." He doesn't make eye contact, and my gut starts twisting.

"This revelation doesn't change anything." Mom glances at me and back at Kyle. "I've spoken to Victoria, and we've agreed to go ahead with the wedding reception at the Titan as planned. Of course, Dragonetti's health problems will make life a little more difficult, but we'll find a way around it. He needs to know what his daughter is, and we need to be the ones to show him."

Kyle shakes his head slowly. He uses the inhaler a second time, and we all wait for it to take effect. "I can't do it. Not now. Not with Sienna in the picture."

His eyes lock onto mine, and it's as if he's transferring his anxiety to me. I feel his heart racing, the shallow breaths, the gut-crippling spasms when he thinks about what might have happened to Sienna.

"But you've already taken the first steps." Mom shrugs. "That's the hardest part out of the way."

"Leave it, Mom." I step in. *Little brother Caleb to the rescue.* "Olivia will receive an invitation. She'll be at the party with or without Kyle's participation."

"But we won't have her exactly where we want her. We won't have convinced her that she still has a chance of winning you back, and without that, she'll just be firing bullets in all directions, hoping to hit a target."

Nice metaphor. But she seems to have forgotten her eldest son's fragile mental state.

"Okay, so we'll find another way to convince her. I'll stage a public argument with Victoria." My fists clench at the thought of dragging Victoria even deeper into this, but having seen her at the last family meeting, I know that she'll understand. "Olivia is so deranged that she'll believe it because that's what she wants to believe."

"This won't work." Mom's voice is firm. "It will jeopardize the alliance with Don Dragonetti. Whatever anyone thinks of him, he believes in strong family units, and your wife has already introduced herself to him privately. He won't look favorably on a public tiff."

I recall Victoria suggesting that she should speak to Olivia, and the way I shut her down without listening to her reasoning. But I already know that I won't put her in that position. I don't think anyone fully understands what Olivia is capable of.

"It's fine." Kyle sucks on the inhaler and holds his breath. "I'll do it."

"No!" I'm on my feet. "Fuck the alliance. We've come this far without it. It isn't going to hold us back now."

Terry's eyes narrow, and he shoots me a look that says I've crossed a line.

"Sorry, Mom, but if Kyle doesn't want to see this through, I think we should respect his wishes. Think about it. There's a reason why Victoria came into our lives and brought Sienna with her. I'm not going to destroy Kyle's chance to put things right because of an alliance that may or may not happen anyway if Don Dragonetti doesn't recover from his heart attack."

Mom arches an eyebrow. "Family comes first, Caleb. You know that. I'm surprised that you would risk this family's future for a woman your brother met once in a nightclub."

I've always known that my mom can be cold, determined, ruthless even. But I never truly believed that she would put family before love. She got lucky when she met Terry—without him, we wouldn't be where we are today—and I always thought that she wanted the same for her children. Right now, listening to her talking about alliances and doing what's right for the family, I know that I would walk away from it all if it meant that Victoria would be safe and happy.

"What if I said that I would risk it for Victoria? I'll cancel the reception and deal with Olivia myself."

Mom stands, her lips stretching into a wide smile. "I would say that I believe you. Honestly, I thought it would take you longer to work out your feelings for Victoria, but I'm glad that you have." She winks at Terry, who smiles in return.

"But this is precisely why we should proceed as planned," Terry adds.

"It's fine." Kyle's breathing is finally starting to regulate, and some color is returning to his cheeks. "I'll do it. On one condition."

We all wait for him to elaborate.

"You keep me updated every step of the way regarding Sienna. I want to know where she is. Who's holding her. How we're going to rescue her."

"Done." Terry nods. "There's an old abandoned cargo airport outside of Lake Placid. My sources intercepted comms between Ivan Petrov and a private aircraft flying into the country from Russia."

"You think he's holding Sienna there?"

His alliance—if that's what it can be called—with Olivia, must've been going on in secret for way longer than any of the other families realized. I'm impressed. I never knew that Olivia Dragonetti was capable of guarding a secret, but this potentially makes her even more deadly.

"If she was in the city, I'd have heard about it," Terry says.

"Okay, what are we waiting for?"

"A distraction."

"The wedding reception." That sinking feeling is back.

It all slots into place. Mom knew the party had to go ahead, but she wanted her sons to commit to it before we found out why. She wasn't putting family before love; she was guiding us in the right direction. She knows us better than we know ourselves, and she wanted to be sure that we accepted our emotions before this went any further.

"Can't we bring it forward?" Kyle asks. "I can't wait until next week. What if... What if they're torturing Sienna?"

"Unlikely," Terry says. "Ivan was sent away for dishing out justice for his girlfriend. Okay, so perhaps his methods could've been a little less violent, but he did it for all the right reasons. He doesn't kill for pleasure."

"A nutjob with a heart," I say.

"Unlike his current partner in crime." Terry stands, bringing the meeting to a natural conclusion. "Ivan might want Olivia on his side, for now, but I don't believe that he sees it as long-term, and he will draw the line at senseless violence to satisfy Olivia Dragonetti's itch."

"He hasn't ruled out an alliance with the Murrays," I add. "Killing Sienna will send that up in flames before it has even left the ground."

"I hope you're right." Kyle stands, pocketing the inhaler.

The urge to see Victoria and hold her in my arms, to finish what I started the evening before, is too great to ignore. "Is Victoria still at your house, Mom?"

"No. After I convinced her that going ahead with the party was the right thing to do, she went back to the Wraith." She stands up and entwines her fingers with Terry's.

She looks older. Still immaculately groomed, but it's almost as if her body is finally telling her that it's time to let go of all this, to find some peace, allow the next generation to take over. Has she been waiting for her sons to fall in love and find their own family unit before she and Terry hand over the business? She'll have a long wait for the twins to settle down, but perhaps she sensed all along that Victoria and I were more than just a mutual agreement.

I smile at them both. Couple goals right there. "I'm heading home to catch up on some sleep."

"Yeah, right." Cash's eyebrows dance independently. "Someone should warn Victoria to get out the baby oil."

23

VICTORIA

I force myself to remain calm when I leave Moira's home. I smile. Tell her that I'm heading back to the Wraith to get a massage and speak to a stylist in the salon. She kisses my cheek, tells me to make the most of Caleb's absence and pamper myself to my heart's content. Abigail is playing video games with Emily in the den, and I don't disturb her. If anyone would be able to see through the smiley façade, it's Abigail.

I'm trembling when I climb into the back seat of Caleb's car.

"Where to?" Martin asks.

Since my little adventure with Abigail after we lost him in Macy's, I feel his eyes on me wherever I go. Even if he isn't with me, it still feels as if his eyes are everywhere; it wouldn't surprise me if he keeps a spreadsheet of my movements and emails a copy to Caleb every hour.

"The Dragon's Den."

I could lie. I could ask him to take me back to the Wraith and try losing him inside, but it's too close to Caleb, who will be following my movements around the building too. Olivia won't like it, but at least this way I'll have back-up, and Caleb will know who's responsible if anything happens to me.

Martin's cell is already out of his pocket.

I lean forward and rest my arms on the partition separating me from Martin and the driver, Kev. "Please don't tell Caleb."

They're both silent, but Martin is prepared to hear me out.

"Olivia Dragonetti has asked me to meet her." True so far. "I think ... with her father in the hospital, she wants to apologize."

"You know I'll have to tell Mr. Murray about this."

I know. I'm just frantically trying to find a way around it that doesn't involve me running around the city like an escaped fugitive.

"I think she would rather speak to me alone first. Woman to woman. With the history between her and Caleb, it would just make things awkward."

Martin's left eye twitches. "I'll let him know that's where we're going. He'll have my head on a platter if I don't keep him informed."

Shit. "I'll take responsibility. I'll tell him that this was all my idea, and I bullied you into taking me." Nothing. "Things are so precarious with Olivia I don't want to rock the boat. We might not get another opportunity to put things right between the families."

"Look..." Martin rubs his jaw with his free hand. "I hear you, but it's more than my job's worth." He doesn't add after he lost me inside Macy's; we both know that's what he meant. "I'll square it with Mr. Murray, and then I'll accompany you to the Dragon's Den."

My heart is thumping. We're still in Staten Island, and the car might not be speeding, but I'm not brave enough to try jumping out of a moving car, dodging the traffic, *and Martin*, and make my way back to Manhattan without incurring the wrath of my husband.

Martin faces the passenger window, phone pressed to his ear.

I wait for Caleb to pick up. He'll be angry. He'll be raging that I even considered meeting Olivia alone after our conversation last night. He made his feelings on the matter quite clear, and here I am going against him at the first opportunity without so much as an explanation.

But Sienna's life is at stake here. Who knows what the crazy woman will do if I don't show up today. I'm not prepared to risk it; I'll simply have to find another way to get there.

So, I almost cry out with relief when Martin lowers the phone without speaking to Caleb. "No answer. I'll fire a message through."

"He's busy," I say too quickly. "Family meetings. He might not respond immediately." Who am I kidding? No matter how important the meeting, Caleb will see the message straight away, and then he'll intercept us before we even arrive at the Dragon's Den.

"We'll see." Martin's thumbs tap away on his cell phone.

I sit back in my seat as the car heads closer to Manhattan and stare out of the rear passenger window. The Dragon's Den, an appropriate name for whatever Olivia is cooking up. But rather than feeling like the wanderer who stumbled upon the den by chance, I feel like the knight on a quest to rescue the princess. Empowered by the knowledge that Caleb tried to find Sienna after the accident, and Kyle didn't leave her to die.

Caleb will be angry when he finds out where I'm going, but he will protect me. No matter what. He gave me his word, and I'm not letting go of it.

I wait for Martin's phone to ring, for the driver to take me directly back to the Wraith, for Caleb to be waiting for me in his private parking lot. But when the car stops outside the Dragon's Den, and Martin climbs out first to open the rear door for me, it takes me a couple of beats to realize that I'm here.

My heart performs somersaults as I climb out of the car. Why didn't Caleb stop me? Didn't he receive Martin's message, or have the Murrays planned yet another twisted scheme to catch Olivia out? I don't know how they live with all the plotting and manipulating, but I guess it's so rooted in what they do that they no longer notice it.

"I'm staying right with you." Martin scans the street left and right, Kev taking up his position on my left.

I nod. My mouth is dry, and I don't trust myself to speak as we enter the Dragon's Den.

Outside, the building is imposing. Not as tall or as sleek as the Wraith, nor as glamorous as the Titan, but the subtle dragons clambering up the façade are impressive, the kind of building inhabited by emperors in fantasy novels.

Inside, however, the décor is dated. The lights in the foyer are dimmed to detract from the shabbiness of the crimson carpet and the emerald-and-gold-flecked wall coverings. The concierge is dressed in a black suit, his waistcoat in peacock colors, the front desk polished mahogany. More dragons cling to huge columns in the grand entrance, and the floral display in the center is magnificent, filled with peacock feathers, arching golden branches, and tiny twinkling lights.

But there is still an air of a hotel that is hankering after bygone days, and I feel a twinge of sadness for Don Dragonetti. Instead of focusing her passions on a man who doesn't want her, Olivia could've been dragging the family business kicking and screaming into the twenty-first century. With some love and attention, the Dragon's Den would rival its competitors, and I don't understand her lack of interest in the legacy that funds her privileged lifestyle.

The bellboy leads us through to the casino and the private room where Olivia is waiting for me in a booth.

Her eyes glitter when she spots my bodyguards. Her mouth turns down at the corners. "They go or this doesn't happen."

"Caleb would tear this place apart if he knew that I was here alone." I shrug and stand my ground.

Olivia relies on fear of her crazy reputation to intimidate everyone she deals with, so I can't let her see that this is all bravado, and that underneath, I'm battling to stop my legs from trembling. Mason might be the most unreliable person I know, but he did teach me to stand up to school bullies by pretending to be confident even if I'm quaking inside. He taught me that all bullies are cowards who belittle other people to make themselves feel bigger.

Maybe it's fear of rejection with Olivia. Maybe she sees other people in happy relationships and is scared that it will never happen to her, so rather than looking at herself, she tries to bring everyone else down.

I look at her properly for the first time. She's beautiful with her long white-blonde hair, large eyes, and perfect heart-shaped mouth, but it's true what people say: this kind of beauty is only skin-deep. Underneath the designer clothes and the expensive makeup and the professionally maintained hairstyle, I think that Olivia Dragonetti is a spoiled, unhappy child.

"Fine. But they wait at the bar."

Martin inches closer to me, his arm brushing mine.

"It's okay." I murmur, keeping my eyes on Olivia. "I'm not going anywhere."

The two men take up their positions at the corner of the bar where they have an unobstructed view of the booth, and I slide onto the bench seat opposite Olivia.

"I didn't think you'd come." She smirks and gestures for the bartender to bring her another drink. She doesn't ask me if I want one. "Honestly, I thought Caleb would keep a much closer eye on you."

"He doesn't need to. He trusts me not to do anything rash."

"Ha! He obviously doesn't know you at all." The bartender serves her drink, over ice, with a slice of lemon and a gold straw. With a glance my way, he leaves us alone.

"What's that supposed to mean?" My voice sounds unexpectedly strong and steady, and for that I'm grateful.

She sips her clear drink, leaving an imprint of her lipstick on the end of the straw. "I know about you and Caleb."

My stomach churns. She's bluffing, I tell myself. She's trying to scare me into walking away from Caleb and leaving the path clear for her to step in.

"My dad told me what he overheard, so don't bother trying to deny it."

Fuck. Fuck. Fuck. When he didn't mention it at Moira's house, I convinced myself that he didn't hear anything. Why did he tell her? He knows that Caleb is never going to marry her, even if I'm taken out of the equation, so why? What was he thinking?

"What do you want, Olivia?"

"I thought it was obvious. But in case you haven't quite figured it out, I want Caleb. He's kidding himself if he thinks that marrying you will achieve anything, whereas a marriage between the Dragonettis and the Murrays..." She smiles, but it doesn't travel as far as her eyes. "It will make everyone happy."

"What about Caleb?"

"What, you think you can make him happier than he will be with me?" She furrows her brow. "Oh my God, you do, don't you?" She sits back in her seat with a twisted smile. "His little plan backfired because you already think that this might be forever."

Don't bite. Don't bite. *Don't bite*. If I react, she's already won.

"What about you?" I try to project more confidence than I feel into my voice. "Will it make you happy?"

"Duh. Caleb Murray and Olivia Dragonetti. What's not to be happy about? The press will be all over us. We'll be the most photographed couple in New York City."

"You didn't answer the question."

Her eyes narrow. She leans closer and hisses, "Fuck off, Victoria. What do you care whether I'm happy or not?"

"I don't." I shrug. "But I do care about Caleb, and if you're unhappy, he will be too."

She opens her mouth to speak and closes it again. Her expression hardens. "Here's the deal. Your brother and your friend in exchange for Caleb."

I sit back in my seat and glance at the two men watching me closely from the bar. What choice do I have? Olivia and I both know that I'm going to accept her deal, but the real problem is getting her to keep her word.

"Forgive me if I don't believe you. How do I even know that you have Mason and Sienna?"

"You don't." She shrugs. "Off you go then, if you don't believe me. Makes no difference to me if they're alive or dead." She gestures to the doorway.

"What's in it for me?"

"I deliver them back to you alive. I would say they'll be in one piece, but I can't guarantee they will be. Sorry."

Sorry, not sorry.

"You'll need to do better than that."

She rolls her eyes, her bottom lip rolling out. "Who told you it was your turn to call the shots?"

"Caleb has offered to set me up for life. Why would I walk away from that just because it's what you want?"

She tips her head back and laughs, flicking her fine hair over her shoulders. I can't imagine her and Caleb together. Thinking of them in Caleb's bed or in the rooftop pool, drinking champagne from each other's mouths, feels like being punched in the gut, and I force myself to breathe, in through my nose, out through my mouth.

"I knew you could be bought," she says. "Everyone can."

"Do we have a deal?"

"Fifty grand."

I don't waste a beat. I stand up and go to walk away, the two bodyguards instantly alert.

"Wait," she snaps, and I turn back around. "A hundred grand."

I shake my head. "I'll take my chances with Caleb. He'll find my brother and Sienna, and then everyone will be happy." I smile, repeating her words.

"He'll be too late. They're safe right now, but I can change that in a moment." She snaps her fingers to prove the point.

I sit back down. "Why would you do that? What have they ever done to you?"

"They know you." Her face is so close to mine I can smell the alcohol on her breath.

"Half a million." My palms are sweaty. Even if she agrees to the sum, I don't trust her to keep Mason and Sienna alive. It isn't even about the money. I'm just trying to buy Caleb enough time to find them before Olivia gives the order to have them killed.

"Done. I'll transfer the money into your bank account today, and then you'll disappear from New York City by midnight tonight."

"I don't think so. I'll disappear once I know that Mason and Sienna are alive and well. Until then, well, I'll just go back to

Caleb's apartment. There are still a few rooms we haven't fucked in."

Her mouth drops open, and her eyes grow small and dark. "I'll take you to them now."

I hold her gaze, drop my voice. "Caleb's men will never let me go."

"Restroom. There's another way out. By the time they realize you're not coming back, we'll be out of the city." Her mouth twists into an ugly grimace. "If you dare."

I stand, catch Martin's eye, and gesture in the direction of the restroom. He responds with a barely discernible nod.

Heart thumping, I enter the restroom and stand in front of the basins. What am I doing? This must be a trap. Olivia probably has someone waiting outside to shoot me in the head, and that way, she gets to keep her money and Caleb, and no one will ever find out what happened to Mason and Sienna.

I turn on the faucet and splash my face with cold water while I wait for Olivia to join me. Before I can straighten, strong arms grab me from behind, forcing my face down against the marble surrounding the basins. My hands are dragged behind my back and my wrists are bound. Someone—a man—shoves a hood over my head and growls at me to move.

The hood smells like stale cigarettes. It's itchy, and I can already feel hives rising on my forehead and neck. I stumble forward and splutter when the guy's hands start patting me down, checking for hidden weapons in my pockets and under my clothes.

I feel sick. Images pop into my head of Caleb shooting him for touching me, and I think that he'll live to regret this.

Something hard is pressed against the back of my skull, and an iron fist grips my upper arm. A different door opens. We walk, and I can feel carpet underfoot. Into an elevator. Outside. Where is Martin? Has he realized yet that I'm taking too long? I try to concentrate on my footsteps, to keep my bearings, but it's hard when I'm so hyper-conscious of my thudding heart and the blood gushing in my ears.

Voices. Hushed urgent whispers. My skin prickles.

"What the fuck, O!" A man's voice, a slight accent.

The hard object pressed against the back of my skull forces my head down.

"Don't get fucking soft on me now." Olivia Dragonetti. "We need her to see it though."

My mind is racing. See what through? Is there more to it than getting Caleb back?

Before I can try talking to her, I'm shoved forward, my face hitting something hard, and someone lifts my legs off the ground, forces me into the fetal position, and closes a lid. I try lashing out with my feet, but the space is so confined, I can't stretch my legs. I slide around, using my knees and elbows to measure the space, then I feel something rumble beneath me.

An engine.

I'm in a car trunk. I only hope Olivia keeps her side of the bargain and takes me to Mason and Sienna.

24

CALEB

I'm almost out of the door when my cell phone rings. Martin.

I know before I even raise the phone to my ear and hear him say, "We have a problem," that something has happened to Victoria.

"Where is she?" I growl.

"Dragon's Den. We lost her."

I kill the call, turn around to find my family watching me with dark eyes. "They have Victoria."

No point venting my anger on Martin. That will come later. No point even asking him how it happened. They disobeyed my orders; they allowed Victoria to walk into the Dragon's Den, and then they failed to keep her safe. My priority is to find Victoria and make sure that Olivia Dragonetti never so much as sets foot in the vicinity of the people I care about again.

Only then will everyone in my employ know what happens when they disappoint a Murray.

"Let me handle it." Terry is already out of the door, flanked by Cash and Bash, cell phone raised to his ear. "You stay here."

"No can do." I follow him into the corridor, everyone else on my heels.

No one asks how—the details are unimportant. We know why, and we now have a location. Sitting around and waiting for more information to land in our laps isn't an option.

"You're too involved," Terry shoots back. "Mistakes will happen."

"Caleb, wait." This is Mom. "You know Terry is right."

I stop and turn around to face them. Terry will handle this his way, and I'm not about to stop him. He always gets results. But Victoria is my wife, and this is personal. No one touches the woman I want to spend the rest of my life with and walks away unscathed.

"The only mistake here is Olivia Dragonetti thinking that she can win." My voice is cold. I'm calm. Calmer than I've ever been, because I have a purpose, and that purpose is Victoria. "Go home, Mom. Keep Abigail safe."

"Caleb." She shakes her head, and I can see the same fear in her eyes that I saw when I was a little kid, and she was scared that our father would hurt us.

"Don't worry about me, Mom." I pull her into a hug, kiss the top of her head, and then walk away.

Kyle matches my stride. "I'm coming with you."

"I'm doing this alone."

"Caleb, for fuck's sake. She has Sienna too. Five years I've wasted wishing that I could go back and change what happened; you can't take this away from me now."

I don't slow down. Terry and the twins have already disappeared, and I'm grateful to have them as backup, but how do I tell my big brother that it's my duty to keep him safe. That I worry he's too fragile to get involved in this situation. That holding a gun to the head of our family's enemies isn't his strength.

"I'll bring her back, I promise. You'll get your chance to tell her everything."

I use portable flashing lights on the roof of the car to beat the traffic. In the basement parking lot at the Wraith, I switch the car for the Harley, fasten my helmet, and head to the exit, the engine thrumming between my legs.

I don't know what makes me stop, but I slide my cell from my pocket and check the tracker on Abigail's phone. My heart skips a beat when I find that it's moving. Heading north, towards Lake Placid. Good girl—she's learning.

It almost feels wrong to be heading out of the city without Victoria behind me. I focus on the moments we've shared in the short space of time since she agreed to be my wife, watching her in the dressing room mirror, tasting her for the first time, burying my face between her legs in the elevator, fucking her in the rooftop pool. But it's when I picture her eating lamb on rice out of greasy paper, the tears in her eyes in the theater, the way she nestled against me on the Byway with the city lights in the distance that my cool resolve almost crumbles.

Fuck the alliance.

Fuck this way of life if it means that I can't have her.

I promised to keep her safe, and I've not done a great job of it so far.

There's no sign of Terry when I stop at the abandoned warehouse in Lake Placid that he mentioned before, but I'm not the first to arrive. Vans with black-tinted windows block the entry points, and half a dozen guns are pointed at my head before I even dismount and remove my helmet.

I raise my hands in front of me, palms facing outward. "I don't want any trouble. I'm here to find my wife."

A man steps forward from behind the weapons. Unarmed. I recognize the thick dark hair, prominent eyebrows, and narrow lips. Lev Petrov. Ivan's father.

"We can't let you through."

There's a pistol in my inside pocket and a knife tucked inside my boot. I'd maybe take down one, two if I'm lucky, before they kill me, but if they wanted me eradicated, they'd have done it already.

"This isn't up for debate." I lower my hands slowly. "I meant what I said: I'm not here to cause trouble between our families. But my wife is inside that warehouse—" I nod in the direction of the building behind Lev and his men "—and I'm not leaving without her."

"My son is also inside that warehouse." Lev remains where he is, protected by the guns still pointing at my head. "You may not wish to form an alliance between our families, but I take no chances when it comes to my son's life. No one enters the building unless I say they do."

"I wish Ivan no harm... So long as my wife is safe."

Lev's mouth twitches at the corners. "My son is hotheaded, but he does not kill without good reason."

Ivan is inside; I have no doubts that Olivia is with him, but Lev Petrov is outside. The exit routes are blocked. He doesn't like this situation any more than I do, but we're on opposite sides of the fence. His son has already been banished once. If —*when*—shit goes down, he wants to ensure that Ivan doesn't take the rap. They might be prepared to sacrifice Olivia Dragonetti to save their own, but I'm not relying on their good nature and mafia code to protect Victoria.

"Then you have nothing to worry about." I step closer.

"Stay where you are, Mr. Murray." Lev's voice is cold, clipped. "I had hoped that we might do business together in the future, and I'm sure you appreciate that no one here wishes to start a war."

"Let me through, and you have my word that I will forget Ivan's part in this."

"Your word." His smile surfaces briefly and disappears again. "Why should I trust you?"

He's stalling. He's wasting time while Victoria is inside his warehouse with Olivia Dragonetti, and my patience is wearing thin.

I walk towards him. I'll be no use to Victoria dead, and I can't take on a Russian family single handedly, but I can prove to him that I don't want a full-scale war.

I glimpse movement to my left, but before I can reach for my gun, something hard connects with my jawbone, and I sprawl forwards, white-hot pain flaring inside my skull. A knee is between my shoulder blades as I hit the ground. I try to roll, the pain crashing through my head with the movement, and swing a punch with my right fist. It connects with the shin of the man standing closest to me before a booted foot grinds my wrist into the ground.

My arms are dragged behind me and cuffed, the metal clinking as they haul me back onto my feet.

Lev stands in front of me, while his men grip my arms with iron fists, the barrel of a gun pressed against my neck. "Your devotion to your wife is commendable. Truly. But you perhaps misunderstood me when I said that I could not allow you to interfere."

I can feel my brain throbbing against the inside of my skull. "Perhaps you misunderstood me when I said that I'm not here to interfere. I'm simply here for my wife."

His expression is neutral. "You and I both know that you would not have entered that building and walked out with your wife without blood being shed."

I blink against the pain. He's right, but I'm not going to give him the satisfaction of agreeing with him. Until Terry arrives, I need Lev Petrov in my corner. "What's the plan?"

He smiles. "The plan is already in motion."

"But you're not going to tell me what it is."

My cell phone rings. It's Terry's ringtone.

One of Lev's men slides a hand inside my pocket, pulls out my cell, and hands it over to Lev. "Mr. Keegan," he speaks into the handset, his gaze holding mine. "Lev Petrov. Your stepson is already here. Seems he beat you to it, but don't worry, he is in good hands." He ends the call and tosses the phone aside; I hear it land with a dull thud in the scrubby borders surrounding the warehouse.

A black car pulls up outside the vehicle blockade set up by the Petrovs. The rear door opens. More of Lev's men appear from inside the stationary vehicles and surround the new arrival. I see a black suit, silver-gray hair, stooped shoulders. The man's movements are slow, head bowed, as he makes his way towards the warehouse entrance, Lev's men providing a safe passage for him, weapons aimed directly ahead.

Don Dragonetti.

My stomach twists. He's the last person I expected to see here. I didn't even know that he'd been discharged from the hospital, but obviously his daughter means more to him than any alliance. She means more to him than his own health, and I have a fleeting vision of him collapsing inside the warehouse and Olivia fist-punching the air in her moment of power-hungry glory when she takes over as heir to the Dragonetti family.

Disappointment settles inside my stomach. He knows that Victoria and I are not married. She'll be expendable in his eyes, especially if it means that I'll take Olivia off his hands and keep her in check.

He disappears inside the warehouse, the door closing silently shut behind him. Lev's men stand guard.

That's when I hear the screeching of tires as Terry arrives with backup.

25

VICTORIA

Two men drag me out of the trunk and into a building. It smells musty, damp. Even through the hood, I can tell that it's dark inside. There are floorboards underfoot. Footsteps in front of and behind me, a guy on either side of me, holding me in case I try to escape.

Then the building seems to open up into a wider space. Heavy hands sit me down on the floor, and the hood is tugged from my head.

I blink at the thugs who dragged me inside, bringing them into focus. They're both dressed in black. They're younger than I expected them to be. Could one of them be the guy who followed me and Abigail into Penn Station? I didn't get a good look at his face, but I remember what Terry said about him, and I shudder.

Then I hear a whimper from somewhere nearby and realize that I'm not alone.

"Sienna?" I crawl across the dusty floor on my knees, losing my balance with my wrists tied behind my back.

Sienna tries to sit up when she realizes that it's me. Her wrists and ankles are bound; her hair is greasy and matted, and her eyes are raw, dark circles smudging her gaunt cheeks. As she slides back against the wall, using it to prop herself upright, I spot the legs behind her.

It's Mason. But he isn't moving.

"Oh my God, Mason!" I lunge sideways and land on top of him, expecting him to roll over and say my name, but he's lifeless. "Mason?" On my knees, I lean over his face, panic hurtling through my veins at his gray skin and blue lips. "Mason, wake up. It's me, Victoria."

Using my shoulder, I smooth his hair away from his face and spot the blood, matted and dark, on his scalp.

Tears streaming down my face, I look at Sienna who is watching me with dark, sunken eyes. "How long has he been unconscious?"

"I don't know." Sienna is crying too.

"Are you hurt?" I can't see any blood, but that doesn't mean that they didn't hurt her when they brought her here.

She shakes her head. "I'm scared, V."

"I'm so sorry." I crawl over to her and brush my face against hers in lieu of a hug. "This is all my fault, Si. I'm so sorry. I never meant for this to happen."

"None of this is your fault." Her voice cracks, and I can see that the skin around her lips is dry and cracked too.

"Have they been giving you water?"

Sienna's eyes flit to a spot behind me at the same time as I hear raised voices. I roll awkwardly into a sitting position, blocking Sienna as if I can protect her with my wrists bound.

"I'm done here." A young guy with raven-black hair who I assume is Ivan Petrov, raises his hands and walks away from Olivia Dragonetti across the room.

I think this must be a warehouse. It's a huge space with a high ceiling. The high windows are so grimy and weather-stained that they let in minimal daylight. Boxes and cartons are stacked up on tall metal shelving against the walls, and there's no furniture, but I can see a forklift pushed up against the far wall. I scan the room for the way out, my stomach twisting when I realize that it's at the other end of the building.

"Ivan, get back here!" Olivia screeches.

Ivan keeps walking. He raises a hand over his shoulder in a kind of salute, but my heart seems to freeze when I hear the click of a gun. He halts at the same time, and I instinctively shuffle backwards, shielding Sienna with my body.

When Ivan turns around to face Olivia, he has a gun in his hand too. "Seriously? You really want to do this?"

"You give me no choice." Olivia shrugs. She's holding the gun with both hands, arms outstretched. "We're in this together, remember?"

"Were. We *were* in this together. I didn't sign up for abducting Caleb Murray's wife." He glances my way, our eyes meeting briefly. "I want out. You do your thing, but don't expect me to go along with it."

Olivia laughs, the sound bouncing off the walls. "Very funny. I'll tell everyone that this was your idea."

"Be my guest and go right ahead."

Ivan makes a circular motion with his gun, and my breath hitches in my chest. I don't know the first thing about guns, but I've watched enough movies to know that you don't mess around with them.

"You think no one will believe me, but they will when I tell them about your boyfriend." Her expression is smug, and I've never wanted to punch someone in the throat more than I do right now.

I expect Ivan to laugh in her face and tell her that everyone already knows, but instead, his face pales. His hair flops forward over his eyes, and he tries to flick it back with his elbow.

"Thought that would get your attention. You wouldn't want Daddy to find out, would you? Not when you've tried so hard to keep it a secret."

She's a nasty piece of work. I don't know why Ivan needs to hide his relationship, but I'm angry that she thinks she can get away with using it against him. I'm angry at Ivan for allowing her to manipulate him so easily. And I'm angry at both of them for dragging innocent people into their fucked-up, messy lives.

I want Ivan to tell her to go fuck herself. But he doesn't. He stands there with a gun in his hand and a defeated expression on his face like all the fight has been sucked out of him.

"That's what I thought." Olivia lowers her gun. I don't even know where she got it from, but she isn't taking any chances and keeps it in her hand. "Watch her while I go speak to Caleb."

My pulse races, and I feel sick when I hear her say Caleb's name out loud. It sounds all wrong when she says it, like she has no right to his name because it belongs to me. Which is ridiculous when I have no right to it either. But if I am growing his baby inside me, I at least deserve the opportunity to tell him.

I watch her walk away and disappear through the door at the far end. Ivan watches her too. As the door swings shut behind her, he raises the gun, aims it, and says, "Bang."

"Fuck, man." The young guy who dragged me here joins him. "Why the fuck did you let her get away with that? I'd have shot her in the fucking mouth and shut her up."

"And then what?" Ivan pockets his weapon. "She'll shoot herself soon enough."

He glances our way, and I realize that he's our only hope of getting out of here. Because I'm not leaving without Mason and Sienna. The other guy will shoot us in the back of the head if we try to escape and ask questions after.

"Will you help my brother?" I call out.

The other guy's eyes narrow, but Ivan checks out Mason who still hasn't moved.

"Please?" I need to talk to him alone, and I need to do it before Olivia comes back.

He mutters something to his friend that I can't hear and then approaches us slowly, his eyes fixed on Mason like this might be a trap.

"He's unconscious," I say, when he's close enough to hear me without raising my voice. "He needs medical attention."

"There's nothing I can do about it right now."

I maintain eye contact. Isn't that what you're supposed to do in hostage situations? Show the abductor that you're a real person, try to find a connection so that they have to think about killing you. I feel like I'm already halfway there because Ivan knows who I am, and he's being manipulated into seeing this through.

"Can you at least bring some water so that I can keep him hydrated?"

Another glance at Mason's immobile form on the floor. Then he snaps his fingers, his eyes never leaving mine, and one of the other men comes forward with a two-liter bottle of water.

Ivan slices the ropes binding my wrists with a small knife and hands the bottle over, and I seize the opportunity. "Please help me get my brother out of here."

His eyes drift back to Mason and settle on his sallow skin. He's thinking about it, now all I have to do is convince him that it's the right thing to do.

"Caleb will help you," I whisper. "He's on his way here. He knows this is all down to Olivia, and he'll see that your name isn't dragged into it."

I'm bullshitting and I pray that he doesn't see right through me. I'm also praying that Caleb will listen to me before he does anything drastic. One bullet is all it will take for Ivan to retaliate, and I can't even think about what will happen next.

"You don't understand." Ivan shakes his head and glances towards the doorway as if half-expecting Olivia to appear with her finger still on the trigger of her gun. Whatever he was about to say, he has obviously changed his mind. "Stay out of it."

"What about my brother?" My voice is laced with panic.

"It will have to wait."

I'm losing him. I'm not like these people. I don't know how to use fear and threats to get what I want, and I'm nothing like Olivia who thinks that she can bully a man into marrying her. Maybe that's all people like Ivan know, but from what Olivia said, it's obvious that, like anyone else, he has issues that can't be resolved with money and bullets.

So, I resort to the only thing that I know how to do: being honest.

"Caleb and I are not really married."

His eyebrows lower over his dark eyes, and I remind myself that he's the one with the gun, the one responsible for keeping us alive right now.

"Don Dragonetti went to Caleb with a proposal: an alliance in exchange for marrying his daughter. Caleb would never have agreed to marry her but, well, her father is persuasive." Ivan is still with me so far. "So, he asked me to pretend to be his wife."

"It isn't real?" His voice is louder than I would've liked, but no one else appears to be listening.

"No." I swallow. My mouth is dry, and I can feel a cough tickling the back of my throat.

His face breaks into a smile. "Fucking brilliant." He releases a breath and rubs the back of his neck. "This is going to tip her straight over the fucking edge."

"She already knows. That's why I'm here: she thinks that she can buy me out of Caleb's life. But she can't." Deep breath. "Because I'm in love with him. It didn't start off real, but I think Caleb feels the same way about me."

There's a long pause. I can see the thought process behind his eyes while he figures out if I'm telling the truth and what Caleb's next move might be. I hope that he has found someone who means the world to him because then he might just be able to relate to what I'm saying. He might just want to help.

"He promised to keep me safe, and I believe him. He won't marry Olivia because he doesn't love her, and what my friend here doesn't realize is that Kyle Murray is in love with her too."

Ivan's top lip curls away from his teeth in a snarl, and I hope that I haven't pushed it too far, but now that I'm on the subject of love, I sense him softening like butter left out of the fridge.

"Five years ago, there was a road traffic incident. My friend Sienna and Kyle Murray were both in the car wreck. The Murrays pulled Kyle from the wreckage, but they wrongly assumed that Sienna was dead. Kyle has never gotten over it because ... because he's in love with her."

"V?" Sienna whispers behind my back. "What are you saying?"

I ignore her. I'm afraid to break eye contact with Ivan and lose our slim chance of getting out of here alive. "So, you see, you won't only have Caleb seeking revenge if anything happens to us, you'll have his brother too."

"They'll have to catch me first."

Fuck.

"Wouldn't you rather have them on your side? They won't use your relationship to blackmail you." I smile. The timeless act of friendliness. "Please, Ivan."

I'm almost there. I think I almost have him when the door opens, and Olivia walks in, her arm linked with her father.

The tiny glimmer of hope flickers out and dies.

26

CALEB

Terry hasn't just shown up armed; he's brought an entire fucking army with him. No one messes with Terry Keegan's family and walks away from the scene.

He approaches Lev Petrov, Kyle a couple of steps behind him while Cash and Bash surround the warehouse. His glance slides my way, noting the men flanking me, and the cuffed wrists, before settling on the man calling the shots.

"That's my stepson you're holding against his will."

"We had no choice. We did it for his own protection."

On cue, the men step away from me, and someone else unlocks the cuffs around my wrists. Terry's eyebrows raise in question at me, and I nod in response. The pain is still reverberating around my skull, but I can live with that so long as Victoria is safe.

"So, you'll stand aside—"

Terry doesn't finish because that's when the gunshot reaches us from inside the warehouse. A second shot follows almost instantaneously. Everyone reacts at the same time.

I run towards the entrance, surrounded by the thud-thud-thud of heavy footsteps. There are men on the roof, impossible to tell which family they belong to, shooting open the skylights. Lev's men shoot the doors open on both sides of the building and storm inside in battle formation.

My heart feels like it's in my throat. "Stay back," Terry yells, but I'm not listening. I can't hear any more gunshots from inside, but one is all it would take to shatter my future to smithereens.

Windows smash as I run along a narrow corridor behind Terry and his guys. I don't often pray, but right now I'm praying that it was a warning shot. Olivia must know that she'll never get away with this. She'll have the Petrovs and the Murrays hunting her down, and she'll never be safe to roam the city streets again.

Terry and his men pause outside an internal door. Their faces are expressionless; this is just another job to them. They're simply following orders: protect their own and shoot to kill. I don't know where Lev's men have gone, but I'm guessing there's more than one way into the warehouse. Terry's eyes meet mine, and then the men are spilling through the door, weapons raised, trigger fingers ready.

Voices. "Don't shoot!"

Another, more familiar voice yells, "Hold fire!"

My stomach lurches upward with an image of Victoria lifeless on the floor of the warehouse, Olivia Dragonetti standing over her with a smoking gun in her hand. Terry won't be able to stop me. He'll have to shoot me himself if he wants to keep my hands off her. My fists are already clenching in readiness to squeeze her neck until her eyeballs pop.

So, it's several moments before my brain can process what I'm seeing when I storm into the storage unit behind Terry. They spread out in formation, their weapons still raised, as the silence settles around the scene in front of us.

My eyes seek out Victoria and find her in a corner of the unit, on her knees between Sienna and Mason. She's so busy scanning the faces of the armed men who continue to spill into the building that she doesn't spot me at first, and for a couple of moments, I have her all to myself. She's searching for me. She knew that I would come, and there's no fear in her eyes, only anticipation of the moment when she finds me.

It doesn't matter that she's on her knees on the filthy floor, or that her hair is disheveled and half-hanging out of a loose ponytail, or that her face is smudged with dirt. She is, and always will be, the most beautiful woman I have ever set eyes on, and when she looks at me, my chest feels like it will explode.

Knowing that she is safe, my pulse settles into a steady beat. We heard gunshots. I scan the warehouse now for a body, blood, the perpetrators. Ivan is flanked by two men with similar dark looks and black clothes. His left hand is clamped over his upper right arm, blood oozing between his fingers. But it's the old man walking unsteadily towards us carrying the body of a woman in his arms that snags my attention.

Don Dragonetti's face is ashen; his cheeks have hollowed out since I last saw him, and deep grooves are etched across his forehead. In his arms, her legs dangling against his thigh, is his daughter Olivia. It's obvious that he is struggling to carry her, but there's a determination, a fire behind his eyes, that prevents anyone from interfering.

Terry and his men stand aside for him to pass. The Petrovs form a line opposite us, and the don keeps walking, accepting the gesture of peace, his pace halting. As he passes, he catches my eye and nods once, and I don't try to stop him. He's a proud man from one of the original Italian mafia families. I don't know what happened to Olivia, but the other families will offer him the privacy and respect he deserves; whatever went down here, Olivia is his sole heir, and he will accept the consequences of her actions.

I watch Lev Petrov open the door for Don Dragonetti to leave. The area was secured by the Petrovs before I arrived, but it's obvious now that the don's arrival was part of the plan Lev refused to discuss with me. He will be free to leave, and the two remaining families will clear up the mess.

"Go get her." Terry places his warm hand on my shoulder before following Lev outside.

Victoria watches me cross the room, her eyes large with tears. I help her onto her feet, run my fingers through her hair, and press her body against mine. I hold her close and breathe in the smell of her and make a silent vow to never let her go. She's trembling, but she pulls away so that she can look at me.

"Caleb, I'm so sorry—"

"Hey." I cup her face with both hands and kiss her on the lips. "You don't have to say anything."

Her eyes grow large with tears. She throws her arms around me and rests her head on my chest, and I hold her while she lets it all out, and the warehouse starts to empty.

Eventually, she pulls away from my embrace and wipes her cheeks with the back of her hands. With a tentative smile, she slips her hand into mine and takes me to Sienna. Ivan and his stalker-friend are already carrying an unconscious Mason outside. I trust that he'll be in capable hands.

Sienna leans against Victoria for support, gripping her hand tightly. Her face is grimy and streaked with tears, her hair matted, and I can see the livid skin above the neckline of her sweater from the burns she suffered in the wreckBut she's a striking woman, and there's something familiar about her that I can't quite place.

"Caleb, this is Sienna. She was in the car crash with Kyle on New Year's five years ago." She hesitates. "Kyle told me all about it."

I don't hear Kyle come up behind us until he's standing beside me. "Ruby?"

There's a tremor in his voice that makes me want to wrap him in cotton wool and protect him from the rest of the world. He's a grown man, a brilliant and intelligent lawyer, and a loyal friend to everyone who knows him, but I will always feel like a superhero in his presence.

Sienna winces as if in pain. "You... You don't look any different."

"Apart from the hair." Kyle rubs his hair self-consciously. He stuffs his hands inside his pockets and pulls them straight back out again, tugging the hem of his jacket. His eyes are all over the place, anywhere but on Sienna.

I step in; someone needs to give him a helping hand. "I'm Caleb, Kyle's brother. Sienna, meet Kyle; Kyle, meet Sienna, not Ruby Tuesday or Wilma from *The Flintstones*."

"Yeah, it seemed like a good idea at the time." She chews her bottom lip in a habit that mimics Victoria's, and eyes up Kyle from beneath lowered eyelashes. "I thought..." Her already raspy voice cracks. "You probably don't want to know what I thought."

"Victoria told me." Kyle seems to jolt to life and takes her hands, folding them between his own and raising them to his chest.

I've never seen him like this with a woman. Nervous. Timid. Frightened of saying the wrong thing. I mean, I know how much he struggled after the accident, but he never once expressed his feelings about Sienna. I thought it was all guilt.

"I never..." he begins. "I would never... I believed that you didn't make it." His voice trails off.

"His brother checked your pulse," Victoria says. "Or rather, he couldn't find one. I believe them, Si."

Sienna closes her eyes, tears spilling over her bottom lashes. When she opens them again, she's shaking her head, and it's as if she has already checked out, already dismissed Kyle from her life a second time, as she snatches her hands away.

"Sienna, I can't even begin to imagine what you went through." I glance at Victoria, who is fighting to hold back her own tears. "My brothers should've pulled you from the wreckage. In hindsight, well, it's as much my fault as theirs. I'm not making excuses for them. They thought they were doing the right thing by calling the emergency services and removing Kyle from the situation. If they'd been able to get hold of me, I'd have told them to stay with you."

Would I have told them to stay with her? Hindsight has a habit of distorting the past to resemble something that doesn't keep you awake at night. I'd have told them to pull her from the wreckage. I hope. But I know Kyle would've been my priority too, as it was for Cash and Bash.

Family first.

"Can you forgive me?" Kyle's voice shrinks almost to nothing.

"I don't know. I can't just erase five years of knowing what you did to me." She inhales deeply, and her shoulders slump on the exhale. "It isn't just about that. It's all this too." She peers around the warehouse. "I don't know if I can ... live like this."

"It isn't always like this," Kyle says. "I promise you."

"How can you promise that?" she snaps. "Victoria meets your brother and the next thing I know, she's married, and I've been abducted along with her brother." Sienna's voice is hardening.

"Why don't you ask Victoria how she feels about me," I suggest.

Victoria blinks, gap-mouthed, like I just told her to stand up and sing opera in front of an audience.

"V?"

All eyes are on Victoria, but she only has eyes for me. "I-I don't know how I feel about this way of life, but I do know that when I'm with Caleb, I feel safe, and beautiful, and desirable. I feel like anything is possible and that he will always be there to catch me when I fall. And if this way of life is the price I have to pay for falling in love, I'd pay it a million times over."

I must be grinning. Victoria comes to me, stands on tiptoes, and kisses me on the lips, and I find myself whispering, "I love you too, mo chroí," without even thinking about how those words will change my life. I should've told her sooner. I had the opportunity on the Byway, and I let it slip through my fingers. Maybe if I'd grown a pair of balls and acknowledged how she'd flipped my world on its axis, we wouldn't be here now, but we don't dwell on maybes. We forge our own paths, and we don't look back.

"Please, just give me a chance," Kyle says. "That's all I'm asking. A chance to prove to you that I'm not an asshole in a dumb wig and costume."

"Yeah, that was all my idea too." I wrap an arm around Victoria's shoulders and hold her against me. It's where she belongs. It's where she's going to spend the rest of her life, if she'll have me. "I was Danny Zuko, and Kyle was Kenickie. I thought it would be fun to be someone else for a night. Incognito. Just two regular guys who wouldn't be recognized."

Only, I hadn't counted on bumping into Sandy. Not that it matters now that I've found Victoria. For the first time, I can think about it without even wondering what Sandy is up to anymore.

Victoria unfolds my arm from around her shoulders and peers up at me. "Say that again," she whispers.

"Which part?"

"The part about being Danny Zuko."

"I knew it!" We both turn around and stare at Sienna. "Black wig, leather jacket. I knew you looked familiar. Danny Zuko, meet Sandy. Sandy, meet Danny Zuko."

27

VICTORIA

THE BALLROOM IN THE TITAN IS EXACTLY HOW I pictured it. There's a raised platform in the center of the room, the fountain spilling gold water into a pond filled with golden fish. The walls are decorated with floor-to-ceiling white and gold feathers, the tables laden with food in gold tureens, and at the far end, on a platform draped in shimmering gold curtains is the band. It's opulent and glamorous and glitzy, and I stand inside the doorway, hardly daring to believe that this is happening to me.

A few days earlier, Caleb and I were married in a small, private ceremony in the gardens of Moira and Terry's property on Staten Island. It was everything I'd ever dreamed of. We made our vows beneath a white rose covered arbor, surrounded by our close family and friends, with Abigail as our flower girl.

There were no photographers. There were no mafia family representatives. The bodyguards maintained a discreet distance.

We took selfies on our phones of happy, smiling faces, laughter, and love. Sienna went around snapping photographs on her camera of us all when we were not watching. Natural photos. Images of me and Caleb dancing around the garden with flowers in my hair, and a rose tucked behind Caleb's ear. Abigail being pushed on the garden swing by Bash. Mason popping an olive into his mouth looking more relaxed than I can ever recall seeing him. Moira and Terry snuggled together on the decking sofa.

Sienna and Kyle... The kind of hurt Sienna experienced after the wreck doesn't vanish overnight. Kyle is patient, and I believe him when he says that making Sienna happy is his life's mission, but I'm worried that her scars run too deep to ever be repaired.

Caleb sneaks up on me from behind in the ballroom and nibbles my earlobe, his hands snaking inside the plunging neckline of my dress. He pinches my nipple, and I bat his arm away as I turn to face him. "The guests will be arriving any moment now."

He pulls me close and wraps his arms around me. "I could lock the doors. I can picture you now, naked behind one of those gigantic feathers." He smiles.

I can feel the bulge in his pants pressing against my abdomen. "Not exactly the outfit I had in mind for tonight."

Caleb wrinkles his nose. "Trust me, it would be for my eyes only. You're mine, remember.?Gach mianach."

I peer into his eyes. "You never did tell me what that means."

"It means that you're all mine. Gach mianach. And don't you ever forget it."

"How could I?"

Caleb picks me up and, with my legs wrapped around his waist, turns three-sixty, kissing me until I feel giddy and a little bit queasy. "Put me down." I can't help laughing though.

Moira and Terry come in with Abigail, who runs over to me and squeals, "I've got a bunny rabbit."

"A bunny rabbit?" I glance at Moira above Abigail's head.

Moira shrugs. "We couldn't resist when we saw her in the pet store, could we, Abigail?"

"Her name is Snowy because she's all white."

I crouch in front of Abigail. "Snowy. I love it."

Abigail is wearing a white dress covered in embroidered daisies that pick out the green and amber flecks in her brown eyes. Her hair is loose and reaches almost down to her waist, and she looks more like me than ever.

She is staying with Moira and Terry while Caleb and I go on a honeymoon to Europe. Mason has gone to Florida to stay with Mom and Quincy for a while. After the abduction, he broke down in the hospital and confessed to his gambling addiction being out of control, so we're hoping that some quiet time with Mom will help to get him back on track. He'd lost his way somehow, lost sight of what was important as the debts started accruing, but I have a good feeling about his future now.

"I know how to take care of her. Emily told me what to do. She's learning to be a vet." Abigail's expression is serious;

looking after a bunny is an important job. "Emily will help me clean out the hutch, but I can move her into the run myself so she can eat the grass."

"I'll have to come meet her when I get back from our honeymoon." I kiss the top of her head and stand up. "What do you think of the ballroom?"

Abigail peers all around, wide-eyed. "I like the fountain," she says before skipping off to join Emily, who seems to be her favorite person these days.

Cash and Bash came in while we were discussing Snowy. They stand on either side of me and kiss my cheeks. "We didn't get you a wedding present yet," Bash says.

I smile. "Guys, you really don't have to. I think Caleb has everything we could possibly want in his apartment."

"Ah, but does he have one of these?" Cash ducks underneath one of the food tables and comes back out with an inflatable unicorn, inflated, complete with golden unicorn's horn on its head.

I burst into giggles and take the unicorn, pretending to inspect it closely. "Indeed, he doesn't. We'll give it pride of place in the pool, and every time Caleb falls off it, I'll think of you."

"My turn." Bash copies his brother, disappears underneath the table, and returns with a curious transparent cube. I chew my bottom lip trying to guess what it is so that I don't make him feel bad. "It's an egg-cuber," he announces proudly.

"An egg-cuber?" Caleb takes the gift and turns it around, his brow furrowed. "Just what I always wanted."

"I knew it." Bash grins. "I thought that if ever there was

anyone who would want to make square eggs it would be my seriously square big brother."

We all laugh as the ballroom continues to fill with guests.

The twins have eased my anxiety a little, but my heart is still drumming dramatically. I've barely known Caleb for a few weeks, and his world and events like this are still so alien to me I feel like a deep-sea diver stumbling upon an underwater city without an oxygen tank.

"Hey, I've got you. You'll be fine." Caleb's arms snake around my waist from behind, and he kisses me on the lips as I lean back against him. "Have I told you how beautiful you are?"

"No." I shake my head, twisting my mouth away from his lips in feigned confusion. "Have you told anyone else?"

Caleb turns me around and places both hands on my shoulders. His face is so close to mine our lips are touching. "You are, and always will be, the most beautiful woman in the world to me, and don't you ever forget it."

I slant my eyes and tease him with a sly smile. "Out of curiosity, what will happen if I forget?"

His lips tickle my ear as he whispers, "I will withhold my cock and make you beg for it. Naked. On your knees with your butt in the air." He pulls away.

My face is flushed, and I can feel my nipples hardening. "I'll bear that in mind."

Sienna navigates her way across the slowly-filling room, and Caleb chuckles. "Saved by your best friend. We'll resume this conversation later."

Sienna looks stunning in a floaty green-and-gold dress with a high neckline and long floaty transparent sleeves. Her red hair is piled up on top of her head, with long curls framing her face, but the first thing I notice about her are the flushed cheeks. She looks happy, and seeing my best friend happy is the best wedding present ever.

"Wow, look at you." She holds my hand and twirls me around. "I can't remember the last time I saw you wearing anything other than jeans. What have you done to her, Caleb?" She smiles. "I mean, wow."

My cheeks flood with heat, and I hold onto Caleb's arm.

Even I see a different person when I look in the mirror now, and I told myself it was because of the designer labels stitched inside my new outfits. But it isn't. It's knowing that Caleb feels about me the way I feel about him. It's knowing that he will always be by my side, and that our future is together. It's like the real me was hibernating until the sun came out, and Caleb is my sunshine. My oxygen. My Prince Charming.

"Where have you been?" I ask Sienna, deflecting the attention away from me. "I haven't seen you for a couple of days."

"I've been busy ... looking at art galleries." She pauses. "I think I've found one."

Kyle wanted to help her start her own gallery, but Sienna refused his offer. She's keeping him at arm's length. It's survival instinct, and I can't blame her for that. She almost died in that car wreck, and I can't even begin to imagine what horrific images appear inside her head when she closes her eyes at night.

But Caleb kept his word and is funding the gallery on the provision that she repays him with one of her paintings when she's a famous artist charging millions for a picture of a sunflower.

"I can't wait for you to see it, V. It's perfect."

"It's the first thing I'm going to do when we get back from Europe."

Caleb smiles. "I'm excited for you too."

Kyle joins us then, and as always, I study their body language, hoping to see a glimmer of something more. Something romantic. That hope fades when Sienna reflexively edges away from him. She barely makes eye contact before grabbing a glass of champagne from a passing server, and muttering, "Oh, well, time to mingle."

Before the accident, Sienna was always the first person to get up and dance at a party, and the last one standing, and it breaks my heart to see her avoiding the dance floor like it's something toxic. Almost as much as it breaks my heart when I see the defeated expression on Kyle's face.

Caleb places a comforting hand on his brother's shoulder, but Kyle shrugs it off and heads outside, his eyes lingering on Sienna's back as he passes by.

"She'll come around in her own time," Caleb says, pulling me against his chest and kissing the top of my head.

I wish I could be so certain. But I want Sienna to be happy, and if that means keeping her distance from the Murrays, then I'll respect her wishes all the way.

I peer around the room at the smiling faces of the guests. I spot Denise with a small group of people, and wave at her from across the room. She waves back and winks at me. She's still reeling from the knowledge that when she offered me a temporary job, she was introducing me to my future husband. She never saw herself as a matchmaker before.

A familiar figure appears in the doorway, young, tall and slender, with raven-black hair.

"Ivan," I say at the same time as Caleb mutters, "Brailand."

We face each other. "Brailand?" I arch an eyebrow when Caleb asks, "Ivan?"

Turning back to the two men who are now accepting a glass of champagne from one of the servers, I realize that this must be the secret boyfriend Olivia mentioned in the warehouse. Caleb had been worried that Brailand Voth had been abducted too, but it turned out that he'd resigned from his job and taken a step back from his regular life to protect the man he loves. Ivan Petrov.

"They make a lovely couple," I whisper to Caleb. "I hope everyone can see that."

"Well, if they can't, it's their loss." He kisses me on the lips. "I'll go and speak to them. Will you be okay?"

"Go. I'll be fine." I watch him walk away. His broad shoulders, slim hips, wavy hair... How did I get so lucky?

"You look radiant, Victoria." The voice catches me unawares, and I turn around to find Don Dragonetti standing beside me holding two glasses of champagne. He offers one to me, and when I take it, he clinks his glass against mine. "To your future."

I smile, sip my champagne, the bubbles fizzing on my tongue. "How are you feeling?"

No one had heard from the don since the incident in the Lake Placid warehouse. We didn't even know if he would come to the wedding reception, so I'm surprised to find him looking ruggedly handsome in a smart black suit and crisp white shirt.

"Weary." He sips his drink. "But don't tell anyone I said that."

"I won't."

"I hear you'll be leaving for your honeymoon tomorrow. I won't spoil your evening with talk of business, but please tell your husband that I will speak to him on his return."

"Is it serious?" I blurt out before I can stop myself. Me and my big mouth.

"My dear," Don Dragonetti smiles, "in this city, everything is serious."

I want to ask about Olivia. I don't know how badly she was hurt, but no one has seen or heard of her since that day, and I'm scared that I'll ask the wrong question, and he'll tell me that the gunshot was fatal. It all happened so quickly that I didn't even see who fired the first shot. Then another went off, and when I peered out from beneath my arms, Ivan and Olivia were bleeding on the floor.

"Please don't look so concerned, Victoria. I think your husband will appreciate what I have to say."

Is he going to offer Caleb another chance to form an alliance? With Olivia out of the picture, it would benefit both families and should be a smooth transition on both sides.

"Is Olivia..." It will eat away at me if I don't ask. "I mean, does she know what you want to speak to Caleb about?"

Don Dragonetti downs half his glass of champagne in one mouthful. "You didn't see what happened, did you?"

"No. I was there when she threatened Ivan before you arrived. He wanted to leave. He didn't like what was going on."

The don's eyes seek out Ivan who is deep in conversation with Brailand and Caleb, a wide smile on each of their faces. "He was worried about the fallout with the Murrays. My daughter unfortunately had no such qualms."

I don't know what to say. Olivia was governed by her misguided desire to be married to Caleb. But she abducted my brother and my best friend to get to me, and although I might be able to forgive her, I will never forget what she did.

"You said that you hoped we might be friends, Olivia and I." Pause.

I don't know how far I can go without being disrespectful to the mafia boss. Caleb has a lot of respect for the older man, and I've learned enough to know that respect is key in their line of business. Without it, they might as well pack their bags and relocate to the other side of the world.

"That was then, and this is now," he says before I pluck up the courage to continue. "My daughter fired the first shot." At my gasp of surprise, he adds, "Fortunately for all concerned, my daughter was more proficient at applying makeup than she was at wielding a firearm."

My eyes instinctively drift across the room to Ivan Petrov. It must've been a surface wound; he doesn't appear to be in any pain, and when our eyes meet, he raises his glass to toast me.

"Did Ivan try to stop her?"

"He didn't need to." Don Dragonetti has been acknowledging other guests throughout our conversation, but now he turns to face me, creating a tiny bubble in which only the two of us exist. "I fired the second shot."

I blink furiously. I'm not sure I heard him correctly with the ringing in my ears as I relive those terrible moments in the warehouse.

"I... I mean, you..." I swallow a mouthful of champagne too quickly and feel it bubble and fizz as it goes down.

"I was aware of a mole within my organization. Agreements were broken. Pressure was being put on my business by the police commissioner. The casinos were losing money. I suspected of course, but I didn't quite believe it until Lev Petrov informed me of my daughter's antics with his son." He drains the liquid in his glass and sighs heavily.

"Is she...?" I can't bring myself to finish the question.

"She has been taken care of. So, you see, you have nothing to worry about on that score."

I swallow, tears inexplicably welling in my eyes. "What about you? Will you be alright?"

He smiles, and his eyes crinkle at the corners. "Yes, my dear. Thank you for asking." He places his empty glass onto a tray as a server walks past, leans in, and kisses my cheeks. "Enjoy your honeymoon. We will meet again when you get back."

"Thank you." Although he is smiling, I sense the heavy sadness resting on his shoulders. I throw my arms around him and hug him closely. "Please take care."

I release him to find Caleb watching us with a curious half-smile. "Don Dragonetti, I'm so glad that you could make it." He shakes the older man's hand.

"I can't stay. But I wanted to offer my congratulations to the happy couple."

I watch him navigate the small groups of people in the ballroom with handshakes for the men and kisses for the women. His spine is straight. He knows everyone, and everyone greets him with respect, and I can't help feeling that an alliance with the Murrays means more to him than he lets on. Maybe he looks upon Caleb as the son he never had. I only hope that we never let him down.

"Happy?" Caleb pulls me into his arms and kisses me on the lips.

"Always."

EPILOGUE

VICTORIA

Abigail comes running over to us as we climb out of the car.

"Auntie Vicky, Uncle Caleb, come and meet my friend, Resh." She grabs our hands and leads us into the extensive gardens of Sudbury Valley.

A boy is sitting high up in a grand old oak tree, tossing leaves down to a girl who is making patterns with them across a boulder. Other children are laying belly-down in the grass reading books. Some are deadheading the flowers in the borders; some are simply running around; a boy is sitting by himself playing guitar, oblivious to the other children around him, while another is performing somersaults.

Resh, when we find him, is sitting in the dappled shade of an apple tree with a tablet on his lap. He's a couple of years older than Abigail with long jet-black hair that flops over his eyes, and a narrow serious face. When he spots us, he stands up, wipes his hands on his slacks and greets Caleb with a handshake. "Nice to meet you, sir."

"Nice to meet you too, Resh." Caleb smiles. "Abigail talks about you a lot."

"She talks about you too. She said that you ride a Harley Davidson, but she didn't say which model."

Caleb hesitates, and I can see it in his profile that he isn't accustomed to discussing motorcycles with an eight-year-old. "It's a limited-edition Anniversary Road Glide." He glances at me, the brief look asking if this is too much information.

"Does it still have the eagle?" The kid's expression is still perfectly serious.

"It sure does."

"I want to own a Harley Davidson when I'm older."

Abigail joins in, "Maybe you could bring it next time, Uncle Caleb, and take Resh out for a ride."

Caleb's expression is like a plea for help. Stick him in a boardroom filled with mafia mobsters and he'll wrap them around his little finger and tie them in knots. But faced with a genius child with a commendable knowledge of Harley Davidson's back catalogue of models, and he clams up like an oyster.

"I don't think that will be allowed." I step into the rescue. "For safety reasons. We would need to get your parents' permission, Resh."

"They won't mind. I've been on a motorcycle before."

Abigail grins at him like he's the only person in the world who exists for her right now. I recognize that gleam in her eye. It's the same gleam I see in my own reflection in the mirror every day since I met Caleb.

She has been attending Sudbury Valley for six months, and she is thriving. We already knew that Abigail was bright beyond her years when we first visited the school, back when Caleb's expectations were low at best. Now, she can hold a conversation about climate change and democracy and The Jonas Brothers like an adult. Her confidence has grown. She doesn't worry about voicing an opinion at home or in school, and she and Resh have been creating their own video game.

An adult approaches us—there are no teachers at Sudbury Valley, only adults who supervise and enhance the children's learning—a young woman with cropped pink hair and a nose piercing. She's wearing red Doc Martens with a kilt and a red sweater, and when she smiles, I notice that her top teeth are a little crooked.

"Hi, I'm Nina. Abigail has been so excited to show you the video game they've been working on. But she has another surprise for you too." She winks conspiratorially at Abigail.

We follow Nina, Abigail, and Resh into the main building.

When we first considered Sudbury Valley for Abigail, Caleb was skeptical. No learning structure, no teachers, no exams, no classrooms, he said it was a recipe for disaster. But when we spoke to some of the older children attending the school, we realized that they were still learning all that they needed to be mature, confident, and well-rounded adults when they graduated.

Emily had been right. A generic one-system-fits-all education couldn't possibly work for every child, and Abigail's needs and strengths didn't lie in a classroom where she would've been expected to complete tasks beneath her capabilities, five days a week. At Sudbury Valley, if she wants to spend a semester designing computer games, then that's what she does. She's still learning, but she's learning the subjects that interest her, the stuff that she is passionate about, and will take with her through to adulthood.

Now, Caleb's eyes and mind are open, and when he and Abigail are together, she surprises him with the questions that she asks about the Wraith. They have the kind of father-daughter bond that I wished she had with Mason, but that I'm starting to realize now might never happen. Mason has the same addictive personality as our mother. If he isn't gambling, he's drinking or experimenting with drugs, and even though Caleb paid to put him through rehab, he checked himself out after a week and disappeared again.

It was Caleb's idea for Abigail to stay with us between semesters. I hadn't believed it possible to love him more than I already did, but when he told me that's what he wanted, my heart was so full I thought it would burst.

The rooms inside the building are painted in bold, bright colors. The children smile at us and say hello to Abigail and Resh as we pass through. They're happy. No one is struggling with Math or reading or science. Every child here is confident that they can achieve whatever target they set themselves.

In what must be the closest the school has to a computer room, Abigail and Resh sit down and demonstrate the video game they designed. Their thumbs fly across the controls, and I can barely keep up with the characters on the screen.

Abigail did this, I tell myself when they complete the first level. But none of this would've been possible if I hadn't met Caleb.

"Are you ready for your surprise?" Nina asks.

"We're ready." Caleb squeezes my hand and answers for me.

I'm more emotional than ever these days, and he is always on hand with a hug and a tissue, and a hot dog smothered in mustard and ketchup. Sometimes I wonder if he hired a hot dog chef just to satisfy my weird cravings during this pregnancy.

In another room, some children are already sitting in bean bag chairs staring at the wooden stage. Caleb steers me away from the squashy cushions and helps me into a seat at the back of the room, his hand caressing my swollen stomach.

"I don't want you getting stuck in a beanbag." His lips brush my ear and send shivers down my spine.

When we first met, I wondered if this passion would be tempered over time, but it shows no signs of abating yet. If anything, being pregnant has made me insatiable. I can't get enough of Caleb. I've even started visiting him in his office at lunchtimes, locking the door, and begging him to lick me until I explode, and Lauren has now added flushed cheeks to the pursed lips and suspicious eyes with which she always greets me.

Maybe one day, Miss Ingram will accept that I'm in Caleb's life to stay.

Abigail disappears behind the stage with Nina and Resh. When she comes back out, she is wearing a blonde wig, a white dress, and a sunny yellow cardigan thrown over her shoulders. Resh follows her in black pants and a black T-shirt, his hair gelled back away from his forehead.

"Danny!" I squeal in Caleb's ear.

"Sandy!"

I don't know how Abigail knew about the first time Caleb and I met, but I watch her and Resh's performance of *Grease* with tears streaming from my eyes.

On our way back to the city, we detour along the Upper Delaware Scenic Byway. We stop at a heritage café in a small town and drink hot chocolate, not coffee—too much caffeine is bad for the baby—from mismatched porcelain cups, our fingers entwined on top of the table.

We talk about the refurbishments currently happening to the Dragon's Den, and my vision for how it will look when works are completed. It was Don Dragonetti's idea for me to get involved in his casino's renovation plans after the wedding reception. Surprised, I'd felt out of my depth. I had no formal qualifications or experience, but he said he had complete faith in me, and Caleb encouraged me to try.

I'm glad he did. I'm decorating the nursery in our apartment now. I wake early every morning, drag on paint-splattered overalls , and spend my days blissfully hand-painting fairy tale scenes around the walls. I've finished Cinderella's castle. Now, I'm working on an underwater scene with Ariel, Sebastien, and King Triton, and when that's finished, I'm going to paint the house and characters from *Encanto*.

Driving back along the Byway, Caleb leans forward and asks Kev to pull over on the side of the road.

We climb out, and I can't believe that we're standing in the exact same spot where we stopped the first time Caleb took me out on his Harley.

"How did you remember this spot?" I lean against him and admire the spectacular view. Caleb's breath is warm on my cheek, and his hands are resting on my pregnant belly.

The last time we were here, I didn't even know how Caleb felt about me. I had hope, but I also had the end of our fake marriage contract looming over my head. Now... I inhale deeply and relax against my husband's chest. Now, I literally have everything that I could ever possibly want, and I still pinch myself frequently to remind me that it is real.

"How could I forget?"

I turn around in his arms and kiss him on the lips as our baby girl kicks him for getting too close. His face breaks into a wide smile that sets him aglow. He has been glowing since the day that I announced the pregnancy, and I can't wait for him to meet our baby. I already know that he will be the best daddy in the world.

"Do you remember what you asked me that night?"

"Uh-huh. I asked you what you wanted."

"And I didn't answer because I received the phone call about Don Mateo's heart attack."

Mateo Dragonetti. Who'd have thought that the mafia boss would've become such a huge part of our lives when his daughter was the reason Caleb married me. "I remember."

"Ask me again."

I smile. "What do you want, Caleb?"

"It's easy. It's the easiest question I've ever had to answer. I want this. All of this, mo chroí. I want our daughter, and all the other children that will follow her. Sometimes, I wonder what I ever did to get so lucky."

He lowers his head to my belly and kisses it tenderly, and the baby responds with a gentle kick.

He straightens, cups my face in his hands, and peers into my eyes. "But most of all, I want you, Victoria."

Thank you for reading my book, I hope you enjoyed it as much as I did creating it. Please leave a review to help me grow.

If you enjoyed Victoria and Caleb's story, you will adore Brandon and Rose in Fake Dar Vows.

Here is a sneak peak.

Brandon

My phone vibrates on my desk, my mom's face smiling at me like a cameo portrait inside a precious locket. She's wearing her favorite pearls in the image, her hair swept back Audrey-Hepburn style, her smile revealing perfect white teeth. I can almost imagine her hissing under her breath, *"Answer the damn phone, Brandon,"* while the photographer catches her still sharp cheekbones in exactly the right light.

I reject the call.

Again.

I hit redial on the landline telephone on my desk and get straight through to Julia, my personal assistant. "Has my mother tried calling today?"

"Wrong question."

"How many times?" I try.

"Ooh, at least a dozen, maybe more. I lost count shortly after I arrived." I can hear her chuckling to herself as I cut her off.

I swivel my leather seat and stare out of the penthouse window at the winking glass of the Chrysler Building in the sunlight. My mother wants to discuss my father's birthday arrangements even though she'll already have everything in hand with zero input from either me or my brother. It will be the same scenario as last year, and every other birthday before that: she'll run through the itinerary that she emailed to me a week ago, and wait for me to say, "I'll be there, Mom."

She knows I can't refuse. It's the big seven-oh, and she'll want everything to be perfect, because there's no room for anything less in Ruby Weiss's life. The decorations will be themed, the food will be gourmet, and the games will be competitive—just how my father likes it—and we'll all be expected to perform like circus animals, raising the bar a little higher with each turn.

I skim-read the email. A week on Ruby Island, the private island in the Keys my father bought for my mom to celebrate their fortieth wedding anniversary, dress casual, cocktails served at six, all arguments to be conducted behind closed doors.

Centuries ago, they'd have given me and my brother Damon pistols, instructed us to choose our seconds and meet at dawn to settle it like men. Winner takes all. Quicker and easier than the relentless tournaments we've been forced to endure all our lives in the name of competitiveness.

When my phone vibrates again, I close my eyes and inhale deeply. I stand, slide my suit jacket from the concealed closet in my office, and shrug it on, retrieving my phone as I pass my desk. Might as well take advantage of the fine spring weather and walk to my next meeting while I avoid her calls.

A glance at the Caller ID tells me that my mom has been shunted down the line—this is not a regular occurrence in Ruby Weiss's life. No doubt it will be noted in her silk-covered journal to be discussed with me when I finally pick up.

I hit the green button. "Sam."

I'm already exiting my office. Julia, my PA, glances up from her own conversation, eyes wide. She covers her cell phone with her hand, too late to hide the personal call.

"Eleven-thirty meeting," I say.

"Will you be back?"

I can't avoid my mother all day, and the anticipated conversation is already causing a headache to brew behind my eyes like I've been reading small print for hours. "Depends."

Julia's smile is fleeting and doesn't quite reach her eyes. She's immaculate in a dark-gray shift dress, her hair tied back on top in a coordinating bow, the kind a child of kindergarten age might wear. We've worked together for five years and in all that time, I've never seen her make a personal call, even discreetly, during office hours.

Her gaze drifts to the phone in my hand. Sam is still hanging on, but he can wait.

"My mother," I say, the lie slipping off my tongue easily. "I'll keep you posted."

My office is on the top floor of the tower that my father had commissioned when he made his first billion. I step into the elevator and glance back at Julia as the doors glide silently closed. She has her back to me, cell raised to her ear.

I follow suit. "You've got thirty seconds," I say to Sam.

"There might be a problem at the source."

I follow the levels on the display in front of me. "What kind of problem?"

"SEC is paying a little too much attention for my liking," Sam says.

"Do I need to step back?"

"No." Pause. "No, I can sort it."

"That's what I pay you for."

I end the call. The elevator stops smoothly, and the doors swish open.

One of my father's old associates is waiting to ride it back up, and I greet him with a wide smile and well-practiced handshake, firm enough to project confidence and control of the situation. Too limp, and you can kiss goodbye to any future business transactions; too heavy-handed and it implies a level of intimidation. It isn't something they teach at Harvard —it's a Weiss family thing. My father is a pro.

"Brandon, you'll be at the family celebrations."

"Of course." I incline my head and keep the smile fixed in place like the dutiful eldest son.

"See you there. My wife and I wouldn't miss it for the world."

Of course they wouldn't. It will provide a conversation starter for weeks after the event. *Did you hear about Harry Weiss's birthday festivities? We were there by personal invitation.*

I turn away to cross the sleek marble-floored lobby and collide with a child.

The infant barely reaches my thighs—I know this because as she lands on her backside, her sticky fingerprints are left behind as evidence on my suit pants. The mouth opens, the chubby cheeks grow pink, and siren-strength wails fill the otherwise silent lobby.

A young woman comes running over clutching a plastic container filled with sandwiches, sliced salad vegetables, and a rosy, red apple. She hoists the child onto her hip, dropping the container in the process.

"I'm so sorry," she says, bouncing the child up and down, oblivious to the sound emitting from her. Her gaze immediately drops to the fingerprints on my pants, and she wrinkles her nose. "It'll wipe off. It's only watermelon juice. She was eating a slice of watermelon on the way here."

Sarah, the receptionist, joins us. She blinks slowly, her mouth a round 'O' of horror. "I'll fetch some tissues." She scurries back to the front desk.

"I'm on my way to a meeting." I'm still staring at the stains—there's no way they're wiping off with a tissue.

"It was an accident." The woman strokes the child's blonde curls and rubs noses with her until the tears dry up and the siren-shrieks morph into the occasional juddering sob. When she looks at me again, her eyes are accusing. "You should've been watching where you were going."

"You do realize this is a private office building, right?" I say.

Sarah is busy dealing with a client while the stains on my pants are drying up.

The woman with the child rolls her eyes around the high-ceilinged, glass and chrome lobby with its white leather couches and carefully chosen artwork. "My mistake, I thought this was preschool, but I can see now that it's far too clean and stuffy."

"Stuffy?" I don't even know why I'm getting drawn into this conversation. This is my building. I should be able to come and go without fear of sticky fingers and bawling kids.

"Yes, I bet there's zero fun to be had in this building."

A retort teeters on the tip of my tongue, the kind I might've spouted as a fourteen-year-old with raging hormones and giant footsteps to fill. Instead, I clench my fists and jut my jaw, the façade that works with everyone else in my life.

Sarah's gaze flits back and forth between the client and our conversation as if realizing she might've prioritized the wrong person.

The young woman's shoulders slump as the child rests her head on her chest and peers at me from beneath long wet eyelashes. "I'm sorry. Look, I'll pay for your pants to be dry-cleaned if it will help."

"Not really," I say. "I'm already late."

I see the hurt in her eyes and ignore it anyway. I don't know why the incident has me so rattled. Scratch that. I do know why it has me so rattled—it has nothing to do with the fingerprints that are already starting to fade, and everything to do with the young woman whose honey-blonde hair, if released from the ponytail secured at the nape of her neck, would curl the same way as Kelly's.

I go to walk around them and hesitate, bending to retrieve the plastic container from the floor. "You dropped this," I say, handing it over.

"Thank you. It's for my dad. It's his lunch; he forgot it this morning. He's careless like that. My mom always said that he'd forget his head if it wasn't—"

"Your dad works here?" I cut her off.

Most people tend to overshare. Ask a simple question, and they'll spill enough information to either incriminate themselves or gain a new friend. It's the reason why I stick to the questions that will give me the answers I'm looking for.

She nods. She has the same color eyes too... "He's the janitor."

I hear my own breath escaping and do nothing to stop it. I couldn't pick out the janitor in a police line-up, but I'd bet my lucky dollar that he looks nothing like his daughter.

"Tell him there's a café across the road if he forgets it in future." I walk away.

Sarah dashes around the desk waving a tissue at me like a flag. "Mr. Weiss. The tissues..."

"Forget it." I don't even glance behind me.

My phone rings again and, distracted, I answer without thinking.

"Brandon, honey," Mom's voice is silky-smooth. "I was starting to think that you were avoiding me."

"I've been busy, Mom," I say.

"Too busy to discuss your father's birthday party?"

"I'll have to call you back, Mom. I'm on my way to a meeting." I cut her off and locate Julia's direct line on my call log.

She picks up before the phone even rings. "What did you forget?"

"The janitor," I say.

I can almost hear her sliding closer to her desk and locating his personal details on the internal system. "What about him?"

"Who is he? Name, background, length of service."

"Jonathan Carter. Came to us from a local high school. References all checked out. Eleven years' service. Squeaky clean." Her tone is professional. "Was granted compassionate leave when his wife died four years ago. What's the problem?"

"His daughter and grandkid were in the lobby when I left. Make sure it doesn't happen again."

"Okay." Julia seems to want to say more, but I don't give her the opportunity.

A sleek black Bentley is parked outside the building, the rear passenger window rolling down as I approach. My mom's face appears, and she calls out, "Brandon!" At least she doesn't pretend that she was just passing by.

The passenger door opens—it's an order not an invitation.

I climb in beside my mother who is looking regal in an ivory Chanel two-piece, her legs crossed primly at the ankles, her favorite subtle perfume filling the back of the car. All that's needed to complete the queenly image is a gentle wave to her subjects through the window. I breathe in the familiar scent and my lips instinctively curl up at the corners. At thirty-five years old, I wonder if I will ever stop needing her praise and approval.

The Bentley joins the slow-moving traffic—it would be quicker to walk.

"Your father's birthday." She dives straight in—Ruby Weiss has never mastered the art of small talk. "You didn't respond to my email."

"I've been busy." I don't add that I knew she'd be angry if Julia replied on my behalf. "I'm not sure I can make it. I might have to fly out to Europe."

She fixes me with the gaze usually reserved for wealthy acquaintances who are about to donate a large sum of cash to whichever charity she's promoting at the time. "I already cleared your diary with Julia weeks ago, Brandon. I've managed to get hold of the Patek Philippe wristwatch your father has admired for so long. The Grandmaster Chime. And I want everyone to be there when he sees it."

"For the grand unveiling," I say.

For his sixtieth birthday, she had my father's portrait painted by a relatively unknown Baltimore artist highly recommended by a close friend. His reaction was somewhat anticlimactic, and the painting has never been seen since.

"You seem a little on edge." My mom's eyes narrow as she studies my face.

I glance at my phone. A message from Julia: *Done*.

I need to get out of the car, walk to the meeting, clear my head and release some of the tightness in my neck and shoulders. Perhaps I'll get Julia to arrange the masseuse for later this afternoon; weekly visits are no longer enough.

"I'm fine," I say tightly.

"You work too hard," she says without conviction. "You need someone to look after you."

"I have Julia."

"You know what I mean. Look how happy your brother is. All I ever wanted was to see you both happy and content."

"I know, Mom."

Satisfied that she has made her point, she sits back again. "I don't want the celebrations spoiled by business talk. I'm relying on you to steer the party the right way if your father is getting drawn into a serious conversation. You know what he's like."

I do, and so does she. If the chat turns to business, a bunch of wild horses won't drag him away.

"Kelly has been helping me with the theme. We're keeping it theatrical. Your father loved *Hamilton* when we saw it on Broadway…"

I tune out. My shirt collar feels two sizes too small, and the back of the car is starting to feel claustrophobic, my mom's perfume clinging to every available surface. Of course, Kelly has been helping her. She's the perfect daughter-in-law, a good mom, a loving wife, and never misses a family event.

"Stop the car." I'm already reaching for the handle as the Bentley draws to a smooth halt. "Sorry, Mom," I say. "But I'm running late."

I climb out and close the door behind me. My mother slides across the seat and peers out through the lowered window. "Brandon, next time you use an important meeting as an excuse to avoid talking to me, can you at least make sure your pants are clean?"

She sits back in her seat as the tinted window glides up and the car moves on.

. . .

Chapter 2

Rose

"Okay, this is beyond a joke." I toss my dinner plate into the frothy water in the sink and wipe bubbles from my cheek with the back of my arm.

I know where the instruction came from without waiting for my dad to elaborate.

Mr. Weiss.

The man in the gray silk suit.

The man who was horrified by a few fingerprints on his goddamned perfectly pressed pants. I'd bet his kids only get to speak to him from a safe distance. I can picture him standing in the doorway of their bedrooms and wishing them goodnight with a relieved smile at surviving another day without getting his hands dirty.

"He looked at Izzie like she was something I'd dragged in off the sidewalk," I grumble over my shoulder. Something smelly. Something that he would no doubt have his assistant remove from the soles of his shoes to save him from getting his fingers soiled.

No, scratch all the above—Mr. Weiss isn't the paternal type. I'd bet he never ate watermelon without a fork either.

I'm angry at myself for wasting any emotion on the guy, but seriously, who does he think he is? He could've asked me politely to take Izzie outside, but instead, he gets his assistant to suggest that Dad use the café across the street the next time he forgets his lunch.

"Hey, Rosie, it's okay," Dad says. "Mr. Weiss has an image to maintain. It's my fault. I shouldn't be so forgetful in the mornings."

"Don't apologize for him, Dad."

I inhale deeply and plunge my hands into the hot water. I don't like it when my dad bows down to his bosses like this. Running a corporation is one thing, and sure, the guy is probably under a lot of stress, but it doesn't give him the prerogative to treat people unkindly.

"He can't dictate what you eat, Dad," I say, swallowing my initial response. "Izzie wasn't even being noisy. Thirty seconds later, and we'd have been out of there, and Mr. Weiss would've been none the wiser."

"Bad timing, Rosie. That's all it was. You can't diss the man for doing his job." Dad cleans ketchup from Izzie's face with a baby wipe and gets her down from the table.

Maybe Dad's right. The guy probably didn't give the incident a second thought while he sat through his dull afternoon meetings, and scrolled through his emails, and added his illegible signature to a ream of classified documents. He probably doesn't even remember the call he asked his assistant to make.

Maybe this anger bubbling inside my chest isn't even about him.

The doorbell rings. I grab a towel to dry my hands and take it with me to the front door, Izzie almost tripping me up along the way.

It's Jess, Izzie's mom. "Sorry I'm so late," she says. She bends down, scoops her little girl into her arms, and smothers her face in kisses while Izzie squirms and tries to push her away. "Have you been a good girl for Auntie Rose?"

"Yes, Mommy." She wraps her arms around her mom's neck and rests her cheek on Jess's.

Jess and I have been friends since middle school.

As eleven-year-olds we became inseparable over our shared love of Fleetwood Mac songs, flared jeans and disco boots, *Scooby Doo* and *Ghostbusters*. As we grew older, Jess became more athletic and captained the high school basketball team, while I grew a pair of breasts the size of melons and realized that winning the 200-meter sprint was never going to happen.

We didn't hang around with the popular kids, but neither were we relegated to the bottom of the school hierarchy, floating along somewhere in the middle with our quirky obsessions and silly sense of humor. I always thought that we were tolerated by the jocks and the trendy girls because of Jess's love of sports, while she put it down to my breasts.

Whatever the reason, our friendship survived high school, relationships with boys, college, and everything else that life has thrown our way since.

"She's been an angel as always." I hold the door open wide to let her in.

"Hmm." Jess wrinkles her nose. "Will someone please explain to me why you get the angel and I get the demon?"

"I don't believe you," I say, tickling Izzie's waist and making her giggle. The child will break hearts when she's older.

"Okay." Jess sets her daughter down and eyes me suspiciously. "What's happened? And before you say 'nothing', I can feel the heat of your wrath from here."

Dad pokes his head around the kitchen doorway and calls out, "Come on in, Jess. I'll make coffee."

We go through to the kitchen where Dad already has the coffee brewing.

"Hi, Mr. Carter," Jess says. "I can't stay long. I need to get this little one into bed. Dave's on babysitting duties tonight, and I'm going out for a couple of drinks with my cousin."

"You should go with them, Rose." Dad's shameless when it comes to forcing my company onto others. "It'll do you good to get out."

Jess's gaze hops between the two of us. "Yes, come, Rose. You can tell me all about what's got you so rattled." Her eyebrows dance independently. "My guess is it's man related."

Dad chuckles, and I shoot him a glare that goes unnoticed. "It's not what you're thinking."

"Oh, sweetie, you tell yourself that if it makes you feel better."

***

"Okay, I take it all back. Sounds like this guy wears his boxers too tight." Jess downs her glass of wine and asks the bartender for a refill after I recount the incident in the lobby of Weiss Tower.

The bar is busy, but not so noisy that we have to shout to hear ourselves speak; it's buzzing, and the urge to run home and hide behind a book in my pajamas is real.

"I just wish Dad would speak up for himself," I say, rubbing my thumb over the condensation on my glass.

She shakes her head. "Rose, your dad is a grown man. He has worked hard all his life, raised a quite spectacular daughter, and he doesn't need you to hold his hand."

I sip my drink, swallow, and feel the familiar sting behind my eyes. Dad meant well, suggesting that I get dressed up in something other than a T-shirt and faded jeans and spend some time with my best friend, but alcohol always produces the same result.

Jess's warm hand covers mine.

"I miss her so much," I say as the first tear trickles down my cheek. I catch it on the tip of my tongue and sniff loudly.

"I know." Jess nods. "You did everything you could for her, Rose. Your mom knew how much you loved her. You even dropped out of college to care for her."

"So, why do I feel so guilty?" I shake my head, swallow a larger mouthful of wine to blur the edges of what's going on in my head. But still the same old emotions drag up from somewhere deep inside like water being drawn from a well.

You go through life smiling at people, trying your best to be a good person, to be kind and thoughtful and compassionate, and it works. At least on the surface. No one sees what's going on beneath the bright smile because they have their own stuff to deal with, and that's okay. It's how it should be.

So, you keep going, tell yourself that you're coping, that finally, you've moved on from grief and guilt and loneliness, and then one glass of wine and wham! It all comes flooding back.

"She never got over it," I murmur. Jess has heard this all before, but she's the kind of friend who listens and doesn't tell me to let it go and move on.

"It isn't something you ever really get over, Rose, losing a baby. But you know what, your parents doted on the baby they did have—you! They poured double the amount of love into you, which makes you a very lucky person."

The bartender slides Jess's drink across the bar towards her, and she flashes him a grateful smile. He looks at my almost empty glass, raises an eyebrow, and I down it in one. He pours another without prompting.

He's good looking, dark hair, olive skin, high cheekbones, the kind of guy I'd be attracted to if my heart was in it. I turn around to face the room which is still filling up.

It's early evening. The place will be busy later, and that will be my cue to leave.

It isn't that I don't like crowds, I'm just out of touch with partying since Mom died and everything started sliding downhill. Robbie. My career. Marriage. Jess says it's because the universe is picking up on my negative energy, and maybe she's right, but I can't seem to drag myself out of it, and the bad news just keeps on coming.

"There she is!"

Jess points out her cousin Mindy who has just stepped through the doorway looking fabulous in an emerald-green pantsuit and strappy silver heels. Like Jess, she's tall and athletic with long raven-black curls that tumble over her shoulders and turn heads wherever she goes.

Even so, I'm not looking at her. I'm looking at the couple walking in behind her, holding hands, the huge diamond on the woman's wedding ring finger casting light signals around the room.

Robbie and his new fiancée.

I'd seen the engagement on our mutual friends' social media posts, but I'd buried that one deep too; in a city this size, you can go through life without ever bumping into someone you want to avoid.

"Rose?" Jess's voice penetrates my thoughts. "Are you okay?"

"Yeah, I'm fine." It's the standard response that spills out with minimal effort.

I have no right to feel jealous or bitter or any other kind of emotion now that Robbie has moved on with his life. I was the one who called off our engagement. There was too much going on at the time—my mom was sick, my grades were falling in college, Dad was a mess—at least that's what I told Robbie. The truth was, we'd been together since high school, and I always felt like something was missing, like I wasn't ready for marriage and kids and a home of our own. So, I handed back the ring and walked away.

I've spent the last few years convincing myself that I did what was right for me at the time, that I wanted all those things, but not with Robbie. Only now, I'm not so sure.

Blurry eyed with tears, I slide off my stool—I need to get away before Robbie spots me. My elbow connects with a glass. I gasp and hold my breath, watching the scene behind me play out in Jess's eyes and the way she flinches.

I whirl around, an apology on my lips, and realize that I'm face to face with the man in the gray suit from Dad's workplace.

Mr. Weiss.

He's still wearing the same clothes, but instead of mucky fingerprints, the front of his jacket is now wet and turning the same shade of red as the wine that was in his glass a moment ago. Recognition dances across his features.

"Do you ever watch where you're going?" I ask.

"Where *I'm* going?" He holds the glass away from him as if preventing the final few drips from landing on his jacket might somehow save it from being irreparably damaged.

Jess steps in and grabs my arm. "What my friend meant to say is she's sorry. She'll pay for your jacket to be dry-cleaned." She waggles her fingers in the general direction of his chest.

"That isn't what I meant." I straighten, facing him squarely.

Twice in one day—how is that even possible? Until this morning, I didn't even know this guy existed, and now he's everywhere, like a bad smell that refuses to blow away even when the windows are opened.

"This is the guy I was telling you about," I say, "the one who knocked Izzie over this morning."

"Okay." His jawline juts like he owns the place. Maybe he does own the place—it would just about sum up my luck right now. "Firstly, I didn't knock Izzie over this morning, she ran into me."

Jess is still clinging to my arm, but now she's watching him carefully, her expression unfathomable.

"Secondly, the kid shouldn't have even been inside the building."

Jess's eyebrows almost slide into her hairline, and I swallow the hysterical laughter that's threatening to spill out of my chest. I've seen that look before, and I wouldn't want to be on the receiving end of it, especially where it concerns Izzie. She's daring him to keep going.

And he does. "Thirdly, the suit is ruined, and I doubt she

could afford to replace it, although I'm tempted to have another one made and send her the bill."

"Let's go," I say to Jess, turning around to leave. "It's not worth it."

Jess doesn't take her eyes off Mr. Weiss. When she speaks, her tone is cold. "Firstly, the kid, Izzie, you know the one who ran into you this morning, is mine. Secondly, if there's no sign on the front door saying NO CHILDREN ALLOWED, then she has as much right to be in that building as the next person."

"BEWARE THE OWNER would be more appropriate," I mutter under my breath.

"And thirdly…" Jess hesitates, a smile tugging the corners of her lips. "You should try buying washable suits, it makes life a lot easier."

I suck my lips in to smother my smile. I bet Mr. Weiss wishes he'd chosen any other bar to walk into tonight but this one.

The bartender has been lingering over the customer closest to us, following our interaction with a lopsided smile on his face. All around us, eager faces are turned our way, sensing the argument brewing.

"Hey, guys." Mindy, looking utterly gorgeous, appears next to Jess. "What's going on? What did I miss?"

"We're leaving," Jess says. "This bar is a little overcrowded."

"But I just got here." Mindy is still talking and glancing over her shoulder at Mr. Weiss as Jess leads her away.

I chance one final look at him before I follow them. Our eyes meet, only it isn't anger I see in them, it's something else. Pity perhaps? I walk away and I don't look back.

. . .

Read Fake Dark Vows Now Free With Kindle Unlimited and available on Paperback.

ABOUT THE AUTHOR

VIVY SKYS the author of Steamy Contemporary Romance novels, featuring smart, strong, sassy and witty female characters that command the attention of strong protective alpha males, from Off limits, age gap, bossy billionaires, single dads next door, royalty, dark mafia and beyond Vivy's pen will deliver.

Follow Vivy Skys on Amazon to be the first to know when her next book becomes available.

Printed in Great Britain
by Amazon